D0058292

The Secret Science of Magic

Published by PEACHTREE PUBLISHERS
1700 Chattahoochee Avenue
Atlanta, Georgia 30318-2112
www.peachtree-online.com

First published in Australia in 2017 by Hardie Grant Egmont
First United States version published in 2018 by Peachtree Publishers

Cover illustrated by Brooke Smart
Design and composition by Adela Pons
Jacket design by Nicola Simmonds Carmack

Printed in March 2018 by LSC Communications in Harrisonburg, VA
10 9 8 7 6 5 4 3 2 1
First Edition
ISBN: 978-1-68263-014-3

Library of Congress Cataloging-in-Publication Data

Names: Keil, Melissa, author.
Title: The secret science of magic / Melissa Keil.
Description: First edition. | Atlanta : Peachtree Publishers, 2018. | "First published in Australia in 2017 by Hardie Grant Egmont." | Summary: Told from two viewpoints, Sophia, seventeen, a Sri Lankan-Australian math prodigy with social anxiety, is panicking about her future when classmate and amateur magician Joshua proclaims his love for her.
Identifiers: LCCN 2017021869 | ISBN 9781682630143
Subjects: | CYAC: Genius—Fiction. | Magic tricks—Fiction. | Social phobia—Fiction. | Dating (Social customs)—Fiction. | High schools—Fiction. | Schools—Fiction. | Melbourne (Vic.)—Fiction. | Australia—Fiction.
Classification: LCC PZ7.K25187 Sec 2018 | DDC [Fic]—dc23 LC record available at *https://lccn.loc.gov/2017021869*

The Secret Science of Magic

Melissa Keil

PEACHTREE
ATLANTA

No performer should attempt to bite off red-hot iron unless he has a good set of teeth.

—Harry Houdini

The greatest card trick in history is known by many names. Sometimes it's called Topping the Deck; sometimes, The Ambitious Card. But most magicians know it as The Trick that Fooled Houdini.

See, the self-proclaimed World's Greatest Magician was so convinced of his own awesomeness that he issued an open challenge to his fellow magicians: show him any trick, three times in a row, and he'd tell you how it was done. Houdini really believed there was nothing in the world he couldn't explain, no illusion he couldn't deduce.

It's possible that Houdini was a bit of a git. And he was clearly unfamiliar with the concept of a giant, karmic arse-kicking.

Dai Vernon, one of the best cardsmen of all time, took up the challenge. He asked Houdini to pick a card from a deck and to write his initials on the chosen card. He slipped it into the middle of the pack. Vernon snapped his fingers and—bammo!—Houdini's card appeared on top of the deck. Houdini made Vernon repeat the trick again. And again.

Vernon repeated it *seven times*, but Houdini could not explain how it was done. Needless to say, the World's Greatest Magician was pissed. Houdini may have aced jailbreaks and underwater escapes, but he never did learn Vernon's trick.

I figured it out when I was ten.

Now, I would never claim this makes me a better magician than Houdini—that would make me sound like a tool. But still, pulling off something the master magician couldn't do is a pretty nice boost to a guy's ego. And anyway, with practice, the Ambitious Card isn't even that hard. Like all my favorite tricks, its brilliance lies precisely in its simplicity: a majorly clever sleight of hand and some skill in palming the cards.

Sleight of hand is critical to most illusions. Misdirection, of course, is vital. But the fundamental key to all magic is simple:

Timing.

Without careful, precise timing, a magician will end up dropping his cards, or, you know, sawing his own legs off. I cannot stress this enough—the most important tool in a magician's bag is timing.

Well, timing—and an audience. A willing participant who chooses to follow your escapades is kinda crucial as well.

I risk a glance at the front of the Biology lab. Mr. Grayson is attempting to load a YouTube clip—I assume it's bio-related—onto the smart board. He's trying to look convincing, but the panicked thumping on his laptop betrays the fact that Mr. Grayson is about as tech savvy as a Franciscan monk. The lab is airless and dim. The class is alternating between somnambulism and unashamed sleep.

Except for one person.

Sophia.

I drop my eyes to my desk.

Sophia. Known to her best friend, the sweet-faced Elsie Nayer, as "Rey." Known to our teachers, who address her with a combination of apprehension and awe, as "Ms. Reyhart." Known to everyone else as "The Genius."

Sophia is staring at the spinning wheel of death on the smart board screen. She's tapping her pencil impatiently against her lip, her body folded over as though she's trying to vanish inside her own skin.

In a moment you'll hear her mention me. Pay attention, 'cause if you blink you might miss it.

I believe she will shortly describe me as "that dipshit who's always smiling at himself."

This is not ideal. But, to be fair, not *entirely* surprising. Sophia glances over her shoulder, black hair bouncing. Her sharp eyes survey the room, passing over me with what I perceive as the faintest hint of distaste.

So, yeah. I'm not exactly Mr. Popular. A guy who spends his spare time installed like a fern in the History stacks of the library does not endear himself to other human life-forms. And maybe I do tend to "loom like a gimp," as I once heard some rando jock-head say. I thought that was a bit unfair. It's hard not to loom when you're six foot three and built like a praying mantis.

Oh. And I *may* have recently been spotted at the train station while wearing a cape.

What can I say? My timing isn't always stupendous.

I sneak another peek at her lab station.

Significant moments meld to your memories in weird, mysterious ways. I remember the assembly was in spring, because the school was canopied by leaves—colossal red maples that seemed to block out the sky. I remember an army of year sevens jammed into the Arts building on the far side of the East Lawn, a hundred gray uniforms cold and damp from drizzle. I clearly remember being herded into a wobbly seat behind some dude who'd won a prize for writing to the Queen—and beside the girl with the thick black ponytail whom I'd been observing from a distance for the better part of a year.

The girl in whom I recognized a familiar skin-shifty restlessness, like her molecules were bouncing between different dimensions.

I remember nothing about the parade of speeches onstage. All I remember is Sophia, sitting aloof and straight beside me. Her eyes were focused on the page she held, which was covered with scrawls like some incomprehensible secret language; the answer to a national math prize that had our teachers falling over themselves.

I remember clearing my throat, an involuntary sound that I'm pretty sure came out as a whimper.

She looked up from her paper, dark eyes unblinking, for just a moment.

And despite the fact that I'd barely spoken a single word aloud that year, a rusty voice bubbled out of my mouth. "What do you see?"

She looked down again, fingers fluttering reverently over

her equation. She smiled, without glancing up. And she said one word—the only word Sophia Reyhart has spoken to me in almost five years:

"Magic."

And I knew my life was supposed to have her in it.

I would bet money that Sophia doesn't remember that moment. I would stake my collection of first-edition Raymond E. Feists, or my super-rare vintage Russian marine watch, still in its box, on the fact that she doesn't see me as anything other than a looming, too-smiley, weird guy—if she ever thinks about me at all. This is okay.

I tap my hand against the deck in my pocket.

I will avoid the obvious pun about playing my cards right.

But, as I have mentioned, timing is everything.

And I think it's almost, just about, time.

♠

Chapter One

The Uncertainty Principle

A basic theory of particle physics states that every atom in existence has already lived a life as a billion other things. Nothing—not a single particle in the universe—is new. So it's entirely possible that the atoms you breathe have passed through the heart of a star or the pee of a dinosaur.

Right at this second, I'm staring at the mole on the side of Mr. Grayson's left nostril and wondering where exactly in the universe that has been. Does his mole share its atoms with one of Jupiter's moons, or a prehistoric sloth, or a piece of ancient gypsum, or Euclid? Christ, is there a more depressing thought than that? One of the greatest mathematicians in history, and his atoms end up in the nostril mole of a balding, year-twelve Biology teacher who, at this moment, is frowning at his laptop screen as if spellbound by the spinning wheel of death.

Why am I obsessing about nose moles? Who knows. I've always assumed there's some kind of rhyme or reason to my brain's meanderings. But lately, I've started to suspect that most of the things I know are just, like, intellectual leftovers—gunk churning in the soup that is my cerebellum and bobbing up to the surface at arbitrary moments.

Mr. Grayson is wrestling with YouTube because, evidently, learning about mitosis must involve an animation and a rockin' soundtrack. The remnants of his lunch are perched on his desk: a sad triangle of cheese on rye and a banana, slick with bruises.

Fact: Bananas are naturally radioactive, containing potassium-40, a radioactive isotope of potassium.

Fact: Every human shares 50 percent of their DNA with a banana. Elsie recently made me spend a Saturday watching an entire season of *Dance Moms* on Netflix. This fact? No longer so surprising.

Fact: The song "Yes, We Have No Bananas," a hit in 1923, was inspired by a chronic Brazilian banana shortage.

Great—now that stupid song is stuck in my head.

Shut up shut up shut—

Under our desk, Elsie gives my wrist a quick, sharp tap. "Sophia. Stop. Freaking. Out," she murmurs. Her voice is that glass-calm she has taken to using on me lately, the sort of calm to which I'm sure potential ledge-jumpers are subjected.

"I'm. Not. Freaking. Out," I murmur back.

Elsie's deep-set eyes are almost imperceptible in the dim room, but I surmise that she is glaring at me with her no-nonsense, stern face. "Yeah, you are. Close your eyes, Sophia. Breathe."

Since my only options are to comply or endure another meditation session with her brother Colin, who has recently discovered the "art of mindfulness," I do what she tells me. I close my eyes and concentrate on slowing the hammering in my chest.

Panic attacks—even the mild ones—suck balls.
Elsie's hand hovers near mine until my breathing sort of returns to normal. Only then does she move away. I don't know how she knows when to do this. When I open my eyes, she winks at me and turns back to the smart board.

Mr. Grayson has mercifully figured out the restart function on his MacBook, and the screen jerks to life—eukaryotic cells, accompanied by music that sounds like the death throes of a defective Dalek. I breathe. And, involuntarily, I glance over my shoulder at the eighteen faces in the dark behind me.

There's Margo Cantor and Jonathan Tran, gazing at each other with their strange moo-eyes, and Lucas Kelly, his school tie peeking through his open fly. In the back corner is the new guy, Damien Pagono, notable only for the fact that he is, once again, picking his nose with his pencil. Beside him is that dipshit who's always smiling at himself. His head is bent over his books, a curtain of dark hair obscuring all but one pale cheekbone.

I flick my eyes back to the smart board. Mitosis. Hoorah.

I'm not a prodigy—not in the true sense of the word. I didn't solve the Riemann hypothesis when I was a fetus or write symphonies when I was two or anything. But I *could* read before I could walk. And I understand numbers like I've been told other people understand regular language. I have no idea what my IQ is because my parents never wanted it tested. And frankly, I've never been that desperate to know.

In the words of my mum, I am "just a bit sharp," not "special" or "different."

In the words of Matt Smith, my favorite *Doctor Who* Doctor, "I think a lot. Sometimes it's hard to keep track."

But, here's the thing—for every former child genius who's attempting to cure cancer or build an intelligent sex-bot or whatever, there's another one living under a bridge, talking to their shoes and eating their own toenails. For every young prodigy winning a Nobel Prize or a Fields Medal, there are a dozen others who've sunk into nothingness, their promise evaporating like those has-been celebrities Mum likes to read about in *Who Weekly*.

And then, of course, there is my very favorite brilliant burnout.

Grigori Perelman should be, like, a math superhero. He should be living in a Russian penthouse with a gaggle of supermodels, or whatever it is that famous boys are supposed to dream of. He figured out the frigging Poincaré conjecture—the first person in history to solve this supposedly unsolvable problem. The Poincaré conjecture helped explain the very shape of the universe. In certain circles, this is considered to be a remarkable thing. In certain circles, Perelman should be a god.

What he should *not* be doing is living in a cockroach-infested apartment with his mum, shunning his career and math and personal hygiene—becoming a hermit who turned down the *million-dollar* prize for cracking a puzzle that had some of the best minds in the world stumped. Not even Elsie, who geeks out over bizarre medical stories, appreciates the magnitude of this.

I read an article about Perelman in a journal over the summer. Strangely, that was around the time my panic attacks began.

I *so* should not have mentioned any of this to my parents. Because now, the curriculum of my final year of high school—on the school counselor's recommendation, after consultation with my mum and dad—includes year-twelve Drama.

It's supposed to be "cathartic."

It's supposed to help my "current mental state" by forcing me to do something that "lies outside my skill set."

It's supposed to be "fun."

So instead of using my free time for useful things like sleeping, or actually trying to *solve* the Riemann hypothesis, I have to stand on stage in the dilapidated Arts building, pretending to be a tree while trying desperately to emote.

Elsie taps her pen on the desk, snapping my focus. "You're okay, Rey," she mutters. I think it's a statement, not a question.

I close my eyes, and I breathe. I am okay. But I'm supposed to be more than okay.

I am supposed to be *extraordinary*.

The bell rings. The lights go on. The half of the class that is awake bolts; everyone else drags themselves blearily to their feet. I shake off my maudlin navel-gazing and swing myself from my stool.

Elsie gathers her things. Damien Pagono passes us while humming the chorus of "Brown Sugar," grinning at Elsie and giving her a wink that she has categorically defined as "skeezy." Evidently, our complete lack of response to the last half a dozen times he has serenaded us with songs about brown girls has not lessened his enthusiasm. Elsie and I have discussed this at length, but we still can't decide whether it's racist. As usual, we both ignore him.

"Another week down. Sixteen to go." Elsie tucks her books into her bag. "So. Are you really okay?"

I struggle into my blazer as the class jostles around me, a swirling vortex of polyester and wool. "Yes. I'm fine. Just... had a moment."

"Sure, okay. Any reason why your moments seem to be happening more frequently lately?" she asks carefully.

"Is this your attempt at an official diagnosis, Doctor Nayer?" I say, straightening out my uniform.

Elsie raises an eyebrow. "When I'm head of cardiology at a flashy hospital, I'll remind you that you used *doctor* so belittleishly."

I didn't mean to sound so crabby, and I don't *think* she's actually annoyed, but just to be safe I say, "I'm sorry, Els. I'm just...tired."

Elsie picks up my chewed pencil, which has somehow ended up on the floor. "Sophia, go home. Watch TV. Tomorrow will still be tomorrow, tomorrow."

I force a smile. "Fortune cookie?"

She grins.

"Nope. Quote-of-the-day loo paper."

"So the best advice you can offer me is from the toilet? Is that supposed to be a metaphor for my life?"

Elsie reaches behind me, briefly, and untwists the strap of my bag. "Metaphorical toilet or not, Rey, I think, all things considered, you should take your inspiration wherever you can find it."

I grab the TARDIS wallet that holds my pens and pull back the zipper.

There is a card in my pencil case.

It is smooth and new-looking, blue with a silver pattern of swirls and stars on one side. A standard poker-sized playing card. (Sixty-three by eighty-eight millimeters. I don't know how I know this fact.)

I flip the card over.

On the reverse is the two of hearts.

Elsie leans across the desk. "Are you taking up blackjack? We could make a fortune with your endetic memory."

"Eidetic. Elsie, this isn't mine. Is it yours?"

She snorts.

"Do I look like my Auntie Amita? I'll start playing cards when I develop that hormonal mustache."

I frown at the card. It stares back at me.

The two of hearts is contained within a finely drawn black hourglass. The top and bottom bulbs hold the red hearts, one pointing down and the other pointing up. In the middle of the bulbs, through the neck of the glass, a trickle of red sand joins the hearts together. It's simple. But sort of beautiful.

"Elsie, seriously, how did this get here?"

She sighs. "Sophia, don't fixate. It's just a card." She tugs at her ponytail, black waves bouncing—her "annoyed" sign that I know means she is ending this conversation. "I gotta get to band practice. You sure you're okay?"

I shake myself out of my stupor. "Yes. I'm fine. I'll see you tonight?"

"Yup. Need help with Physics homework. And Math. And I've got more brochures for campus accommodation that we *need* to evaluate. Seriously, if we don't choose wisely, I'm gonna end up in a dorm with a bunch of toothy American cheerleaders. Or worse—the Bible kids." She throws me one of her wide smiles and skips out of the lab before I can respond.

Donkey balls. I am *so* not in the mood for Elsie's future planning tonight.

I glance at the card again.

It really is pretty. I guess the sand is supposed to be spilling from one side of the hourglass to the other, but there's no way to tell in which direction. It's a perfect palindromic image: mirrored hearts keeping some impossible, immobile time. But...

My pencil case has been sitting in front of me, zipped shut, for the entire hour and twenty minutes of the class. I have not moved. No one has approached me.

Fact: This card is not mine. This card is not Elsie's. It was not here at the beginning of the lesson. There is no logical way it could have slipped into my pencil case.

I flip the card over.

The two of hearts...

Intriguing.

Chapter Two

The Paradox of Time Travel

I bolt home from the bus through one of those sideways rainstorms that no amount of umbrella calisthenics can thwart. I've lived in Melbourne my whole life, but the weather still freaks me out; blue-sky mornings that descend into gusty gray by lunch, as if the city is suffering from some chronic mood disorder.

I stumble through our side door and into the freezing kitchen. My brother is camped at the dining table, skinny frame huddled inside his parka. I can see condensation in his breath; his lips are tinged blue. Toby recently acquired a Finnish exchange student as an Economics study partner, and he's been filling my big brother's head with all sorts of nonsense about memory conversion and thermoregulation—nothing with much scientific basis that I can find, but regardless, thanks to Viljami, we're no longer allowed to use the heater during exam time.

Toby's books are spread in front of him. His black hair is slipping slightly out of its side part, and a third of his polo shirt has come untucked from his pants. I suspect that he must be extra-stressed. My brother, normally, would never let himself look so rock star.

He startles as the door slams behind me. For a second, I almost think he looks pained, like that time Dad accidentally clipped him in the nuts with a mini-golf putter. He quickly rearranges his expression into unreadable blankness.

"Hey," he says. He opens his mouth, then closes it again.

"Hey," I reply. I drop my dripping things on the kitchen floor, swiping wet hair from my eyes.

Toby straightens his pens. "Good day?" he mumbles.

"Yes. Fine. It was...school." I glance at Dad's souvenir magnets and photos of the Sri Lankan cricket team on the fridge. They don't seem to have anything to contribute to this conversation.

My brother and I have always been useless at sports, but Dad likes to say that if there was a doubles division in the Awkwardness Olympics, Toby and I would be gold medal shoo-ins. Dad also likes to say that comic relief is the best cure for hostility and tension. I am fairly certain no one else in our house is on board with this theory.

Toby taps at his laptop. "Did Mum text you? She and Dad are at Auntie Helen's again. Apparently there's some new crisis with Nisha's wedding decorations. Mum's left, like, eight kilos of chicken pasta in the fridge. And money for pizza." He sniffs. "Just in case I'm incapable of working the microwave, I suppose."

Toby tugs an exercise book toward him, and I think this is my cue to leave. Thing is though, I've never been able to resist a puzzle. And despite my efforts, the conundrum of my brother remains frustratingly unsolved.

"So you staying in? Whatcha working on?"

I glance at his upside-down notebook. I'm not sure what "competitive equilibrium" is, but, upside-down, it's obvious that his last answer is totally wrong.

Toby does this double take when he catches me peeking. I'm useless at deciphering body language, and when it comes to my brother's, I have only the vaguest of theories. Elsie is convinced that one day we're going to arrive home to catch Toby decked out in leather and Viljami trussed up like a Christmas ham, but—ignoring the disgustingness of imagining my brother engaged in any sort of sex antics—I think the only thing we're in danger of interrupting is one of Toby and Viljami's marathon debates about tax law.

"Gonna tell me where I've messed up?" he asks without looking at me.

The correct answer is on the tip of my tongue, before I run another set of calculations in my head. Factoring in Toby's tone of voice and the scowl he is aiming at his papers, I conclude that his question is probably rhetorical.

"No," I answer. "Your last three steps are wrong. I'm sure you'll figure it out."

I congratulate myself on my diplomacy as I grab a pear and drag my feet to my bedroom.

I love my room. It's my only real haven, my very own isolation chamber that hasn't changed much since I was five—a yellowing prime numbers poster stuck to the wall beside my bed; glow-in-the-dark stars in constellations of the southern sky that Toby helped me stick to my ceiling a lifetime ago; a brilliant picture that reads: *Time Travel Club*

Begins Yesterday. And my favorite find of all—a faded canvas of van Gogh's *Starry Night* with a cobalt TARDIS swirling among the stars, even though both Mum and Elsie claimed it was "tacky."

My bedroom is *mine*, unlike the rest of my life, which feels like it was built for a person whose existence is, at best, theoretical.

I haul my bag onto my desk and collapse into my chair. The movement jolts the mouse, kicking my computer to life. I notice, with a little heart-jump, that there is a solitary email sitting in my inbox.

With a deep breath, I click on the message from the St. Petersburg Steklov Institute of Mathematics. The subject line is in choppy Cyrillic: Grigori Perelman.

I glance at the printout on the pin board above my desk, the most recent photo anyone has managed to capture of Perelman. It's grainy and slightly out of focus. Dark eyes under bushy eyebrows peer hopelessly into the distance of a gloomy Russian street. He looks like a lost, bearded yeti.

Like so many of my kind, the prevailing opinion is that he is both brilliant and batshit crazy.

I *need* to talk to this guy.

Although I've been studying it for a whole three months, my Russian is still a bit sketchy. I open my Russian dictionary in a separate window on my screen, switch to the Cyrillic function, then read through the email.

Dear Ms. Reyhart,

Thank you for your continuing interest.

Unfortunately, I'm afraid that we still cannot help.

Perelman has not worked with us for years. He does not talk to academics. He does not talk to other mathematicians. He most definitely does not talk to journalists. I think we can surmise that he will not talk to high school girls.

It is his choice to remain incommunicado, and we must ask that you, like us, respect this decision.

Best of luck with your future endeavors.

Balls. I don't know what else I was expecting.

I push my chair back with a sigh.

Music from Toby's easy listening playlist drifts down the corridor, muffled by the rain on my window. I examine my room and consider my options: do the last bit of Calculus homework from the first-year college course I've been allowed to take online, or battle my way through the end of a romance movie Elsie lent me, even though the little I'd watched made my brain hurt. I know that the theoretical underpinnings of time travel are beyond most Hollywood movies, but even so, a time-traveling mailbox at a random lake house is just stupid.

Stacked on my desk are my last two issues of *Pi in the Sky* magazine, still in their shrink-wrap. And on top of the pile, my nemesis: the *Drama Solo Performance Examination Guide*. I pick it up. My chest heaves. I put it down again.

I change into my old flannel shirt, then stretch out on my bed and take a nap.

I'm not sure how much time passes. But when my eyes jolt open, the last of the daylight has disappeared, and elephantine feet are thundering down the corridor. Elsie bursts into my bedroom, arms loaded with books.

She's swapped her school uniform for a black coat over her favorite Starfig Soles T-shirt and a tiny red skirt that could, conceivably, pass as a belt. She dumps her things on my desk and collapses onto my bed.

"I see Tobias is having another spectacular Friday night," she says breathlessly. "Rey, does your brother even have working parts down there? 'Cause the evidence would seem to suggest he's smooth, like a Ken doll."

I shake myself awake. "Elsie, can you please stop making me imagine my brother's junk? My counselor already has plenty to work with." I glance sideways at the goose pimples on the dark skin of her legs. "What are you wearing?"

Elsie struggles out of her coat. She hands me a box of apple juice. "New skirt. You like?"

"Sure. Did you lose the other half?" Elsie rolls her eyes. "Yeah, thanks Auntie Lakshmi. Should I expect a lecture about cows and free milk next?" She reaches over and tugs off the school tie that I didn't realize was still knotted around my neck. "Besides, where else can I wear it? It's either your place or Sunday lunch at my nana's." She yanks her hair out of its ponytail, waves cascading over my bedspread as she flops onto her back again. "Though, now that I think about it, I did hear that Trevor Pine is having a party tonight. Feel like getting wasted and Snapchatting pics of your duck lips?"

I shudder. "Can you imagine?"

Elsie giggles. "Yeah. You and I would walk through the doors, and it'd be like a bad western movie. The piano would stop. Guys would leap out of their chairs, hands grabbing their guns. Ugh—did that sound like a willy metaphor?"

I groan. "And now I'm imagining Trevor Pine's willy. Thanks, Elsie."

Elsie laughs again. She taps her feet, her wriggly body settling into place. "We *could* consider it a social experiment," she says eventually. "You know, study the locals in their natural environment and all that? It's...been a while since we've done that." Elsie grins, but this doesn't make her eyes crinkle at the edges like her normal smiles do.

The idea of enforced socialization makes my toes start to sweat. I've evaded enough family events lately that my parents now only insist on weddings, funerals, and christenings, and I usually spend those hiding somewhere with my cousin Oscar, who is obsessed with fantasy podcasts and only speaks Dothraki. What do people even do at normal parties? The last one I remember semi-enjoying involved face painting and a morbidly obese clown.

"Yes, well, it's lucky we weren't invited," I say. "I don't think I'm up for partying with a bunch of people who hate my guts."

Elsie sits up. She smooths back her hair and proceeds to braid it into a rope. "They don't hate you. They think you're a giant freakazoid, true, but otherwise? They're probably just scared you're some sort of mechanized fem-bot from the future." Elsie gives me a wide, proper Elsie-smile as she leaps off the bed and grabs my Drama guide. "So, how's this going? You figured out how to mime a convincing tree yet?" She dissolves into snorty laughter.

"I'm glad you find my pain entertaining."

"Oh come on, it's a bit entertaining. I mean—" she opens the course book to an arbitrary page—"'Create a solo performance based on the character of Pinocchio.' Is this a life skill that's in demand?"

I bury my face in my bedspread. "Elsie, I know! Why did I agree to this?"

The bed dips as she sits down beside me, a careful hand-width away. "You agreed because your folks gave you hopeful-eyes, and you are secretly a giant sap." I peek at her through splayed fingers. Elsie's face is suddenly serious. "Sophia, the average female lifespan is, what, about eighty-four years or something?"

"Barring congenital defects or getting hit by a bus? Yes, I think so. Why?"

"Because the solo performance is seven minutes long. Seven minutes, Sophia. Not enough time for a shower or even a decent kiss."

I snort. "How would you know?"

"I shower," she says dryly. "And seven minutes is, like, .003 percent of your year or something."

"More like point-oh-oh-oh-oh-two," I answer. I have a feeling I may be missing her point.

Elsie rolls her eyes. "You are willfully missing my point, Reyhart!"

I can't help but smile a little. "So what is it then, Nayer?"

"My *point*, oh obtuse one, is that in the grand scheme of the universe, the exam will be a breeze. You'll do it, you'll either ace it or not, and then it'll be over."

I close my eyes. "Elsie, I've started dreaming about that stupid Arts building. Is that normal?"

Elsie stares at me for a long moment. Her expression suggests that perhaps she is worried, though it's a bit hard to tell under the layers of after-school makeup. She finally points to the juice in my hand. "No psychoanalysis tonight. Drink. Help me find a place to live next year that's not straight out of a *Girls Gone Wild* video."

She jumps off my bed again and grabs a pile of brochures, fanning them out on my bedspread. A booklet on top features a bunch of people in matching jerseys and a banner that reads, somewhat portentously: *The First Year*. And the gloom that's been threatening to envelop me all week settles with a thud in my stomach.

Years ago, Elsie's favorite uncle moved to America to take up a residency at some small research hospital. Ever since Elsie visited him when she was fourteen, Emory University School of Medicine, Atlanta, Georgia, has been her unwavering goal. I know how single-minded my best friend can be. But still, I think part of me has always expected her to change her mind.

"Els, don't you think it's premature to be looking at dorms? You're not in yet."

"Technicality," she replies cheerfully. She eyeballs me again, then sighs. "Fine, okay. Anyway, unless I ace this Physics exam, the only place I'll be doing pre-med is at the online university of suburban Tajikistan. And since we're clearly not partying or Snapchatting any duck faces tonight, I guess we're studying."

I swap the brochures for books, trying not to smile too triumphantly. It occurs to me that—barring a few of my

Friday-night college seminars and Elsie's band recitals—this is pretty much how we have spent most of our Fridays for the past ten years.

"Thanks, Elsie."

She sits cross-legged on the end of my bed. "Yeah. You're lucky Bernoulli's principle sucks both arse *and* balls. But I am calling dibs on the movie after. Be warned, there will be *tons* of kissing in it."

I open my book to the homework I've left unfinished. It's not like I ever deliberately slow down so Elsie can keep up or anything; it's just, every now and then, it's really nice to have someone to work alongside. I can't explain why, but the blustery squall that my thoughts can whip themselves into just feels *quieter* when Elsie is around. Since we were kids, Elsie has accepted all my strangeness the same way she responds to any of the random strange factoids she collects—with cheerful objectiveness. It's one of the things I love most about her.

Fact: Elsie Nayer is the smartest non-freak I know. And even though she sometimes checks her answers with me, Elsie rarely needs my help.

So we work. Figures and formulas occupy the only segments of my brain that, for the moment at least, I know I can truly rely on. It's like wrapping myself in a well-worn blanket, comfortable and familiar and certain. The ever-present tension between my shoulder blades lifts; the sensation of being somehow misaligned inside my skin disappears. As the stubborn patterns in the numbers resolve into answers before my eyes, for the first time today I feel the sparks of something like happiness. Because I may be hopeless at life in general, but *this* thing I can do.

From the corner of my eye, I watch the hands on my wall clock, pacing myself so as not to fill our time too fast. I try to steer our intermittent conversation to safe ground—rumors of our Chem teacher's plastic surgery, possible future developments on *Doctor Who*—but Elsie, like always lately, keeps drifting to America and her plans for next year. I see her eyes flick to her brochures more than once, and before the ink is dry on our final equation, her hands reach for the glossy pile. I have no desire to ruin my precarious contented mood, so I chime in quickly with the only game that I know will reliably distract my best friend.

I polish off my apple juice and give her my best attempt at an irreverent smile. "So what am I going to be when I grow up, Elsie?"

Elsie stares at me with her faux thinking face. "Labrador trainer," she says decisively. "You'll have your own TV show in Japan, one of those wacky ones where the audience gets to throw food and eels at you. It'll be great!"

"Dog whisperer could be fun," I reply vaguely.

Elsie closes her textbook with a thump. "Look, Sophia, I have a crazy idea. Just hear me out, okay?"

"Ugh, you're not going to make me try out for band again, are you?"

"Nah, I can live without hearing you attempt 'Purple Haze' on the recorder again. No, what I was going to say is: Melbourne University's open day is tomorrow, and I think we should go. I mean, I'm not applying, but maybe it'd be good for you? A bunch of people from Augustine's are going. Mr. Peterson drew the short straw of supervising a group. He was grousing about it at lunch, but I think he's secretly excited to be showing off his old stomping ground."

"Els, I've been to Melbourne Uni plenty of times. I don't need to—"

"You don't need to hang out with mere mortals? Yeah, I get it. But think about this—you get out of the house and make your parents happy, and we get dumplings on our way home. Win-win."

"Elsie—"

Elsie's eyes flitter away. "Hey, Rey? Listen, I know I don't exactly get what's going on in your head lately. Maybe I've been caught up with my own stuff or whatever, but it feels like I blinked and, well…" She smiles, a little too brightly. "Your charmingly weird self has *kind of* taken a turn in the direction of eccentric-ville." She touches my arm, not even wavering when I flinch. "But, see, this doesn't have to be a big deal! I mean, Sophia—it's not like you can be any *less* inspired."

I don't know why the idea of doing one stupid university open day makes my heart beat faster than it should. I don't know how to explain to Elsie that *inspiration* isn't exactly my problem. And I *really* don't know how to explain that I am fully aware I'm veering in the direction of "eccentric-ville," but I feel like I'm on a one-way road, and I can't seem to find an off-ramp.

But I also don't know why I keep forgetting that with Elsie, the path of least resistance is usually the path least painful.

"Okay. You're right, it's not a big deal. Let's go."

Elsie bounces on my bed, her tiny skirt hitching even further upward. "Hooray! Chinatown dumplings, cute college boys. It's going to be great!"

I force a smile. "Yes. Great. Hoorah," I say weakly.

We finish our homework, then heat up leftover pasta and watch one of the romance movies that Elsie loves, the plot of which I find somewhat questionable, though it *still* makes infinitely more sense than Keanu Reeves and his time wormhole inside a mailbox. I can't help but feel this curious relief that I can still, albeit unintentionally, make Els crack up laughing with my movie commentary. Not that I always understand what she finds so funny, but every time she giggles, I'm convinced I've been imagining the weird new undercurrent of tension between us.

And then Rajesh, my favorite of Elsie's brothers, picks her up at eleven, and I am left alone in my silent, changeless bedroom.

I shower and climb into bed. At some point I hear my parents' cars return home and pipes creak in the bathroom. Toby's door clicks shut across the hall, and silence settles over the house. Meanwhile, me and my brain are locked in our nightly battle:

So. College. This should be interesting. Wonder if we can induce that impending mental collapse ahead of schedule? You could be, like, the Phantom of the Opera of the Math faculty.

Shut up. Shut. Up.

Sixteen weeks, Sophia! Sixteen weeks—that's two thousand, six hundred and eighty-eight hours. Goodbye, high school.

Damien Pagono almost got expelled for posting a selfie of his testicles on the school webpage, and even he's probably better prepared for the world than you.

Sleep. Sleeeeep.

Do you know that "forty" is the only number with its letters in alphabetical order? Do you know that the average person spends six months of their life on the toilet? Do you know that the King of Hearts is the only king in a deck of cards who doesn't have a mustache?

I sit up.

I climb out of bed, robotically, and slide the mysterious playing card from my pencil case. The sand seems to waver in the watery moonlight, an illusion that almost gives the impression of movement. I turn the card over. The weak light glimmers across the silvery stars on the other side.

I will never understand what makes me do this, but I move my Perelman photograph a few inches to the left and pin the card on my board, just below my ticket for last summer's seminar on Deutsch's theory of time travel, which seems a strangely appropriate place for a suspended hourglass.

I crawl back into bed and tuck my blankets around my face, my eyes lingering on the two of hearts. From this distance, Perelman's inscrutable eyes seem fixed on the card too. In the dark, I can almost imagine that his eyes are just as perturbed.

I'm not completely crazy. I mean, I understand that even if any of the most obscure quantum mechanical theories of time travel were possible, you'd most likely end up as your own grandmother or, like, triggering a universe-unraveling paradox—at best, getting trapped in a ridiculous causality loop, a hapless billiard ball bouncing in an eternal circuit through time and space.

I am not crazy. Not properly.

Not yet, anyway.

But the ability to know where I'm going? Having more than one chance to get it right?

That would be nice.

♦

Chapter Three

The Theory of Gravitation

I've spent heaps of time at Melbourne University over the years, but I don't think I've ever seen it buzz quite like this. Elsie and I step off the tram in front of the main entrance, Rajesh bouncing behind us. Elsie and Raj stand aside, presumably for me to catch my breath, but before I can recover from the press and mash of the tram, I'm smacked in the face by a giant spray of balloons. The color, the college's signature almost-TARDIS blue, should probably be comforting, but somehow it's anything but.

"Sorry, mate," the guy attached to the balloons says. "Latex injuries are an occupational hazard." He smiles at me, all facial scruff and confidence. Under his jacket he's wearing a T-shirt with a picture of a pipe and some French words in cursive. My head is light and my French is rusty, but I think the slogan translates as: *this is not a hipster shirt*. Although the thought of catching the crowded tram again makes me queasy, it takes every bit of my willpower not to bolt back onto the idling behemoth and head home.

Elsie and Raj hover beside me, a Nayer on either side. Balloon-guy's eyes travel over Elsie's tiny denim skirt under her black winter coat. "Lemme guess, you're a Life Drawing model? Arts building's thattaway," he says to her legs.

Raj whistles. Elsie gives balloon-guy a wide, toothy smile, even as her eyes narrow. "I'll keep that in mind," she says sweetly, and loudly, in French. "If I ever need to brush up on deviant sexuality in film noir, or whatever."

The guy looks at her blankly. Elsie points to his shirt. "*Tu ne parles pas français*? Sorry, I just assumed that someone with your deductive reasoning skills would understand his own shirt."

Elsie pulls me away before he has a chance to respond. "Remind me again why we have no friends?" I say, biting back a smile.

Elsie shakes her head with a lopsided grin. "Because you're a socially inept freakazoid, and I think everyone's annoying. Besides, that doofus looks exactly like someone who'd be buddies with Colin. Pretty sure he took that film noir course last semester, right Raj?"

Raj throws an arm loosely around her shoulder. "Does watching Netflix with no pants on count as studying? Dunno whose genes for slothfulness our big brother inherited."

"Who even knew it was possible to fail Cultural Studies?" Elsie says with a laugh. "Only Colin could get watching TV wrong."

At a glance, Raj and Toby could easily pass for siblings. They're both skinny, with skin the same shade of brown, and the same inability to competently kick, hit, or throw any kind of sporting projectile. Yet unlike my taciturn brother, Raj has never been anything but warm. He's always chatty, and, apart from me, he is Elsie's best friend in the world. There are moments though when I still find their relationship... confusing.

"'Kay, Raj, time to piss off," Elsie says. "I believe you said you had some books to borrow, and I need a few hours away from your ugly face."

Raj grins. "Sure you don't want my expertise? Or a chaperone for all those skeezy Engineering dudes? My giant guns gotta come in handy for something." He flexes his spindly arms where no guns of any kind are apparent.

Elsie snorts. "Yeah, and if you'd spent your first year here doing anything remotely cool, I might've taken you up on that. I'll call you if we need help finding the 'Magic: The Gathering' fan club, otherwise, I think we'll be all right."

Raj zips his jacket up to the neck. "It's on the second floor of Union House. But whatevs." He drops a fleeting kiss on Elsie's cheek. "Text me when you're heading back. Have fun, ladies."

Raj disappears into the crowd. I am still blinking at the space he has vacated when Elsie makes a grandiose gesture toward the entrance. "Your future awaits, Sophia! Come on."

We walk through the tangle of people, grabbing a couple of showbags on our way in. Elsie immediately starts stuffing them with brochures gathered from various stands. Music is booming from somewhere on campus. To me, it sounds like it's coming from every direction at once. As Elsie pauses in front of the Math building, I resist the urge to cover my ears.

"So the Augustine's crew are meeting at the main library. We're late, but I'm guessing Peterson will still be boring everyone senseless with his complete history of everything. Should we head over?" She grabs a flyer from a volunteer. "Hey, there's a statistics seminar on soon. Isn't that, like, crack to you?"

I wrap my scarf around my face, the biting cold numbing my nose. A guy jogs past, followed by an older lady. "Most of my subjects will be in here," he tells her as he passes. I can't help but wonder what he's applying for, what path he has mapped out that lets him move with such conviction.

I have no idea why I let myself get talked into this. "Elsie, can't we just wander around? Just you and me?"

Elsie glances at the building. Her eyes linger on a group of laughing people tossing a Frisbee near the doors. She turns to me again and smiles, but I think I also hear her sigh a little bit.

"Sure, Sophia. Let's just hang out on our own. As always." She brightens. "Hey, Raj said the Medical Museum's open. Want to go check out cadavers?"

I dig out the activities program and reach into the depths of my new drama skills for some sham enthusiasm. "There's food on the South Lawn. And, hey, the clubs and societies tables are there as well. Maybe we can check out the mahjong club or, oh, how about the breakdancing club?"

Elsie barks out a laugh. "Sophia, I would happily donate a kidney to see you breakdance."

We wander toward the South Lawn. The campus is congested with people and marquees, a bandstand in the center. Behind us, the beautiful Old Arts building looms, its Gothic clock tower completely out of time and place with the smartphone-juggling multitudes.

I pause where the path meets the mushy, crowded lawn. Inadvertently, I have looped my arm through Elsie's showbag, and I'm holding onto it like it's a life preserver. I am crap with crowds, and this loud mob is making my stomach twist and tumble.

Elsie looks at me through one narrow eye, like she's considering me through a microscope. It's the same look she gave me in grade-four music, when she tiptoed into the corner where I was peacefully hiding and snuck a pair of maracas into my hands. I know how to interpret that look. It means her brain is circling through something that I am not going to appreciate.

"Okay, Sophia," she says slowly. "I know you're not really interested in biology, so I am going to go look at sliced dead people, and you are going to explore and try your best not to have an aneurism."

I balk. "But Elsie—"

"Rey, look around! There's music and food, and, see there, some juggling guys. And have you even noticed that the sky is clear for the first time in ages?" She plants her hands on her hips. "You're going to be fine. Just breathe. I'll be half an hour, and then we can find Raj and get those dumplings. But this is important, Sophia."

My eyes travel frantically over the chaos. "Why, Elsie? Because I'm suddenly going to decide that juggling is a skill I need to master?"

"No. Because I need to know that you'll be okay on your own after I'm gone." Elsie nods decisively. And then she gives me a brief one-armed hug before she takes a few steps away and is lost in the crowd.

Neither one of us is a hugger, nor a crier. But for some reason, Elsie's fleeting grip makes me want to sit right down on the boggy grass and wail.

Of all my options at this moment, a mental collapse would probably not be the most productive one. I step into the mire and look helplessly around me.

There's a guy with a beard who's signing people up for the Juggling Society and a girl dressed inexplicably in a panda body suit. For a second I'm distracted by a guy standing in front of her. He's taking in the scene around him with this wide-eyed, out-of-his-depth look that, somehow, I recognize instantly. He's nice-looking, with curly hair and holey canvas shoes. He looks panda-girl up and down, then turns the badge she has flung at him over with a sharp burst of laughter. He shows it to the tall girl tucked beside him and she rolls her eyes, even though she's smiling. The girl is wearing a dress covered in prints of pink cupcakes and a red scarf wrapped elaborately around her hair. Even from a distance she projects that tangible confidence that typically makes me shrink. I watch them for a moment. I can't tell if they're a couple—unless two people are sucking face, I rarely can—but there's something about the two of them together that makes me feel inexplicably...lonely. I turn away as the girl grabs the curly-haired guy's hand and tugs him, still chuckling, past the panda.

To my right there's a line of people waiting for free popcorn and, as I turn, a group with Chinese Student Society sweaters pushes past, arms laden with pizza boxes.

And there is a boy staring right at me.

I glance over my shoulder. The band is behind me, a crowd milling in front of the stage. I turn back, but it's not the band he is looking at; he's staring, unmistakably, at me.

My brain registers the following:

Tall. Too tall, really, at least six- three or four. A battered leather satchel slung over his body, under a blue showbag, its flatness indicating that it's all but empty.

Brown corduroy pants, long-sleeved blue shirt, gray vest, tweed hat. I'm no fashion expert, but I'm pretty sure I've seen the busker near the supermarket wearing something similar.

I almost don't recognize him out of uniform. And for a second, I have the strangest suspicion that he is a bit startled. Then he sort-of-but-not-quite smiles. That vaguely familiar half-smile, not directed at anything perceptible in the universe around him.

Elsie and Raj are nowhere to be seen. The indifferent crowd near the stage seems to have decided that this is, in fact, the greatest band in history and should be venerated with frenetic dancing in the mud. When I look back, busker-boy is walking toward me.

Balls balls *balls*. Okay. Preemptive strike followed by a quick escape.

I hug my jacket tightly around me. He comes to a stop a few feet away.

"I know you," I say quickly. "Are you here with Mr.

Peterson? I thought he was with the Specialist Math group. I haven't seen you in Specialist, though."

He doesn't speak. The silence stretches far enough for the rising warmth in my cheeks to become perceptible, even through the chill. He folds his hands behind his back and does this wriggly maneuver, like he's subtly adjusting his shoulders. He drops his gaze from the place where it's been hovering above my head. He takes a deep breath.

"Well, I'm barely scraping a passable grade in Finkler's Further Math. I mean, science I don't mind, but I've never really had a head for numbers. It's like, have you ever stared at one of those awesome illusion pictures? You know, you blur your eyes and, if you're lucky, a picture jumps out. And maybe you see a spaceship or the face of Albert Einstein or a dinosaur, but then, you look away for a sec and when you look back there's nothing but colors again? That's kinda like me with math. An occasional stegosaurus. But mostly, it's mangled chaos that I'm pretty sure was created by a guy on 'shrooms."

I stare at him.

He clears his throat. Then he grins. "Ah, yeah. I was with Mr. Peterson's group," he says brightly.

I tuck my hands into my armpits. "Right, well," I stammer. "Don't let me keep you. I'm just—"

"—Sophia." He takes off the hat and tucks his dark hair behind his ears. "You're Sophia," he says, as if this statement holds some significance that I should be aware of. He smiles as he settles the hat back onto his head. "I'm Joshua."

He holds out a hand, formally, like he's Mum's accountant here to discuss my taxes.

I glare at his hand, warring with panic over touching a stranger, worried that my shoes are now encased in mud and I will be stuck in this situation until Elsie comes to rescue me. With limited options, I take his hand, just the tips of his fingers, for a handshake that seems to last less than a unit of Planck time.

"Ah—it's nice to meet you?" he says.

The icy wind is doing nothing to cool my cheeks. Even with an eidetic memory, I can't recall the last conversation I had with someone from school who wasn't Elsie; probably because anybody who isn't Elsie tends to avoid me like I'm lugging a chunk of plutonium in my pocket.

Busker-boy—Joshua—tilts his head, his feet shuffling slightly in the mud. I note, dimly, that the fingers of his left hand seem to be tapping out a shallow rhythm on his leg, a pattern that is only noticeable because his right hand seems to be drumming a totally different beat.

He tucks his hands into his pockets. "You know, a bunch of scientists have managed to teach apes some basic language skills. Okay, their conversations weren't exactly profound—and involved more feces-hurling than I'd be comfortable with—but I reckon if Washoe the chimp can learn to carry a conversation, anyone can." He beams at me.

I gape at him. His words tap dance over one another, smooth and practiced, but like a song played at slightly too fast a speed. And I can't be sure, but I think I catch the tiniest hitch in his pronunciation.

"Who is supposed to be the ape in this scenario?" I blurt.

His cheeks redden. "Ah, I didn't mean…I mean, neither.

Or both? I don't think it's offensive. I can easily be bribed with bananas."

There it is. His deepish voice carries a shadow of a lisp.

Across the lawn, the band kicks into a song the crowd seems to know, and a strident cheer snaps me out of my fugue. Suddenly, I've run out of steam. I'm cold and abruptly aware of just how loud it is here—how the chaos pervades even the edges of my vision. I can feel the wash of prickles traveling over my skin, and the tiny fingers of doom emerging from that place somewhere deep beneath my breastbone. I bury my face in my scarf and pour all my mental energy into breathing.

Joshua's eyes flicker over my face, his expression more baffling than is customary for me. He rocks back on his heels, widening the distance between us.

"My dad, unfortunately, read about this thing in the school newsletter," he says offhandedly. "So I kinda got browbeaten into it. But then, like, only four other people showed up, and Peterson launched into this diatribe about the 'cavalier attitude of youth,' which I think might've been a bit much even for my dad. So I ditched them. I was just checking out the Society for Creative Anachronism. It's a medieval club. They have some awesome clubs and societies here. It's like, the future leaders of Australia need to be prepared to drink beer in an organized manner, and, you know...joust."

"Juggling also seems to be heavily featured," I say absentmindedly.

He glances at the juggling guy and chuckles. "Yeah. You'd be surprised at how popular that is."

Joshua is rocking on his heels, backward and forward, long fingers still tapping. I'm not sure if his movements have had some kind of hypnotic effect, but even though my stomach still feels sketchy, the fight-or-flight response has dissipated a little.

I hug my bags. "Okay, well, I should go—"

But Joshua is looking over my shoulder. His face contorts. "Uh-oh," he mumbles, that swish of color emerging across his cheeks again.

The breeze has picked up, sending pamphlets careening past us. Joshua shifts his empty showbag from one shoulder to the other.

"Look, I know this is a weird thing to ask, but do you think you could hang here for one sec? I could use some backup."

"Backup? What—"

An older guy, his windswept hair streaked with gray, appears from behind me. His hands are laden with course guides and bags.

"Jeez, this place has changed. I was trying to find the spot where the gang used to play hacky sack, back in the day. Can you believe they actually have a KFC now? My friends would have been apoplectic."

The man clasps Joshua on the arm with a big, bright smile. Joshua shoots me a look of desperation—one that I recognize only because I've seen it in my own face, most recently in the Drama room mirrors when I was forced to read Bottom in *A Midsummer Night's Dream*.

The old guy beams. "Hey there! Are you a soon-to-be

Augustine's alumni too? We never get a chance to meet Josh's friends."

Joshua turns those pleading eyes on me. Christ. Like my own issues aren't enough to deal with.

"Yes. I'm Sophia. It's nice to meet you, Mr., um...?"

The crevasses at the corners of the older guy's eyes deepen as he smiles. He holds out a hand, not seeming too fazed when I look at it without shaking. "It's Alex. Mr. Bailey is my father." He winks. "Give me a heads-up if you see a misanthropic old man ranting about the Boer Wars in my vicinity."

I look to Joshua for further direction, but he seems to have become fascinated by something behind my head.

Alex—Joshua's father, I'm going to take a stab at inferring—glances around. "Gillian?"

Joshua gestures with his head. "Skulking in the art gallery. She said she'll text me when she's done."

"Right. Hope you confiscated her Sharpies?"

Joshua grins. It doesn't seem forced or fake, as far as I can tell, but then his smile wavers as his dad passes him the handful of brochures. "So I've been checking out the Arts faculty. Do you know there's *eight* different first-year History subjects you can pick from? How cool is that?"

"Cool," Joshua answers. He shuffles his feet, two small scuffs for each foot. But then he smiles at his dad again, and his dad smiles back. I'm not picking up anything hostile; nothing to account for Joshua's oddness, or the need for my presence.

"So, Sophia," his dad says cheerfully. "What are you applying for?"

Joshua gives me a cryptic look.

I swallow. My standard answer is that I plan to study mathematical physics and then specialize in Riemannian geometry, which is generally a safe answer as hardly anyone I meet understands what that is. But when I open my mouth the words that tumble out are:

"I don't know. I have no idea."

Joshua's dad's smile seems to dim. "Right. Well, I'm sure you'll...figure it out."

Joshua looks at me for a long moment. "That makes sense," he says simply.

I stare back at him. "Are you being sarcastic? I can't really tell."

He gives me a faint smile. "Nope. No sarcasm."

His dad's eyes bounce between us. "Well, I should go find my daughter before she incites a riot in the gallery. Nice to meet you, Sophia. Josh—meet you at the Law talk?" He thumps Joshua on the shoulder before walking away.

I shake myself out of my daze. "Okay, I *really* need to go now. There's, ah, a lecture in the Statistics department I want to catch." I have zero intention of attending a stats lecture. I do have every intention of going home and crawling into bed with *Doctor Who*, the Patrick Troughton years.

Joshua glances at his watch. I hadn't noticed it before, though I don't know how I managed to miss it. It's huge—a thick leather band with a chrome face full of pulleys and gears. "I should go too. I guess Dad's waiting. And I'm meeting some friends in a bit."

"From school?" I say, scrambling for small talk.

"Nah. Not from school. I don't have friends at school." I don't think he's embarrassed or wistful. Just, like, it's not a big deal at all.

The breeze picks up, and I'm suddenly enveloped by the cold that I seemed to have forgotten.

Joshua tips his hat, long hair billowing around his face. "And all Washoe managed was 'hello' and 'please give shoes.'" He steps away. "See you later, Sophia. I think I heard your phone ring."

I whip my mobile out of the pocket of my jacket, but I have no missed calls or messages. I slide the phone back, and my hand closes around something else.

It's a coin, but not any coin that belongs in my pocket.

It's large and bronze and weirdly smooth, like someone has run their fingers across its surface over and over again. It's American, if the Abraham Lincoln face and the word "Liberty" are any indication, but it's of no currency that I can decipher. I flip the coin over. The severe Lincoln face and the "Liberty" inscription are mirrored on the other side.

I spin around, eyes traveling over the laughing, smiling people.

But when I turn to the space where Joshua last was, there is nothing but a lone girl in a soggy panda suit and a giant pile of course guides stacked neatly in the mud.

♥

Chapter Four

There is nothing worse than good magic at the wrong time.

—David Roth

I show up late to work, after jumping on the wrong tram and then almost walking face-first into a lamppost. It's one of those awesomely awesome winter days, all clear skies and crisp, chill breeze, and it kinda feels like the whole world is smiling. A cute kid in front of me turns around and giggles, probably 'cause I'm whistling a song from *Frozen*. I tip my hat and sing the chorus at the top of my lungs. The kid cheers before his laughing mum bundles him away.

My boss has just about finished setting up our stall. Not even her face, as murderous as if someone blow-torched her favorite Doc Martens, can dampen my mood. The smell of coffee and sugary doughnuts hangs in the air. Behind the market, the medieval buildings of the Abbotsford Convent loom.

Amy nods at me as I make my way behind the stall. She's sporting a heavy fur coat that kinda looks like wildebeest hide and a giant bruise on her right cheek.

"Josh. Nice hat."

I dip the cap I inherited from my grandpa. “Amy. Nice bruise. Should I even ask how the game went?”

Amy sighs. “Yeah. We lost again, and our best jammer’s gonna be out for months thanks to a dislocated knee. I’m scheduling extra training on the off chance it might mean we start sucking a little less hard. You free to work Wednesday?”

I grab a box of juggling batons and start stacking them on the table. Vaguely, I remember that I’ve got a paper thingy due on Thursday for Legal Studies that I haven’t even looked at yet. Or maybe it was a test. Man, was it even for Legal?

“Sure. Wednesday? Can do.”

Amy gives me the hint of a smile. “You’re a superstar, Joshua Bailey. Let no one tell you otherwise.”

Amy Avril—who also goes by the roller derby name “Avrilla the Hun”—has been my boss since year ten, when I took a gamble and dropped my résumé at her magic shop in the city, the kinda distastefully named Houdini’s Appendix. Amy has Cleopatra hair, which this month is dyed a sweet shade of blue, and tattooed arm sleeves that feature, among other things, a lady with the words “hell on wheels” underneath. In skates, she stands almost a foot taller than me and can pull off a Two Card Flight trick faster than anyone I’ve ever seen. Needless to say, she scared the living bejesus out of me when I first met her. Although we’ve been known to lose hours discussing the finer points of prestidigitation, I dunno if I would exactly call us friends. I’m *almost* certain she no longer wants to bludgeon me to death with a roller skate, though.

I yank the cape out of my satchel and swing it over my

shoulders. Yeah, I'm aware it's dorky, but Amy insists it's "ironic." I really don't have the guts to argue.

"Nice," she says. "A bit of hair gel and some glitter and you may yet pass for David Copperfield."

I close my eyes. "Seriously? Do you want me to quit?"

Amy shrugs with poker-faced evilness. "Just sayin'."

I wouldn't claim there's anyone I truly hate; mostly 'cause I think it's bad karmic juju to put that out into the universe. But if there's anyone on the planet who I dislike—*intensely*—then David Copperfield, with his douchey hair and overblown showmanship, would be number one with a bullet. I'm not a fan of "extreme magic" under most circumstances. Real magic shouldn't need cameras and helicopters and a few gazillion bucks behind it to be impressive. Also, the leather pants really piss me off. And the giant forehead. David Copperfield is first on the very short list of gits I'd like to smack in the head.

I know, I know—bad karmic juju.

Amy nudges my arm. "Look alive, Joshie. Mama needs a new pair of Brass Knuckle PowerTracs with Atom Poison Wheels."

I'm pretty sure only half those things are proper words. Still, maybe I should focus on the task at hand. It beats the other thing I could be obsessively running through my head, like the replays in those ice hockey games Dad likes. I reorganize Amy's chaotic side of the stand, my mind drifting to Sophia. Those piercing dark eyes, that guarded, heart-shaped face, the low, raspy voice that's indescribably captivating. Then the breeze catches my cape, and one tasseled end billows up and slaps me in the eyeball.

I focus on the task at hand.

I love working at Houdini's, but the markets are my favorite days of the month. The Convent has a really cool, villagey vibe; take away the hipster beards and organic coffee, and it could be anyplace in medieval Europe. And all I have to do is keep people engaged while Amy works the stand. I stick to simple stuff—classic cards, coins—nothing super challenging, but I usually manage to hold a crowd, and it gives me the chance to test-drive some tricks of my own.

Business is awesome today. Our juggling sets are big sellers, and Amy manages not to get in a smackdown fight with anyone, which is a rare and glorious event. The day is cold, but the blue sky has brought out the crowds, and by mid-afternoon our stand has an audience three people deep. A row of kids huddles in front as I talk at them while executing my version of a Hollingworth Reformation trick. It never fails to get a couple of really good gasps from the little guys.

I love performing for kids. Adults seem to feel this need to remain, like, stoically un-wowed, but kids don't ever bother hiding their excitement. They ask a billion questions, true, but they're mostly happy to *not* fully understand how illusions work. They get—better than most grown-ups—that the mystery is half the fun.

I finish my last cup trick with a flourish, and the little guys at the front applaud madly. I even get a few polite claps from some parents before they hustle their kids away, presumably before the idea of tipping occurs to anyone.

"Nice," Amy says as she rings up a set of Christopher Plover books. "I'm liking that spin you've added to the Tear and Restore. You gonna show me how you do that?"

"Nope," I say happily as I drop my coins into my pocket. As the audience clears, I recognize a couple of familiar faces hovering at the back—or rather, I recognize a mophead of hair even more disastrous than mine, and a yellow bouffant that stands in an atmospheric zone all of its own.

I'm not exactly sure how I became friends with the English guys whose band plays here on market days. I recall a urinal conversation being involved, but I've never brought it up. I don't get normal guys at the best of times, but I'm guessing that making friends with other dudes while semi-pants-less is generally frowned upon. Regardless, Jasper and Ethan were the first cool people I'd met in ages, and their circle of friends have quickly become some of my favorite people in the world.

Jasper waves at me, then grunts a hello and scowls at Amy, who scowls a hello back.

"Hey, Jasper," I say as I restack some card boxes. "How goes? You guys on soon?"

He ruffles a hand through his hair. "Yeah. Fecking nightmare. I swear, if I get one more request for Taylor Swift, I might actually go ape-shit and pitch an amp into the crowd."

His bass guitarist, the aforementioned yellow-haired Ethan, shrugs. "But we can buy food this month. And toilet paper. I'm choosing to view toilet paper as a good thing."

"Can't believe I let you talk me into selling out," Jasper growls.

"Yeah. A regular, paying gig, versus spending another

winter turning my undies inside out to save on laundry detergent—"

"You are a fecking musician!" Jasper yells. "Go home to mummy if you're so hung up on clean knickers—"

"Jesus, will you take it somewhere else!" Amy bellows. "I can't think with you bleating in my ear!"

Jasper looks like he's about to say a whole lot of something elses, but he catches Amy's eye and the two of them suddenly seem to find the ground and the sky equally mesmerizing.

"Whatever," Jasper mumbles. "We're on next." He shoots a glance at Amy. "Come check us out. If you feel like it. Whatever."

"Maybe. Whatever," Amy says.

Ethan gives me a sneaky eye roll as he and Jasper walk away. I keep my face averted to hide the smirk that's making its way across it.

"Shut up, Joshua," Amy snaps.

I stretch my hands over my head with a yawn, catching a glimpse of another familiar person skipping toward me.

"You still need me, Ames? Can I clear out?"

Amy grabs some juggling batons and tosses them deftly into the air. "Nah. Get out of here," she says distractedly.

I wave at the girl bounding toward me, who gives me an enthusiastic wave back. Her long hair bounces under a purple beanie, and with her red jacket, green corduroys, and happy smile, she kinda reminds me of a Dr. Seuss character. Totally crush-worthy, if I was remotely that way inclined.

"Joshua the Magician!" she calls out in her lilting British accent. "We missed you last Sunday!"

I stuff the cape into my bag. "Camilla the Chanteuse—nice to see you too. And yeah, had to bail last week. Turns out I had an assignment due Monday that I kinda forgot about. How are you? Is everyone here?"

"Nah, not today. Too many family events and other minor crises. Speaking of crises—did you see Jasper? He really needs to get off this family-event circuit soon. 'Cause I'm not sure that 'Frustrated Rock Star Throws Jumping Castle Into River' is the sort of headline he's looking for."

She gives Amy a salute that passes for hello. "What I can't work out is, why is he still showing up here? I've known Jasper for ages, and I've never seen him this committed." She smiles sweetly at Amy. Amy's rhythm splutters, and her batons crash to the ground.

Camilla winks at me as I choke back a laugh. "So. You done?" she says.

"Almost. Although I can't stick around for long." I feel the edges of my good mood curl. "Dad dragged me to open day at Melbourne University this morning. Pretty sure I'm expected home for discussion and analysis."

"Yeah? I have a couple more months before Conservatory auditions. A couple of months to get my head into a not-going-to-give-myself-a-stroke state." She shudders.

I've seen Camilla perform a couple of times now, and she's really great, but she also tends to twist herself into a bit of a stressed-out mess before going on stage.

I swing my satchel over my shoulder. "Hey, you're talking to a guy who once upon a time would have chosen death by a thousand toothpick stabs over having to talk to another human. But, you know, I got over it. Eventually."

"I know, I know," she says, sighing. "Hey, I'm a billion times better than I used to be. You didn't know me back when even the idea of being in front of an audience would make me puke. Good times," she says. "Anyway, I'm doing a cupcake run. The guys are in the usual spot."

She skips away as I amble toward the bandstand. I see two guys I recognize sprawled on the grass, and they wave as I walk toward them.

Adrian fist-bumps me as I drop onto the lawn and waggles his fingers through mine in a gesture that's either a *Star Trek* sign or a signal to his mothership. He's kinda short, and a bit odd, but also one of the most good-humored guys I know. Just looking at his guileless face is enough to make me laugh.

"Joshua! Dude, you should have been here last week—Jasper got so pissed with these guys, he tried to hit one of them with his mic and almost fell off the stage. It was awesome!"

The guy beside him sweeps his blond hair out of his eyes and leans over to shake my hand. "Yeah. I think the Annabel Lees are shaping up to be the first band in history whose fans might need bodyguard protection from them."

Sam isn't as big a history nerd as me, but we're both taking the same Revolutions course, and he's mega-smart and doesn't find talking history as dorky as most people. We chat idly about our essays, which I will be starting sometime soon, and the dozen Creative Writing courses he's applying for next year; a conversation that I manage to sidestep through some nimble verbal misdirection. And then Sam leans back on his hands and raises an eyebrow.

"Dude, you've gone almost five minutes without mentioning the girl. I think this might be some kind of record."

I laugh. "I'm not that bad."

He snorts. "Ah, ha. And Adrian is not a candidate for the remake of *Willow*."

"Hey!" Adrian yelps. "I like that movie."

Sam grins. "Well?"

"Well, so, I guess—progress? I think. Maybe?"

Sam turns around. He's trying to hide his astonishment, but doing a piss-poor job of it. "Seriously?"

I fail miserably at masking a smile. "Yeah, it wasn't exactly part of my plan—"

"The plan, the plan," he mutters. "Dude, have you thought about just, I dunno—being direct? Or even vaguely normal?"

"Sam, Sophia isn't that kind of girl! She is not *normal*. I can't just tell her that I'm...that she..." The words tumble out in a rush. "That she's the only person I've ever wanted, the only person I've thought about since I was thirteen—"

Sam grimaces. "Jesus. You're right, you can't tell her that. You might actually want to keep that completely to yourself. 'Cause Josh, objectively, it makes you sound a bit... irrational."

I shrug. "It's how I feel. And Sophia deserves something better, something *bigger* than some rando guy asking her out for coffee or whatever."

Adrian nods. "One does not simply walk into Mordor," he says gravely.

"Exactly! That is—well, sort of—exactly it."

Sam shakes his head. "If you're taking tips on girls from

Adrian via *Lord of the Rings*, you're in more trouble than I can help with."

Camilla pushes her way through the crowd, catching the tail end of our conversation. She drops a paper bag on the ground. Adrian pounces on it eagerly.

"Seriously, Josh, do not tell me you're accepting romantic advice from this guy?" she says, pointing at Sam with her thumb.

Sam squints up at her. "What's wrong with accepting romantic advice from me?"

Adrian spits out a mouthful of cupcake as Camilla dissolves into laughter. "Sammy? You giving romance advice is like…Freddy Krueger sharing insomnia tips." She drops into his lap. "Maybe Joshua would like progress sometime this century?"

Sam kisses her forehead. "Yeah, okay. Point taken," he says with a grin.

Camilla huddles into him as the wind whips around us. "I, on the other hand, am possibly competent. News, please?"

I fill the guys in on my morning, trying for my most unbiased, facts-only manner. I leave out the bit where the unexpected sight of her almost sent me tumbling right back into prepubescent voicelessness. I also leave out the bit about my lucky coin. I'm not even sure why. Though I realize, after I've accidentally relayed my entire conversation with Sophia word-for-word, that I am smiling again like a massive tool-face.

Camilla chews the inside of her cheek. "Josh, I'm glad you've made contact. That's progress, you're right. But—

and I've said this to you before, and I know it's none of my business—but don't you think that your idolizing, as cute as it is, might be, well, a little bit unfair?"

I glance at the stage where Jasper is either hastily rewiring an amp or attempting to garrote his drummer. "I don't *idolize* her, Camilla. I know her. And I think, if she just got to know me—"

"Look," she says gently. "I'm sure Sophia's great, but have you ever thought that maybe it's, like, the idea of her that you're infatuated with? She's a real person, Josh. Not a... theory."

I bristle. "That's not true. I know her. I mean, okay, so, I don't *know her* know her, but that doesn't change the fact that she's special. I *see* her, Camilla."

Sam's chin is resting on Camilla's beanie-covered head, his eyes studiously focused on the stage—the giant coward. Camilla untangles herself from him and drops onto the ground. "You do?" she asks sharply. "You know her favorite milkshake, and, I dunno, the first cartoon character she had a crush on?"

"Those things don't matter. They're just details. You can't tell me you know all that stuff."

"Lime spider. And Raphael, the red Ninja Turtle," Sam says lightly. "A fact that I still find disturbing, by the way."

She leans backward. "Right. 'Cause your Princess Leia thing is not at all nerdy?"

Sam shrugs, grinning. "She wasn't animated. Or reptilian."

Camilla rolls her eyes at me. "Look, Josh, my point is—Sophia is a person. She'll either like you or she won't. You can either ask her or you can continue to sit in your room, pining and listening to Air Supply."

I dig up a damp handful of grass. "Who's Air Supply?"

Sam groans. "Dude, don't ask. I'm pretty sure knowledge of hair-metal bands has pushed some actually useful stuff out of my head."

Camilla punches his thigh. "Samuel, don't even pretend you haven't got a file of power ballads on your computer." She giggles. "Lucky I find your off-tune Whitesnake weirdly sexy."

I doubt there is any part of that sentence that could be considered sexy. But then Sam pulls her backward and kisses her, and I'm pretty sure they've forgotten about the existence of other humans.

Adrian nudges me, his chin covered in cupcake icing. "Think you've got about as much useful advice from 'Samilla' as you're gonna get. Unless the advice you're after is related to the mechanics of being joined at the face. 'Cause I think 'Camuel' might be, like, working toward a PhD in that."

"Shut up, Adrian," Sam murmurs.

Adrian snorts. "Next time I'm bringing the spray bottle we use on the cat."

I can't help but laugh. It's not like I'm the sort of guy who cries over Disney movies or anything. I mean, not anymore. But I like being around people who are happy. It gives me hope. Meeting these guys, seeing how Sam and Camilla are together—hell, it's given me enough hope to get off my cowardly arse and do something.

The Annabel Lees finish their sound check and Jasper grunts something into the mic. It could be a hello, or could be a curse on the crowd and their firstborns. It's hard to say.

The drums thunder through the ground. I lean backward and let my gaze float to the sky, thinking about Camilla's questions. I know she's wrong. It's not like I've spent the last five years obsessing over Sophia. It's just that, in the background, I've always known she was there; this steady, fascinating presence in my peripheral vision. But it's more than the idea of Sophia.

It's—well, I can't describe it in words. That's the whole point. It's intangible, indefinable. Like the best sort of magic.

My phone buzzes with yet another message. Crap on a stick. I yank it out of my pocket, but I don't even need to look at the screen.

"Problem?" Adrian calls over the music.

"Nah, man. Just my dad. I think he's a bit excited. I should probably go."

Adrian gives me another fist-bump as I stand and dust off my butt. Sam manages to extract his lips from Camilla's long enough to shoot me a distracted "good luck" before supergluing their faces together again.

I wave at Amy, who's at the back of the crowd, staring at the stage with one of her eighteen variations of a scowl. I head to the tram, pushing aside the jumbled thoughts jostling for room inside my skull. I ignore Dad's texts, and the image of his expectant face, waiting with questions I have bugger-all answers for.

I focus on the task at hand. I have a plan. For now, anyway. The rest—it'll take care of itself. I have faith in my good karmic juju.

The future will be fine.

I'm fairly confident of this.

Chapter Five

The Laws of Thermodynamics

School. Another Monday. The same people dragging themselves to the same classes, the same background noise about weekend parties and hookups and breakups. Like being stuck in a perpetual time loop—an infinite Bootstrap paradox, all events fixed and predictable.

Monday morning's double period is Drama with Ms. Heller, in the building on the edge of the East Lawn. Which is why I'm somewhat perturbed to find myself walking through the blue year-twelve corridor, scanning the mental map of locker inhabitants that seems to have been inadvertently stored in my brain.

He has a top locker, but he still needs to bend down to rifle inside. It's the locker that used to belong to Stephen Shilling, and it's still covered with the remnants of his brief but memorable blaze of glory through St. Augustine's—multiple Sharpie sketches of wieners with smiley faces and the lingering smell of weed.

I hover, clutching my Drama books to my chest.

"So I found something, Saturday," I blurt.

He startles, smacking his head on the locker as he straightens and spins around. Someone has drawn an elaborate sign with the words "depressed vampire support group" above his door. An arrow points into his locker. Just in case the depressed vampires find themselves lost, I suppose.

Joshua's eyes widen. He straightens to his full height, school tie in one hand.

"Good morning," he says eventually, his nimble fingers looping the tie carefully around his neck. "How was your weekend, Sophia?"

"Huh? Fine. It was whatever," I say impatiently. I fish through my blazer pockets. I've been obsessing about this since Saturday, but now, staring at Joshua's face, I'm starting to feel somewhat foolish.

He smooths down his tie and tucks his hair behind one ear, then reaches back into his locker, emerging with a dog-eared novel and a Further Math textbook, the spine smooth and uncracked. I can see that he's attempted to cover some of the more pornographic graffiti inside his locker with printouts of old posters. A sepia-tinted Harry Houdini ad is stuck to one side. I frown at it.

"So what did you find?" he says.

I thrust out the two-headed Lincoln. "Do you know anything about this?"

He places his books at his feet and takes the coin. He runs a thumbnail over the surface, then flicks it into the air and catches it between his long fingers.

"Well, I know these aren't actually minted this way. They're made by hollowing out a coin and then shaving down a second one so it fits inside. But, see, you can't even tell where they're stuck together. It takes awesome metalwork skills to do that."

"Well that's pointless." I grimace. "I mean—why would anyone do that?"

He shrugs. "Cheating at coin tosses? Annoying the Math teacher when they're demonstrating Bayes' theorem?" He glances at me. "Some people consider them lucky," he adds lightly. "A talisman or something."

"Like a rabbit's foot or some other piece of nothing that's supposed to have mysterious power? You know that's nonsense, right?"

He shrugs. "But it's not the thing itself, is it? I mean, I've worn the same pair of socks into every exam for the past two years, and they've served me pretty well. Well, okay, the socks aren't doing all that well. But it hasn't hurt, right? Isn't it just about belief? Like, I dunno, psychological reinforcement when you need it, or a corporeal something to focus on?"

Some guy jostles past with a snort as the word *corporeal* floats between us. I'm busy fending off a too-thick feeling in my brain, like the time Elsie's brother Ryan accidentally shot an eight ball off their pool table and gave me a mild concussion.

I cast another glance at Joshua. He is resting his hip against the edge of the locker bank; his posture indicates that he is relaxed. The top third of a palm-sized notebook peeks from his blazer pocket, the Moleskine cover scattered with scribbles in a tiny and strangely ornate script that seems far too flamboyant for this nondescript boy. I run an exploratory eye over him, all milk-pale skin and dark hair. I can't put my finger on why, but something about his long-limbed frame in the Augustine's uniform just seems, somehow...*discordant*. On closer inspection, he isn't even all that pale; his skin has adopted a slightly uneven pinkish hue, which deepens the longer I stare at him, like he's just been for a run.

"Numismatists," he says quickly. "Numismatists would be totally into this coin. People who collect—"

"Coins. Currency. Yes, I know that." I blink at him. "So, then...you're into coins?"

He tilts his head, like he's thinking extra hard. "Define 'into'," he says with a faint grin. "'Cause it sounds like you're asking if I have some sort of coin fetish. Like I sleep with a fresh pile of twenty-cent pieces under my pillow or something."

Balls. Why the hell am I having this conversation? And, more to the point, why am I not walking away?

"You just seem to know a lot about coins," I say weakly.

He walks the bronze coin between his knuckles, right down to his pinkie and back again. "I know a bit. For instance, did you know that archaeologists have found ancient Greek statues with coins hidden in their hands? I mean, think about it—there were Greek dudes who were awesome enough to be immortalized, and in mid Classic Palm no less—"

"Mid classic what?"

"—and yet," he continues, switching the coin from his right hand to his left, "guys like Aristotle and Archimedes get to be glorified and remembered, while the illusionists are mostly forgotten."

He flicks his hand over, the coin now sitting snugly in his palm.

I meet his eyes again—well, as best I can, considering my eyeline is somewhere around the middle of his tie. Trying to decipher his too-fast words is only intensifying that woolly sensation in my brain; less mild concussion and more like what I imagine my Uncle Roshan experienced after he was kicked in the head by a horse.

I stare instead at the coin, inert in his waiting hand. "So it's yours?"

His eyes flicker between mine. The first-period bell chimes. The tempo of footfalls around us swells.

"No," he says, holding the coin out to me. "It's yours."

I think there was a time, once, when I was capable of acting without weighing up a thousand alternate scenarios of disaster and doom. I'd wave my hand in the flame of a Bunsen burner and sneak a taste of phenylthiourea in Chem lab, just to know what it felt like on my tongue. When I think back, I can barely recognize the me who was so reckless.

I reach out and take the coin from his hand. "There's a penis under your Houdini," I blurt.

He wrinkles his nose as he looks at his locker, where an oversized wang is peeking out from under the edge of the poster. "Yeah. Whoever's locker this was had some pretty unhealthy fixations."

We stare, silently, at a sketch of a weiner with a top hat and a mustache until the warning bell dings, and Joshua clears his throat. "Don't you need to get to class?"

"Yes. Class. I have Drama," I say. I also wave my

monologue book, just in case he has forgotten the English language in the last thirty seconds.

He gathers his things. "That's not going well?" He seems to be examining me extra closely, like I'm a particularly puzzling bacillus under a microscope.

"It's not really in my wheelhouse," I manage to say. He's still giving me that considering look, apparently in no rush to fill in the gaps. "It's not great," I continue, my mouth moving of its own accord. "Knowing no matter how hard you try you're going to end up being...disappointing." I look up at him, but his face is trained on his locker door now. "I hate Mondays," I mumble.

He slips his books into his satchel. His fingers are tapping out a loose rhythm, and his eyes are focused somewhere far away. I don't *think* he looks weirded out by me. More like... contemplative?

I shuffle backward, the coin still tight in my palm. "I should go."

"Hey, um, Sophia?" Joshua fiddles with his satchel straps. "Do you like milkshakes?"

My brain pokes at the question. It flips it over and examines it again. My brain is capable of calculating falling factorials and multiplying huge numbers without a calculator, which, as Elsie points out, is really only useful as a party trick for a very sad party. Yet it can't seem to parse this sentence.

"No. I'm lactose intolerant."

"Oh," he says. "Okay then." I don't know why, but I have the strangest suspicion that he is disappointed.

Behind him, Mr. Finkler, our year-twelve coordinator, is waddling down the corridor, shooing stragglers to class. My feet seem to be cemented to the floor.

"I like banana smoothies," I say, my voice projecting as if from a great distance. "With soy milk. And honey. Sometimes nuts."

The shadowy lines on Joshua's forehead disappear. The corners of his eyes crinkle in a smile. "Cool. Don't worry about Drama. I'll see you round." He turns and disappears, leaving me with a head full of data that I suspect would take more brainpower than I possess to unravel.

The walk to the Arts building, at an average human speed, takes about nine minutes. Considering that I typically drag my feet toward it like I'm heading into a nuclear accident sans hazmat suit, I almost always arrive late. Today, I creep into the theater long after the bell, damp from the drizzle and even more frazzled than usual. No one notices or seems to care.

Built in the 1930s, our Arts building is a double-story brick monstrosity that smells permanently of wet dog, with a peeling facade that Elsie likes to say would make the Bates Motel look welcoming. It's tucked on the edge of the empty East Lawn, a row of identical pine trees behind it. It's far enough from the rest of the school that the screeches from the year-eleven production of *Rent* are mercifully out of earshot. It was once the home of a contingent of Carmelite nuns and used to be known simply as "The Convent" until someone had the bright idea to rename it the "St. Augustine's Visual and Performing Arts Center." Strangely, installing a sign stenciled in *ye olde* lettering above the doors failed to make the isolated nightmare-house more hospitable.

Inside, the theater is a cacophony of sound. The year-ten music club is tuning up in the shallow orchestra pit, and my class is scattered in clusters around the room. Chairs are stacked against the walls, leaving space for seventeen year twelves in various states of faux emotional breakdown.

I slump onto the brown carpet, pain immediately searing through my frontal lobe. I suspect the acoustics in this room *could* be more excruciating, but only if they'd been designed by North Korean torture specialists on one of their grouchy days.

Ms. Heller is up on the stage. Her ponytail swishes behind her, animated as if her hair were starring in a performance all of its own. In front of her are Romy Hopwood and Trevor Pine, who are, apparently, still trying to nail the emotional resonance of a clown and a sad-yet-hopeful circus elephant.

Romy stares into Trevor's eyes. She reaches out to cup Trevor's face in a way that, to me, looks like she's about to give him a dental exam. Then Trevor stands and unleashes a plaintive cry that reminds me of the sound Elsie's Auntie Nirmala made that time she won fourth division in TattsLotto.

Ms. Heller beams. I can't even pretend to be contemptuous, because really? I can barely muster the talent to mime a proper sneeze.

I try to quell the low-grade nausea that I habitually

experience in this class. I'm convinced that my pulse is visible in my throat.

I have no idea why I hate this so much. I think it's because there is no clear theory, no facts or data I have managed to glean that make anything here comprehensible. There are no constants, no fundamental truths. It's not like I'm not trying—I've read every book Ms. Heller has assigned, devoured hours of articles on performance techniques. I've even sat through multiple insipid episodes of *Inside the Actors Studio*, in which celebrities discuss their profession with an earnestness that should be reserved for the discovery of the Higgs boson particle or the invention of toilet paper.

"Yo, Stephen Hawking," a voice crows beside me. "Sup?"

Damien Pagono throws himself on the floor and immediately occupies himself by digging at his teeth with a protractor. "Got ya, you little bastard!" he crows. The pointy end of his protractor holds an unidentifiable glob the color of brain matter. "Huh. When did I eat souvlaki?"

"Congratulations," I mutter. "Your parents must be very proud."

He waggles an eyebrow. "Side of wasabi with that snark?"

"Piss off," I mumble, shuffling away from him and his teeth-fossicking.

I sink lower, vaguely hoping that the laws of physics will rewrite themselves for the next forty minutes and render me invisible behind my backpack.

Tucked inside my Drama folder is the slim Penguin classic of Richard Feynman's *Six Easy Pieces* that I've taken to keeping with me in case of emergency. I slip my hand inside, feeling the reassuring shape of the small orange paperback. I close my eyes, visualizing the pages filled with Feynman's basic, beautiful introduction to Physics that I first read when I was ten. I run the tips of my fingers over the edges of the waxy cover, drawing tiny crumbs of comfort from its well-worn pages, like an amulet against my current situation, like a cheap paper talisman—

Oh. *Shit.*

"Ms. Reyhart!" Ms. Heller crows. I tear my hands out of my folder. "Nice of you to grace us with your presence."

She strides down the stage stairs, ponytail whipping behind her, one hand held out toward me, palm up. I have seen her make this gesture to appease nervous performers, and I think it's supposed to be comforting, but all I can think is that it's the exact same pose as the statue of Jesus that hangs above the stage. Any moment now I'm expecting Ms. Heller's head to spin around while expelling green vomit, which I think is something that Jesus did? Maybe I should start paying attention in Mass.

A cold drop of sweat runs down my spine. "Yes, Miss," I mumble as I stand. Her face keeps moving, all shifting eyebrows and rapid blinks, always too many expressions for me to decode.

"I'm going to assume you're prepared to workshop your practice exam today?" She smiles widely. I think it's meant to be kind, but I can't seem to interpret it as anything other than the smile of someone about to toss a puppy under a bus.

Damien leans back on his hands, smirking. He's the only one who ever bothers talking to me in Drama. I have no earthly idea why. He of the pallid face and ill-fitting uniform, of the public testicle-selfies, who pronounces "Macbeth" with an "f" at the end—is actually a surprisingly good actor. He may be, as Elsie says, a "giant bag of dicks," but he is acing this class.

Ms. Heller steps right into my space. I clock a hint of Lady Grey tea and the sweet perfume that follows her like a cloud, and I have to fight the urge to hold my breath. Someone in the orchestra pit hammers out a drum roll. It may be a coincidence—the music nerds rarely pay any attention to the drama geeks—but the sound just compounds the sensory overload. My stomach contracts.

"So. How have we gone with the exercises we were set?" she asks.

I swallow. "Exercises. Right. Well, we tried them. But I'm not sure we really understood the point."

In fact, I spent several hours on Sunday immersed in a Sense Memory task, whereby I was instructed to sit, breathing deeply, while staring into a cup of coffee. According to the instructions Ms. Heller had given me, this assignment was supposed to help develop "emotions as a reaction to familiar stimuli." What I learned after contemplating Mum's Blend 43 for half an hour is that coffee is damp and brown. I'm not sure how that's applicable to my practice monologue from *All's Well That Ends Well*. I'm writing it off as yet another unfathomable mystery of this hellish class.

Ms. Heller sighs. "The point, Ms. Reyhart, is that we need to work on unlocking some of that *fire* I know you have hidden away!" She closes her eyes, her fingers fluttering near her temple, and I brace myself to be struck by a motivational quote to the face. "The best and most beautiful things cannot be seen or even touched. They must be felt with the heart." She taps me on the chest. "I *know* you have things to share. Don't be shy!"

I resist the urge to remind her that I am not *shy*. That's always been the conclusion most people draw about me, the simplest and least demanding diagnosis, which I rarely bother to correct. "Shy" is a label everyone can get on board with. I contemplate Ms. Heller, her soft eyes and earnestness. I think about her nonsense quote. Anyone claiming that beautiful things can't be seen has never encountered a perfect Pythagorean proof.

I can't stop my mouth from moving. "Why?" I ask. "I'm not being difficult, Ms. Heller. Not on purpose, anyway. But why is this important? Why do you think it's something I'm missing?"

Damien snorts. I haven't failed to notice that he's the only person in class who seems interested in this conversation. "What are these human 'emotions' of which you speak?" he craws in a staccato robot voice, complete with jerky hand movements. He makes a couple of meeping sounds, then falls backward onto the carpet, laughing.

Ms. Heller glares at him. She turns back to me, brows knitting. "Sophia, performance is not just about learning lines and memorizing facts and such." She glances up at the stage, which has been taken over by Joseph Cheng who's rehearsing his solo. "Accessing your emotions, being able to express them clearly—making yourself *understood*—it's such a fundamental part of getting along in the world." She hesitates. "Isn't that something you'd like to improve on?"

Huh. I wonder if anyone interrupted Richard Feynman's quantum electrodynamics research to tell him he ought to spend time getting in touch with his feelings? Or if Turing's invention of the computer was waylaid by a demand that he stop to evaluate his emotions? Despite all my questions about Perelman and his mental state, I seriously doubt his problem was not being demonstrative enough. And yet, the collective minds responsible for my life have apparently decided that nothing I do is meaningful unless I can smile while I am doing it.

I move past my teacher and stomp forward. If I had to name my current emotion, Ms. Heller, I think I'm feeling a little pissed off.

Heavy blue drapes conceal the windows and the outside world. Beyond them, in the middle distance, lie the stark grounds and outdoor amphitheater, with its tiers of sunken seats and its mechanized central stage, out of order for years now. I guess the idea was a "theater in the round" or whatever, but it's never worked properly, and after an unfortunate production of *Joseph and the Amazing Technicolor Dreamcoat* in which Sanjay Khan's pharaoh wig got caught in the stage gears, the amphitheater was quietly decommissioned and has since disappeared under a carpet of weeds.

Dust, thick and dirty, floats before my eyes. I wonder, distantly, if there's a way of calculating the odds I'll slowly asphyxiate in this room while the music club practices an all-brass version of "Funky Town" in the background. I can't even tell if I'm experiencing a freak-out, since I can never breathe properly in here.

I take a seat on the stage stairs while Joseph wraps up his scene.

I drape my hands over my knees, then worry that I'm trying too hard to appear relaxed, so I cross my legs and clasp my hands lightly in my lap. Then I start to worry that my hands are in a ridiculously contrived position, but moving them again is going to make me look fidgety and agitated. I start to feel my focus tunneling down into my hands, like every molecule of skin is lit with a glow that's probably visible to everyone in the room—

"Ms. Reyhart!" Ms. Heller chirps. "You're up."

I force my wobbly legs to stand. Joseph gives me what I think is a sympathetic smile. I clomp across the floorboards to the place under the spotlight that he has just vacated, my heart jackhammering in my throat like it has detached itself from my pericardium and is trying to beat right through my skin.

I hunker down on my knees at the edge of the light and take a few deep, futile breaths. Then I open my mouth and let forth a torrent of words.

"Then I confess here on my knee before high heaven and you that before you and next unto high heaven—"

"Okay, relax your shoulders, Sophia," Ms. Heller calls from somewhere to my left. "You're supposed to be professing undying love, not taking a knee in the locker room at halftime."

I shake out my shoulders and try to relax my hands, but my extremities seem to have lost all feeling. "Um...*my friends were poor but honest, so's my love, be not offended for it hurts not him—*"

Ms. Heller moves into my line of sight. She grimaces. "Okay…sure. How about we slow down a bit and maybe try it a tad less…murdery?"

There is a snigger in the auditorium, followed by a chorus of *shushes*. I think the laughter might have come from Michelle Pham, though I'm not sure what she's finding so funny. I mean, this is the girl who cried when she couldn't figure out binomial expansion in year-ten Math—far more justifiable grounds for eye-watering mirth, if I were prone to that sort of thing.

Ms. Heller clears her throat. "Come on, Sophia. You're doing…great."

I close my eyes. I know the words I am supposed to say. It took me all of three minutes to memorize them. I am not shy. But I can't do this. *I can't.*

I shuffle onto my feet again, imagining that the heat of the spotlight is causing my molecules and atoms to vibrate faster and faster, the space between them expanding—

"*That he is loved of me—*" I toss one hand skyward, having seen the gesture in a YouTube clip of this monologue, though I have no idea what it is supposed to signify. "*I follow him not…not…*"

I can't fail at something so simple. Something that Damien Pagono, who is now cleaning his shoes with his teeth-protractor, can excel at with apparently no effort. What does it say about me if I can't take one tiny step outside my comfort zone without falling in a heap? What does it say about my potential if I'm incapable of mastering something new?

I can't breathe. The next line of this goddamned ridiculous monologue is stuck somewhere in my vocal cords. My feet feel like they have adhered to the stage, that one hand still pointing incomprehensibly to the sky. I'm so busy sinking into a tangle that I almost miss the officious-looking junior who has walked into the room. He strides up to the stage and thrusts something at Ms. Heller. "From the office," the kid barks, before marching out again.

Ms. Heller frowns at the oversized red envelope in her hand. It's shiny and fancy-looking. I'm close enough to see the small, elaborate writing on the front, ornate curlicues drawn with a thin black marker, like a wedding invite from a fairytale giant.

"Maybe Finkler's finally gonna ask you out," Damien says from the edge of the orchestra pit. "Check if he's sent a photo of his dong."

Ms. Heller shoots him a glare. Someone in the orchestra pit plays the first few bars of "Don't Stand So Close to Me" on the viola, and a few people giggle.

Ms. Heller blushes. Whatever mysterious aura of authority that surrounds her wavers as she looks at the envelope. Her indecisiveness prompts all activity to come to a slow halt.

She places her monologue book on the stage steps, then digs her car keys from her pocket, sliding the tip of one beneath the flap of the envelope.

"What on earth," she mutters as she withdraws her hand. In it she holds a small, irregularly shaped piece of red paper, only slightly larger than her palm.

I'm distantly aware that my feet have regained some

feeling and that I have drifted down the stairs. On closer inspection it's not a single piece of paper at all; rather, it's what looks like some kind of flat, elaborate origami, the edges razor-straight and pressed into a complex series of folds and creases.

A small, white tag is attached to the bottom of one of the folds.

I peer over Ms. Heller's forearm. The tag bears an inscription in minuscule writing, a pretty script that matches the lettering on the envelope. The writing reads simply: *here*.

Ms. Heller's fingers flutter over the instruction. I've seen her face adopt that same glazed expression before, usually when she's quoting chunks of Chekhov. She holds the red shape delicately in her fingers. Then, almost impulsively, she gives the tag a swift, precise tug.

The sharp-edged creases of the origami become softer before my eyes. Segments of crimson move and unfold in the direction of the tag. It's too convoluted for my eyes to follow. However it has been created, the mechanism is impressive.

The paper shape rearranges itself, pieces blossoming outward and upward as Ms. Heller tugs at the tag, her other hand clinging tightly to the bottom. Between the thumb and forefinger of her stationary hand, red segments coil around on themselves, a slow-moving paper vine, forming seemingly of its own volition.

Remaining in her fingers is the stem of a small but perfectly shaped crimson paper rose.

"Oh," Ms. Heller breathes. She glances around, a dusky blush staining her cheeks.

Someone whistles. Someone else *awwws*. Romy's eyes well with unshed tears; a reaction that I find almost as perplexing as the paper rose itself, until I remember that I've seen her sob at a picture of an orphaned baby sloth on someone's Instagram. Romy Hopwood is probably not the most reliable barometer of conventional human emotion.

Ms. Heller twirls the rose slowly in her hand. Several people yelp and point excitedly as they spot the thing that I have just seen. Another tiny white tag has unfolded partway along the stem.

My nose twitches. The faintest hint of an almost-familiar smell tickles the edge of my senses.

I give up all pretense of being surreptitious. I grab Ms. Heller's sleeve, pulling it, and the flower, toward me. The tiny script on the second tag, in urgent caps, reads: *HOLD AWAY*.

"Ms. Heller," I begin, "um, maybe, I think you should—"

There is a sound—a faintly effervescent hiss. It's followed by a soft fizz and a barely audible *pop*, like the crack of kindling in a very tiny fireplace.

For a moment, the entire class and the people in the orchestra pit and even Damien Pagono freeze.

A dot of blue appears at the base of the rose bulb. It's sparked by nothing I can see, like someone has touched the paper with the tip of an invisible match. The smudge of light seems to hang suspended, so faint that for a moment I can't be sure it's really there.

Ms. Heller recoils. She thrusts the rose away from her body, the stem still pinched between the tips of her fingers.

The paper rose ignites. Fingers of fire creep leisurely, steadily upward, enveloping the petals in a bright mini-inferno. The flame has the strangest glow, blue, almost green, clearly some kind of chemical fire.

It's mesmerizing; a too-bright torch in the dim, dusty room. There are a few alarmed gasps alongside a smattering of applause, which turns to animated exclamations as the entire bulb of the flower is engulfed in cobalt flame. The color of the fire seems to be changing now, emerald with a halo of purple. Curiously, it also seems much smokier than a fire of that size should be.

The pretty flame dances in Ms. Heller's extended hand. And then two things happen at once.

As quickly as it ignited, the fire extinguishes, leaving Ms. Heller staring open-mouthed at the charred remains of a red paper stem. Tendrils of thick blue-gray smoke curl toward the ceiling, followed by a chorus of affected coughing from a few of the more melodramatic members of the class.

Ms. Heller looks up. I follow her eyes to the smoke alarm that sits snug between the lighting rigs.

"Oh, dear," Ms. Heller says.

She drops the rose remnant and crushes it under her foot, just as the piercing shriek of the fire alarm howls through the building.

Amid the resulting panic—the fleeing Music Club members, Damien Pagono's maniacal *whoop!* and Ms. Heller's desperate attempts to instill calm while enacting the emergency evacuation procedure—I find myself immobile. My eyes are glued on the crimson envelope, still balanced innocently at the edge of the stage, the tiny lavish script pinging something in an alcove of my memory that does the oddest thing to my stomach, like being airborne the instant before turbulence. I disregard the sensation impatiently as my brain clicks through the various scenarios that are likely to ensue.

The fire alarm is deafening. Yet I hear it as though I'm underwater, as if from a great distance away. An inexplicable flare of adrenaline is pumping through my bloodstream. I feel kind of intoxicated with it.

I take the three steps to the stage and grab the calligraphic envelope, folding it in half and securing it hastily inside my Feynman book. Using a handful of tissues, I gather what is left of the paper rose and squash it inside my blazer pocket. And then I follow Ms. Heller and the rest of the class out into the freedom of the damp morning sunshine.

♦

Chapter Six

The Magnetic Moments of Elementary Particles

Suffice to say, word of the incident spreads like magical wildfire. By morning break, half of St. Augustine's is gathered on the East Lawn, drawn like hounds to the scent of a spectacle. Elsie makes a beeline for me; apparently, by the time word reached her side of campus, the story was that the Visual and Performing Arts Center had been overrun by zombie terrorists wielding flamethrowers and exploding vials of smallpox or something.

I hover at the back of the crowd, the faltering gears of my brain spinning. I have no idea what I should be thinking, but I *can* now confirm one previously untested hypothesis—that triggering a smoke alarm on campus automatically alerts the fire department. There's a fair bit of ogling at the three trucks' worth of firemen milling aimlessly on the lawns. I think most people are just disappointed that the building hasn't been burnt to the ground. The hysteria is not helped by the fact that the story is in the hands of the year-twelve Drama class, the vast majority of whom are, well, dramatic.

Questions are asked, hands are wrung, and an assembly

is hastily convened. We are instructed to "grow up," and urged to "encourage the responsible party to take ownership of their actions." We are harangued to "not take this critical year lightly," and solemnly reminded to "start acting like the adults we are soon to become." No one, apart from the three girls in the Socialist Club, seems to question why the sprinklers in the building aren't working. But later that afternoon the East Lawn is out of bounds, and a Jim's Plumbing van is parked behind the pine trees.

The whole episode is fodder for too many conversations, until someone posts a video on YouTube of Mr. Grayson, drunk in a 7-Eleven on Saturday night, and the burning rose is all but forgotten.

I am disturbed by two things. One—the momentary insanity that possessed me to cover up evidence of what our principal described as an "irresponsible, foolish act." I disposed of the red envelope in the bins behind the science labs as the first of the fire trucks roared onto campus, feeling like a bad guy from one of Dad's *James Bond* movies, yet unable to alter my course of action. And two—why I haven't said anything to Elsie about my new, somewhat tenuous suspicions.

I had every intention of talking to her. I'd resolved to spill everything I'd hypothesized, these odd and mysterious developments, and let my best friend, as always, make sense of the nonsensical.

But then the second strange event of the day occurred, and all my resolutions flew out the window.

It's lunchtime, and I'm heading toward our spot on the steps of the old library when out of the corner of my eye I spot

Elsie. She has her phone in hand, so I assume she's killing time with her head in a science article, or the *WTF* pages on BuzzFeed. But then I realize that Elsie actually appears to be engaged in a conversation, including eye contact and everything, with some other human beings, none of whom are me. Nina Pierce is leaning against a locker, Marcus Hunn hovering inanely. This tableau makes no sense. Nina and her group were kind of friends with us way back in year seven—these weird extra wheels who emerged briefly on our periphery and then disappeared as quickly as they had come. They never had much to do with me, though they seemed to like Elsie well enough. I don't know why, but one day they just stopped hanging around. As far as I was aware, Elsie hadn't spoken to them in years.

Nina sees me first. Her brows scrunch. Elsie turns around, lips twitching, before her face quickly settles.

"Hey, Rey!" she chirps. Something is going on with her voice. It's higher than normal and just a little too fast.

"Elsie. I didn't know you guys were friends again," I say, nodding toward Nina and Marcus.

I've never understood why simple, factual observations can make people turn all twitchy. But Nina rolls her eyes, and Marcus mutters something I can't decipher in a sardonic tone that I remember well. He hasn't changed much since I last paid attention: hands still buried in the sleeves of an oversized jumper, darting eyes. As bland and unremarkable as a skinny floor lamp with the bulb half-dimmed.

Elsie gives me a sharp look, all tight jaw and laser eyes, and I know I'll be getting a talking-to as soon as we're alone.

She turns her back on me and mumbles something to the others. Nina tugs at Marcus's sleeve, and after a moment of hesitation, he follows her, melting into the crowds down the corridor.

Elsie rounds on me with her hands on her hips. "Sophia, there's nothing to talk about. Just leave it, okay?"

"Okay," I answer. I reshuffle the questions in my head. I also downgrade my alert level, since a lecture doesn't seem to be forthcoming. I dig through my backpack for the extra apple I threw in this morning and hold it out to Elsie. "Did you finish your Bio homework? I'm worried Mr. Grayson is going to keep padding out his phenotype variations unit with more stuff on animal husbandry. I mean, how many YouTube videos on horse semen can there be?"

Elsie shakes her head and makes this sound that could be a huff or a laugh or a sigh. Then she takes the apple and motions down the corridor.

"So any clues on this pyro?" she asks as we walk. "Everyone's buzzing, trying to work out who he could be."

I glance over her shoulder, but the goings-on in the corridor are typical and uninteresting. "Why do you assume it's a he?"

She takes a bite of apple. "Good point. Could be a she. But with the fire thing, I'm leaning toward a dude. And the rose thing is totally a dude move."

"What 'rose thing'?"

Elsie laughs, spraying a few chunks of apple. "Rey, what is the point of supplying you with hours of romantic dramedies if you fail to absorb even the most basic elements? Have you learned *nothing* from my movie collection?"

I snort. "I've learned that the only redeeming feature of any movie featuring Keanu Reeves and time travel is the dog."

We walk through the double doors and head outside. This part of the school, with its covered walkways and maple-lined paths, is like a sonic funnel that amplifies the sound from the surrounding quads. It's like being shouted at from all directions at once, and it always makes my brain feel squeezed. Not for the first time, I wish that industrial earmuffs were part of our school uniform.

"It's a grand gesture, Sophia," Elsie continues, picking up her pace. "And it's clearly designed to impress someone. It's *ro-man-tic,*" she says, enunciating the word with an exaggerated eye roll.

I come to a dead stop. Elsie continues walking. "D'you think Jeremy Forrest finally decided to put the moves on Romy? Or maybe Oliver Osborn is ready to admit his undying love for Joseph Cheng? *They* have been dancing around each other for months—"

Elsie turns around, finally realizing that I am not following. I make my legs move, even as my brain stutters and stalls.

"How do you know so much about these people?" I ask, to buy myself processing time.

People push past, jostling in and out of the building. For a moment, Elsie seems lost in thought. "Lots of stuff plays out here," she says, looking around us. "So many people who've hung out in the same place for years and still manage to stumble across someone they didn't think could be...significant." She shrugs. "I know we've never been in the middle of any of it, but that doesn't mean I don't pay attention." She tosses the half-eaten apple in the bin and tightens her ponytail. "Anyway. We were talking about our mysterious Romeo. Any ideas who he could be?"

I'm not sure what happens to my words on their journey from my brain to my mouth. It's the strangest compulsion; like the exhilaration of puzzling out half a differential equation, coupled with the almost superstitious fear that the answer might vanish if I voice it before I'm ready.

"No. I have no idea."

Elsie shrugs. "It'll probably just turn out to be some wang trying to bunk on a test." She wraps her scarf tightly around her neck and leads us away from the crowds.

I feel guilty, and confused, and all kinds of wrong for hedging with Elsie.

And, for some unfathomable reason, a little bit energized too.

♥

Admittedly, I'm operating at half capacity in the afternoon. My brain, freed from the shackles of Drama-class anxiety, can't seem to stop puzzling through increasingly more baffling and unlikely scenarios. But the morning's brief reprieve is neutralized in the afternoon, when I'm forced to attend my after-hours session with the school counselor.

Through some combination of my nondescript personality and, I think, sheer blind luck, I have suffered only fleeting encounters with Ms. Shellburn for most of my high school existence. To be honest—up until very recently, anyway—I've managed to handle my issues fairly successfully all on my own.

Today, we are working on strategies for coping with "anticipatory anxiety." Ms. Shellburn is nice and everything, but I find these conversations irritating to no end. I don't know why my "catastrophic predictions about future events" are presumed to be merely the product of some neat syndrome, a collection of diagnostic criteria, and not, say, a logical response to the statistical likelihood of future events sucking whopping great arse. My breath always seems too shallow in her office, and I feel claustrophobic, like my skin is contracting with every minute I'm trapped there. Also, I might not be the most receptive person, but I fail to see how role-playing with puppets is supposed to help me.

I'm unbelievably tired when I'm finally set free. My body feels drained, too, which is mystifying, considering I have spent the last hour silently cocooned in an armchair. But everything is achy, like someone has taken to my body and brain with a mallet.

The grounds are wet, the black clouds ready to burst. But for a moment the rain has stopped, and St. Augustine's is as quiet and gloomy as a graveyard.

I'm scouring through my bag for my bus pass, wondering if ennui is a good enough excuse for a sick day tomorrow, when I see Joshua Bailey sitting near the school gates.

He's perched on the wooden bench at the edge of the parking lot. A wide wedge of grass and a tall iron fence borders the school, sequestering us from the world, like we're uniformed exhibits in the world's dullest zoo. A couple of cars are still in the lot, but the school buses have long since left.

Joshua looks like he is attempting to take half his locker home. He's wrestling a bunch of books, trying to shove them into his overflowing bag. He has a tweed cap on, the same hat he was wearing when I saw him on the weekend. I wonder if it's a small act of rebellion against our draconian uniform policy. I wonder if the hat has some significance, if it's one of his lucky talismans. Perhaps he suffers from an unusually cold head? I fear that I may be distracting myself from asking the right questions.

He looks up, but if he's surprised to see me I can't detect it on his face. He stops fiddling with his books, and the mess settles into his bag like it was waiting for a signal.

"Hello," I say as I come to a stop in front of him.

"Hello, Sophia," he answers. "You're here late."

"Yes, well. So are you."

He scuffs his feet on the asphalt. "History study group. The irony is that Revolutions is, like, the one subject I'm coasting in, but Mr. Kilby had a bit of a tantrum after he got the results of everyone else's practice exams and now—after some tears on his part, I reckon—bammo, compulsory once-a-week study session."

"Oh. Okay then. I usually have a…thing on Mondays too. I haven't seen you here before, though?"

He smiles. It's just a smile—the contraction and expansion of facial muscles that can be rearranged in thousands of different combinations, transmitting mixed signals and information, most of which pass me by—and yet it's the oddest thing. I am almost certain that his smile is a little wistful.

"Yeah. I know," he says.

I consider his face for a moment. But then I realize that I am staring at him, unblinking, in a way that Elsie has gently told me people find weird and creepy.

My eyes drift down the wet road. If I don't leave now, I'm going to miss the bus. Toby and his study partner have a revision session planned, so our place will be in full Arctic mode, complete with soft-rock radio and the occasional math problem that a leery Viljami will bark at me, apparently in an attempt to catch me in a mistake.

I gesture at the space beside him. "Can I sit?"

He leaps up quickly. "Of course. Ah, just wait one sec."

He fishes through his bag and emerges with a crumpled piece of black fabric. He folds it in half and places it on the wet bench.

"Thanks," I say as I sit, somewhat primly. The material is soft velvet, thick and plush. "Do you carry this around in case of emergencies?"

He perches on the very edge of the seat. "Well, you never know when your expertise might be called upon," he says, enigmatically.

I clasp my hands in my lap. He is sitting several handwidths from me, a relatively safe distance away. He unsticks a wet maple leaf from the side of the bench and twirls it in his long fingers. In the brief time I have been aware of this boy, I don't think his hands have stopped moving.

"So today was an odd day," I say experimentally, not prepared to give voice to any of my formless theories just yet. "Admittedly, there have been times when I've hoped for a fissure to open up beneath the Arts building and suck us all into oblivion, but this morning was...unique?"

"I heard," he says evenly. He holds out his hand, and a sprinkling of red maple pieces flutters to the ground. "Sounds eventful."

"Eventful. Sure, that's one way of putting it." I fix my eyes on him, but he seems to be intently scouring the ground. He reaches down for another leaf but freezes midway when I drop my bag with an annoyed thud. "Another way would be to say that someone constructed an elaborate prank. A *pointless* elaborate prank, because if it was aimed at anyone in particular, the recipient has no way of knowing that she or he was the target."

His eyes flicker to mine. "It didn't sound like a prank. It sounded like someone went to some effort, although, now that they think about it, maybe they're worried their motives could be considered...questionable?" His eyes remain on me, more direct than flighty. His cheeks are pink, though that could just be a result of the chill evening air. "And if the *recipient* chooses to remain in the dark, well, does that make it any less clever?"

I stare openly back. I don't know what comes over me, but I feel suddenly reckless, bolder than I have all day. "I'll admit, it was technically adept. But fire isn't miraculous alchemy. Our Paleolithic ancestors managed to figure it out, and those guys found the wheel confusing." I shrug. "There are plenty of people who could have pulled that off."

"Oh really?" he says. He turns, facing me straight on. One eyebrow is raised, his mouth turned up at the corner. I believe the descriptor for his expression is *incredulous*. "Explain it then, if it's so simple?"

I rarely have the occasion to feel smug, you know, on account of the whole freak-brain thing. But Joshua's expression makes the cogs in the corner of my head start to whirr. I narrow my eyes.

"Potassium permanganate and glycerin can induce spontaneous combustion, or maybe sodium chlorate and sulfuric acid with a sugar starter, although that probably would have burnt a hole in Ms. Heller's fingers. Obviously it used some sort of incendiary chemical or compound that reacts with oxygen and possibly friction, or homemade flash paper of some kind—"

He is grinning widely at me, his dark eyes sparkling even in the fading light.

"You know that pyromania is considered an impulse control disorder?" I blurt.

He leans back. "Wouldn't know. Fire doesn't really do it for me," he says lightly. "It's kinda show-offy. Even if you could, say, stand in the middle of a tornado of fire and, you know, the gallon of hairspray on your head didn't melt your face off."

I frown at him. "That's very specific?"

He chuckles. "It's a David Copperfield thing. You know, the Vegas guy? Too much makeup, permanent git-face."

Joshua folds his arms on his bag and rests his chin on his hands. "But maybe the thing itself isn't what's important," he says, that small glitch in his voice making an appearance again. "Maybe the *how* isn't the point."

I find myself staring at his perpetual-motion hands, which are now tapping a rhythm against his school bag. I test, and discard, a few questions before settling on the most pertinent problem.

"So, all right, theoretically then, *why* would someone do that?"

Joshua shoots me a brief side-eye, and suddenly I'm not at all sure if I want him to answer.

I stand up quickly. "Um, I should go. Home, I mean. I should go home now."

He stands as well and digs his hands into his pockets.

"Okay. Sure. It's late."

"Yes. Late. I'll see you," I say with a half wave as I head toward the main gate.

"Sophia?" he calls out.

I turn around again, compelled somehow by the odd urgency in his voice. He's still standing, fidgeting with the brim of his cap. He pushes it up slightly so that his eyes are exposed.

"Yes?"

"The how is easy," he says in a rush. "The how is just a Google search, a bit of library research or whatever. It's not the most important thing. The why...the why is much more interesting. It's the question, isn't it?" He smiles and gives me a brief, shy wave.

I leave him standing in the drizzle as I walk to my bus. I'm thinking about questions, and I'm thinking about fire. But in all the calculations that my brain is capable of factoring, I think I may be overlooking a few very relevant variables.

Chapter Seven

The Extra Dimensions in String Theory

I arrive at school the next morning with a new, fluttery feeling of anticipation. I want to attribute it to this morning's Physics class, because today we are starting a unit on particle accelerators, and really, who wouldn't be excited? But then I find my eyes drifting down the year-twelve corridor. And I realize it's *possible* that I am, in fact, assigning my anticipation in totally the wrong direction.

After morning break I have double Biology, where I take my usual front-row seat. I think I've been a bit preoccupied at break. Part of my brain was focused on Elsie's description of this Rosalind Franklin documentary she watched last night, the rest sliding sideways into untested territory.

He is two minutes late, sneaking in just as Mr. Grayson trips over his laptop cable and sends his Mac crashing to the floor. There is a chorus of guffaws from the class. I use the distraction to cast a quick look over my shoulder. I'm not sure what to do when Joshua catches my eye as he folds his long body into his seat. The hair shielding his face makes it even harder for me to tell what he is thinking, but he holds my gaze with a fleeting smile before dropping his eyes to his books. I do notice that he shuffles his chair over, as far away as he can get from Damien, who has just discovered the diagram of a naked woman in our textbook and is protesting loudly about the apparently disappointing size of her breasts.

Elsie gives me a look as I turn back. "You're in a weird mood," she says without preamble.

"What? Why? I'm in a normal mood, Elsie. A normal, third-period Bio mood, just hoping I can make it through class without catching a glimpse of Lucas Kelly's wiener." I gesture behind me, where, due to the unfortunate height of our stadium lab desks, Lucas Kelly's open fly is once again on display.

Elsie peeks behind us. "Jesus. That kid needs a bathroom buddy. Doesn't he feel a breeze down there?" Her brow is still furrowed when she looks back at me. I smile widely, flashing some teeth. I hold the smile in place for what I hope is a reasonable length of time, but judging by the look Elsie gives me, it's as unconvincing as it feels.

"Yeah. Okay, Sophia. You're in a perfectly normal mood," she says with a snort.

I decide to keep my head in my work, despite the fact that I finished this unit's exercises over last semester's holidays. When I do look around, with eight minutes of class to go, Margo Cantor and Jonathan Tran are swinging their joined ankles beneath their desk like they're holding hands with their feet, and Lucas's fly remains persistently open. Joshua has his head buried in his pocket-sized notebook, seemingly ignoring whatever Damien is babbling in his ear. He uses the end of his pencil to push a strand of dark hair behind his ears, exposing one side of his face. I wonder if it's a conscious gesture or a habitual tic.

My normal and perfectly reasonable behavior continues until lunchtime. When the bell rings, I purposefully pack my bag without looking anywhere else before walking calmly to my locker. I don't even descend into an irritated fugue when some guy with a soccer ball under his armpit grabs me briefly by the shoulders and moves me out of his way.

A tingling on the back of my neck makes me turn and scan the space behind me, but I see nothing of interest.

I open my locker. My books are just as I left them, my Feynman wedged beside my Physics notebook, my chicken-on-whole-wheat sandwich and pear in front. I slot my Bio folder and school diary inside, then grab my sandwich.

I'm juggling my lunch and books when a crisply folded piece of paper slips from between the pages of my diary. It flutters to my feet.

I look around quickly, but no one seems to be paying me any attention. I unfold the paper, heart hammering. In the center of the page, in small, familiar handwriting, is a basic parametric equation:

$$x = \sin t \cos t \ln|t|$$
$$y = |t|^{03} (\cos t)^{1/2},$$
$$\text{where } t \in [-1, 1]$$

I grab a scrap of blank paper. With my head inside my locker and the paper balanced on my diary, I scribble out a quick Cartesian plane. It takes me about a minute to plot out the answer, and another thirty seconds or so with my graphing calculator to double check what I am seeing.

"Oh, you have got to be kidding," I mutter.

Ava Dawson, the hockey captain, who has the locker above mine, glances at me suspiciously. She hasn't uttered a word to me all year. Then again, I don't think I've seen her pay attention to anything that doesn't have a puck or stick in hand.

Ava strides off, muttering something about *strange birds* under her breath. I'm left staring at my hand-drawn parametric solution, a curve plotted across an *x* and *y* axis, which looks like this:

It is the most ludicrous thing I've ever been given. It's the sort of thing the boys at primary school Math camp pass to girls, all sweaty hands and eager smiles, crinkly notepaper encased within Valentine's Day cards featuring kissing swans and too much glitter. It's absurd and super cheesy.

I turn the paper over. There is a tiny inscription on

the other side, the same familiar neat calligraphy, that reads:

You'll probably find this super cheesy. But I remembered this quote, and I thought of you.

And beneath that are the words:

In Mathematics, the art of proposing a question must be held of higher value than solving it.

There is no signature.

I fold the Cantor quote and the scribbled answer within the page that holds the equation and slip them blindly into my pocket. My expression is reflected in the shiny metal as I slam my locker shut. I see confusion coupled with a hint of panic, which I'm guessing is customary when I'm confronted with the unfamiliar. My first thought is that I need to put a stop to this—only, I have no idea what exactly "this" is.

I walk numbly down the corridor and out into the chilly air. I briefly acknowledge then quickly discard the something else I thought I saw in the background of my mystified expression.

It was faint, but I think it might have been the shadow of a smile.

The rest of the day passes without incident or further... encounters of any kind. Elsie and I eat lunch between the lichen-covered concrete lions that bookend the old library steps, huddled together as the wind whips wet leaves around us. There are probably more sensible spots to hang out. But it's quiet and isolated here, and that, to my mind, makes it the best spot at St. Augustine's. I think I manage to behave somewhat normally, or at least no stranger than usual—nothing that draws comment from Elsie. Every now and again I think about the parametrical heart in my pocket and blush behind my school scarf. It's on the tip of my tongue to blurt out everything to Elsie, except she's in the middle of a diatribe about the road trip to Nashville she's planning for her first "college vacation." So I let her steer the conversation to her hypothetical future and remain quiet.

I arrive home in the evening desperate for a shower and pajamas. The walk from the bus is so cold that my skin feels prickly, tiny icicles jabbing beneath my blazer. I may not be looking forward to my future as an eccentric shut-in, but living permanently in fluffy pajamas could be kind of a bonus.

The kitchen is quiet. A half-finished puzzle sits on the table, scattered pieces of tulips and a windmill that Mum and Dad abandoned last night.

I drop my bag, ears straining. I register the sound of rhythmic thumping from somewhere beyond the kitchen. Then, there is a thud and what sounds like a grunt of exertion.

I pause, my brain cycling through a series of alarming visions, courtesy of Elsie—the image of Viljami wearing a bikini and a Spiderman mask flashes behind my eyes.

Sometimes, I really wish my best friend was less evocative with her theories.

There is a crash and a yelp from the hallway. I wipe my brain clean and hurry through the kitchen.

The foyer between the front door and the living room usually holds only Mum's small statue of the Virgin Mary and a side table overflowing with photos of various aunties and uncles and cousins. These things have been pushed to one side, and in their place is a noisy, wobbly treadmill. Toby is running—or at least his legs are moving in a fashion that resembles running. It also vaguely resembles the gait of a gawky gazelle that's had one leg mangled in a hunting trap. The ladder from the shed sits in front of the contraption, and one of our chopping boards is slotted through the rungs. Toby's laptop is balanced precariously on top, along with a stack of books, one of which has clattered to the floor.

"What are you doing?" I call out.

Toby shrieks and stumbles, and for a second I am convinced he's going to face-plant on the moving conveyer belt, a comic pratfall I've seen in half a dozen of Elsie's movies. But then Toby slams a hand on a console button and both the treadmill and Toby's lame antelope-jog jolt to a stop.

My brother jumps down and wipes his face with his jumper, an old Movie World sweatshirt with the face of Sylvester the Cat on the front. His sweaty black hair is plastered to his forehead.

"Why are you here?" he gasps, chest heaving. His glasses immediately fog.

"I live here. Remember?" I reply. "Where did that come from?"

Toby plants his hands on his hips, still breathing hard. "Rented it. Need to start working out." He looks hesitantly at me and smooths back his hair. I'm never sure what is passing through my brother's mind, but I have the oddest suspicion he's struggling with more than just regaining his breath. "Supposed to help boost brain power," he says, whipping off his glasses and wiping away the mist. "Exercise, I mean."

"Well okay, sure. You know, there was this study that said people who exercise a lot have a larger hippocampus—that's the part of the brain most associated with long-term memory conversion. I remember reading that in a journal."

"Of course you did," he mutters.

"Do you want it? I think I still have the issue somewhere."

For half a second I think my brother might actually respond, or at least, that he might briefly forget that he can't stand being in the same room as me. But instead he gathers his laptop and books, perspiring face wiped blank, and stomps to his bedroom.

"Should I take that as a no, then?" I say into the empty, sweat-tinged space.

The only response is the click of Toby's door at the end of the corridor.

I retreat to my room with a sigh.

Perelman stares down at me from his place above my computer. His eyes are shadowed, but even if I could see into them, I have no reason to believe I'd have any clue what he is thinking.

And yet, there's something on the edge of his expression that is almost familiar to me. A glimpse, through his thick Muppet eyebrows and out-of-control beard, of bewilderment that's at odds with his giant brain. I can just imagine how he must have felt in this moment, stunned by the unwelcome flash of a camera while on a brief, rare foray into the world. No doubt he was on some mundane mission, probably going to the store for pencils or bread. I wonder what he did afterward. Did he scamper back to the safety of his tiny apartment, heart hammering, or did he soldier on, marching forward despite the intrusive, unsympathetic eyes upon him? Was he thinking about saddle surfaces in Euclidean geometry, the boundlessness of three-dimensional space, or just trying to make it to the shops without tripping over his own feet or stepping in dog poo?

I sit tiredly at my desk and withdraw the parametric equation from my pocket. My heart thuds wildly, curiosity at war with trepidation. I feel like I've fallen into a daydream not entirely of my own making, like I'm an unprepared companion on an unscheduled TARDIS trip.

I toss the mathematical heart into my desk drawer and slam it shut, then close my eyes, shivering in my too-thin uniform. I can feel Perelman staring down at me. I doubt there is any judgment in his eyes, though.

I pull the flannel shirt from the back of my chair over my lap as I turn on my computer and compose another quick email to the St. Petersburg Steklov Institute. I'm sure I've messed up my syntax, and a few of my verbs are conjugated arse-backward, but it doesn't seem important. The only thing that matters is the question.

Hi Professor Kowalevski,

I understand that Doctor Perelman does not wish to be contacted. I think I probably understand why, though I'm still hoping he will make an exception for another Alexandrov geometry fan. I will try again later.

I don't want to be a nuisance, but I'm hoping you can answer just one thing for me. On the last day that you saw him, did Perelman seem satisfied?

I tug my flannel blanket tighter around my legs.

That word, *satisfied*, in either English or Russian, isn't quite what I want. Satisfied implies that it were possible for someone like Perelman to have found the answers to all his questions, that his brain could finally be at rest. It implies that his curiosity had ceased; that he'd discovered everything he needed to and could therefore be content spending the rest of his life with his feet up in front of the TV.

But then again, what if he *had* reached his limits? Even someone as brilliant as him had to run out of ideas eventually. Maybe in the end what made him run from the world was the realization that he'd done the absolute best he could, but his skills could stretch no further. His life was supposed to be an endless series of achievements. It was supposed to be extraordinary. Maybe, after all those expectations, all that potential, he simply couldn't face the ordinary.

I scan over the email again and hit send.

Then I lie down on my bed, still in my uniform, and fall into a nap until Dad wakes me up for dinner.

Later, Toby disappears to the library, and Mum and Dad park themselves in front of the TV to watch one of the cooking shows they're obsessed with. They try to include me, as they always do, but there's only so much conversational mileage I can get out of tears and kale, and it's not long before I lapse into silence.

Eventually, I find myself sitting alone in the kitchen with a microwaved slice of apple pie, reading an article on my phone about the latest failed Riemann hypothesis proof. This time, it's a German mathematician with giant sideburns, who has spent the last seven years of his life working on something that was immediately proven to be a waste of time.

I feel the last of my energy fade. My eyes fall on Dad's souvenir fridge magnets, little reminders of seemingly every place we have been. Some of our vacations have been okay—like our trip to the Sydney Observatory, and that time we went to Rottnest Island and Toby coaxed a baby quokka right up to my hand. But a lot of our trips have been unmemorable, and some unequivocally disastrous, like that time we went to Cairns with Auntie Patricia and her family, and everyone came down with the stomach flu.

I push away my pie and turn off my phone. I briefly consider my buoyant mood from earlier in the day, and it's possible, probable source. And then I quickly relegate both to the far archives of my brain.

I know there is an axiom in experimental mathematics—out of everything you try, most things don't work.

But how useful would it be to know, before you set out on a journey, if the destination was going to be worth the effort?

Chapter Eight

The Eccentric Orbits of Binary Stars

I sleep badly, jerking awake whenever I start to drift, my thoughts becoming more erratic as the house settles into silence. Needless to say, I feel like balls the next morning. My skin is a sallow shade of day-old coffee, the blue circles under my eyes evidence of a night spent staring at the ticking hands of my clock.

I do manage to make one decision, though. Whatever faltering social experiment I have been conducting needs to stop immediately. I have enough uncertainty in my life. There is no room for another ambiguous variable.

Of course, this resolution is predicated on said ambiguous variable behaving in a logical manner. The limited data I've gathered to date should have been evidence enough that this wouldn't be the case.

Because on Wednesday, as I'm deflecting Elsie's probing questions while struggling to keep my eyes open in Biology class, Mr. Grayson's vintage movie projector at the back of the room starts to whirl. It floods the dreary lab with flickering light—and then begins broadcasting a *Doctor*

Who Christmas special. It's the really great one where David Tennant and the TARDIS materialize on the space-liner *Titanic*. The projector is shoved on top of the grimy shelves at the rear of the lab, and as far as anyone knew, was for decoration only. It's still covered in a thick layer of dust and doesn't look like it's been touched, and it's not connected to a power source that anyone can see. No one can figure out how it is working. David Tennant's pretty face bounces among the projected stars, smiling at me through the dust motes. Mr. Grayson has a bit of a meltdown when he can't make it stop, eventually yanking the safety switch and cutting the electricity to the entire wing. It doesn't help. Through the darkness, the Doctor continues grinning at me for another thirty seconds before fading into the ether.

Joshua vanishes from the lab before I can catch his eye.

I hold the pieces of this incident in my head, but shuffling them around and evaluating them in varying orders does not help it make sense. What's even more puzzling? When I do bump into Joshua in the hallway near the water fountains, our brief exchange somehow segues to the relative merits of cheese sandwiches, with or without Vegemite (Fact: Joshua does not like Vegemite), and NASA's latest theory on the bright spots of Ceres.

On Thursday in Physics, I open my pencil case to discover that all of my pens have been capped with tiny felt fez hats, tassels and all. It's unbelievably useless, but it makes me involuntarily laugh out loud. Mrs. Angstrom glances up in alarm, presumably at the foreign sound coming from my desk. She asks me if I am feeling okay and threatens to send me to the nurse's office.

I start catching Joshua in these odd fleeting moments, snatched conversations filled with the strangest small talk, irrelevant, but somehow never dull. I see him for a couple of minutes at the lockers before Chemistry class and bump into him in the hallway a few times between bells. I notice that Joshua rarely seems in much of a hurry to get to class, and that he's never without his battered notepad and a novel, but only intermittently carries actual schoolbooks. Twice after school I notice him perched on the damp park bench near the main gates, and even though I need to catch my bus, my feet linger there for just a few extra minutes, always curious to see what direction our conversations will take.

Like a nebulous element in the atmosphere that has suddenly become perceptible, there he is: in the background in Biology, frowning as Damien waves something on his phone at him; disappearing behind the Humanities building as Elsie and I hurry across the wet grounds to lunch; hunched in his long jacket and tweed cap as he treks through the parking lot, heading who knows where. Whenever I turn around, it feels like he's hovering just on the edge of my vision, his hair covering most of his expression, half-smile always in place.

I'm not sure I want to deal with any more surprises. But part of me continues to look over my shoulder. Perhaps I'd just forgotten what it's like to walk these corridors with any sense of...anticipation? At least, that's my reasoning for why my eyes are constantly scanning the space around me.

Friday lunch, and I'm waiting for Elsie near the Careers office. Even though Elsie has a solid ten-year plan, my best friend's sessions with the careers advisor are a mystery to me. I have no idea what she finds so useful amid the motivational posters of soaring eagles and baskets of cats. Elsie doesn't have anything in her future to stress about. I said as much to her on our way to homeroom this morning, but I'm not sure she appreciated it. In fact—judging from the stiff set of her shoulders and her one-word responses to my questions—I'm guessing she was a bit annoyed with me. I've wracked my brain, but I still can't figure out why. And when I mentioned it to Joshua in the thirty seconds we had between bells, his face became kind of odd and scrunchy, and he rushed off down the corridor, leaving his Legal folder balanced on the water fountain.

I'm huddled against the wall as a tide of lunch-going students presses past. I'm fidgeting with my sandwich bag, to give my hands something to do, when I notice that my watch is missing. I retrace my steps down the corridor, eyes on the floor, then check through my locker and bag, just in case it's fallen off, but the thin, black Swatch with my initials on the back is nowhere to be seen. I know I put it on this morning—right after brushing my teeth but before knotting my tie—because I have put it on at the same time every morning since year seven. It was a birthday present from Elsie, bought with money she'd saved herself, and the leather strap is solid and unbreakable.

I finally make my way back toward the Careers office, my heart feeling kind of wobbly. I don't know why. It's just a stupid watch. It's generic, and replaceable, not a family heirloom or a priceless relic. But I still feel its empty place on my wrist, heavy in its absence.

Elsie is standing in front of the office, her arms crossed tight. When she sees me, her face breaks into a smile.

"Rey! Heya!" She skips toward me. "Thanks! I don't know where you found it, but it's great. Really."

I stare at her blankly. "Huh?"

Elsie reaches into her bag. She emerges with a small, flat tin, roughly the size of her palm. It looks old, the metal worn and dented. The front has a painted picture of a handful of bright peaches, with a banner reading *Peppermints from the Peach State*. A giant flash in orange font, splashed across the top, reads *Georgia*.

Elsie glances down at her feet. "I know you haven't exactly been down with my plans. But this means a lot. You know. That you're trying to be supportive, in your own way. I just...thanks, Sophia."

And then she rolls her eyes and ferrets around in her pocket. "Though, you know, the watch inside was a bit much. I get it, though, I think. Sentiment? Suppose it's as sentimental as you get, huh?" she says with a grin.

She holds out her other hand. My black Swatch dangles from her fingertips.

"Elsie, I didn't...I mean, it wasn't..."

I have no idea what is happening. But then I catch a glimpse of her face, more open than I've seen it in ages. She is looking at me with nothing but fondness, in a way that I suddenly realize she hasn't done in a really long time. And I find I can't finish my sentence.

"Sure. It's fine. Um, thanks, Els," I say as I hastily retrieve my watch from her hand.

I follow her to our lunch spot, bewildered and disorientated. Elsie seems back to her normal, chatty self. Meanwhile, the wheels in my brain spin and spin. It's tougher than trying to comprehend the Meisner technique in Drama, as incomprehensible as the self-actualization exercises the school counselor once made me do.

I fasten the watch tightly around my wrist, and for a brief instant I'm convinced I can feel the memory of the ghost of a hand there. I can't for the life of me decide if it's welcome.

♥

Another Friday night, and Elsie and I have come back to her place. This decision was made after we arrived at my house to find Mum and two of my aunties giggling over glasses of ginger wine in the living room and Toby scowling down the hallway. He'd managed to cover the entire hall runner in a carpet of notes, a loose-leaf flow chart of cramped writing. Toby was perched on one of the breakfast bar stools, overseeing his handiwork like a sullen lifeguard.

Elsie dissolved into guffaws. Toby gave her a sneer. I tried to intervene, asking him some innocuous questions, but my stock of fake cheer seemed to have finally been exhausted. Not that I think it would have made any difference. Toby's reaction was to lock his jaw and shove his glasses even further up his nose, at which point Elsie wedged herself in front of me and asked Toby if the green-eyed gnome who lived up his butt was making him constipated. Toby's response was to ask Elsie if her fingers were getting sore from hanging on so hard, to which Elsie replied, "My day was great, thanks, and oh, by the way, I'm *still* in the top percentile. Wow, it's nice not hovering in the middle of the road." Their laser-eyed stares were enough to give me a stomach cramp, so I quickly changed out of my uniform and rushed us both out of the house again.

We're side-by-side on her bedroom floor now, having spent a couple of hours on our books, sporadically chatting, and watching romantic-dance-movie compilations that Elsie has saved on YouTube. Elsie's brothers are blasting Xbox from the rec room, and the sounds of explosions reverberate through the walls. Strangely, the noise at the Nayers' doesn't actually bother me. Maybe I have become habituated, but the shouts and body slams rarely make me cringe anymore.

Eventually, Elsie and I head into the rec room, slumping on the couch with a can of Pringles. Raj sprawls on the floor, reaching up occasionally to steal a chip. Elsie and Raj are absorbed in the third season of *Gilmore Girls*, while I am giving one of their dogs a belly rub and contemplating whether Perelman ever had to deal with the intricacies of Alexandrov spaces while simultaneously navigating a weird new... acquaintance? Friendship? Is that even what this is?

I wonder if Perelman would be any more adept at this interpersonal stuff than me? I think about the perfect, unembellished writing in the first part of his Poincaré proof, *The Entropy Formula for the Ricci flow and its Geometric Applications*. I think about his out-of-control beard and his apparent obsession with bread. Somehow, I think interpersonal stuff might be low on his list of priorities.

The Nayers' dog, Chuck, rolls onto my lap. He's a giant ball of scruff with no regard for personal space, yet nothing about the crushing warmth of him makes me anxious. Not even when he shoves his face into my belly and pokes me in the eye with a paw.

Elsie's house is the best; a menagerie of strays from her mum's veterinary clinic, some of which have found their way to the Nayers' fur-covered couches and never left. So many cats have passed through that Elsie and her brothers now bestow only generic names upon them: a stream of Whiskerses and Snowys and Mittenses. Battles for naming rights are reserved for the dogs. Elsie, always science-obsessed, and Raj, who likes obscure fantasy references, have owned a beagle named Elizabeth Blackwell and a Shih Tzu called Orm Embar. Colin sticks to action movie stars, and their eldest brother, Ryan, in a period of cultural pride, once named a litter of abandoned Rottweiler puppies after members of the Indian cricket team, until he got accepted into medical school and decided he was too cool to care about dog names anymore.

The upshot is, Elsie's house currently hosts an incontinent pug named Isabeau, an ageing Rottie named Sunil Gavaskar, and an English springer spaniel, presently drooling on my lap, called Chuck Norris.

When I was little, I was desperate for a tiny piece of the Nayers' life. There's something nice about being around animals; they convey only the most basic of information, and they demand nothing but food and belly rubs.

"Yo, whadup Pinky?" Colin calls out as he wanders in from the kitchen, teetering plate of food in hand. "How's life?"

"Hey, Colin," I say with a wave. "Whatcha doing home?"

Colin shoves a steaming pakora into his mouth. "Ran out of food," he says around crunches. "Share-housing sucks, man. Gonna invest in a lock box for the kitchen, army-style." He flops onto the floor beside Raj and hands him the plate. Colin has adopted another new hairstyle this week, shorn at the sides and swept up on top in a buoyant, swooping curve. His broad shoulders and giant gym-arms make Rajesh look like a strange deflated twin beside him, but Raj and Colin are actually a lot more alike than their stoic eldest brother, Ryan.

Elsie throws a Pringle at him. "You have to actually buy food for someone to steal it, dumb arse. Why don't you just hoard mee goreng under your bed like a normal student?"

Colin collects the Pringle from the floor and shoves it into his mouth. He stretches out his long legs. "Aw, but then I'd never get to see your *sundar* face, Elsie-bean. I'm using it as inspiration for my next short film. I'm gonna call it *The Attack of the Crabby Five-Foot Brown Woman.*"

"Shut your face-hole, Colin," Elsie says, reaching over and grabbing a pakora. She doesn't give me one. I can handle my dad's milky curries just fine, but Doctor Nayer's volcanic creations are way out of my league. "Be nice," Elsie says through a mouthful of food. "One day when you're serving fries and wondering what happened to your life, I'll be the sibling who lets you sleep in my pool house."

Raj laughs, and Colin clips him across the head. He peers over his shoulder at me. "See what I have to deal with, Pinky? Can you believe I emerged from the same uterus as these losers? I don't even know why I bother coming home."

Elsie grins. "It's the open fridge and stellar company."

To the boys of the Nayer clan, I have always been known as Pinky. It's a legacy from the time Ryan referred to me as "The Brain," and Elsie immediately took offense. I don't understand why it's so amusing—I've seen the cartoon, and it seemed kind of silly. Elsie has told me that they mean it with nothing but affection, but still, Pinky is as much as she will tolerate. I've never understood the Nayers' dynamic, all the teasing that never slips into actual fights. But part of me has always been just a little bit grateful to be included.

Eventually, the boys wander off. Colin heads home laden with Tupperware, and Raj heads upstairs to do whatever it is Raj does for hours on his computer.

Elsie scrolls through the Netflix menu. "Want to watch a movie? Rajesh'll drive you whenever you want to go. I'm guessing you're not in any rush, though?"

I shrug. "Toby should be in bed by now, so maybe it's safe."

Elsie sighs. "Yeah, god forbid he gets less than the regulation eight hours," she mutters. "I'd say sleep deprivation couldn't make his personality any crappier, but I think we both know that'd be a lie."

I watch as Elsie selects *The Real Housewives of Atlanta*. "I don't think Toby's personality is the problem. He just doesn't like me, Elsie." This is hardly news, so it shouldn't be cause for the ripple of hurt in my chest.

Elsie sighs. "You know your brother is a giant a-hole, right? A giant, jealous, self-involved a-hole?"

"Toby isn't jealous," I say incredulously, as a gaggle of women on TV shriek about something. "Not everyone is going to like everyone. It's statistically impossible. Even if we did emerge from the same uterus."

Elsie's eyes remain on the screen. Her jaw twitches. "Your brother is a pest, Rey," she says eventually. "I'm the last person in the world who'd defend him, but maybe... you shouldn't just write him off like that. You don't know everything that's going on with him. Not everyone has it as easy as you do."

I keep my face averted. "You think I have it easy," I say flatly. I grimace at the irritation in my voice, but I can't seem to wind it back. "What exactly about your life is hard, Elsie?"

Elsie turns with a sharp bark of laughter-that-doesn't-sound-like-laughter. "Oh yeah. You're right. Everything's just cruisy, Sophia. Well, it's not like you're even interested. Are you."

I give Chuck a rough scratch. On the TV, a lady with a tiny backpack throws a stiletto at a waiter's head. "Interested in what? I know what your plans are. You've spent years talking about them. Eidetic memory, remember? What else do you want me to say?"

Elsie grabs a fistful of Pringles. "Nothing. Never mind," she says, shoving the chips into her mouth. "Let's just watch TV."

"Elsie—"

Elsie waves a hand. "No problem, Sophia. When I have everything all sorted, I'll be sure to let you know."

I hug one of the Nayers' couch cushions to my chest. Chuck's drool pools on my kneecap, and he whines, possibly also burnt by the heat of Elsie's annoyance.

"Well, okay," I say, deflating. I know immediately that I've said all the wrong things, because Elsie's entire body is stiff, and she's chewing salt-and-vinegar chips like she's offended by Pringles themselves. I want to say the right things, but I have no idea where to find the words she seems to want from me. I feel like I've been stuck on this track for months, and I can't seem to change course.

So I sink into the couch, feeling every uncomfortable lump and knot. On the screen, a woman in a dress hurls a vase at another woman in a bikini, and then both of them burst into tears. In the darkest corner of my mind, mismatched thoughts crawl, restless and conflicting. I glance at Elsie's mum's collection of Royal Doulton animal figurines on the side table. I wonder if it would help if I just gave up on my fractious mind and hurled something instead. Ms. Heller would probably be thrilled.

I sneak a glimpse of my best friend. Her body is stiff, but her face betrays nothing that I can read. Elsie's silences are pointed, but rarely aimed in my direction—not since the legendary "why-can't-we-go-to-the-formal?" fight of year eight. And it goes without saying that I am useless at conflict.

No vase-hurling for us, then. But I wish I knew how to bridge this divide that seems to be widening between us with each day that passes.

Chapter Nine

Caught in the difficulty of mystifying, magicians often forget that the first role of the artist is to communicate a beautiful idea.

—Joseph Teller

I pry open an eye as a fuzzy tail thumps against my face. Ginormous blue eyes, ringed with goopy, black stuff, are hovering above me, squinting with a familiar combo of edginess and angst.

"Argh, Gillian—if you're gonna murder me, can you at least have the courtesy to let me sleep through it?" I croak, tugging the blankets over my head.

Gilly yanks my quilt down again. With a scowl that contains no small measure of panic, her tiny hands form two fists and unleash a flurry of thuds onto my forehead. She's kneeling on top of me in her school skirt and tights, still paired with her Bikini Kill pajama T-shirt, her cropped hair smushed into a structure like a piece of abstract art. She's reminding me more and more of a punky pixie, or an evil sprite from one of those confusing Japanese horror movies. Narda turns in a few circles on my pillow before flopping down with a huff, fluffy arse in my face.

I haul Narda down beside me. My cat yowls plaintively, and my sister makes a sound that's almost the same. I close my eyes with a moan, but sleep is obviously not going to be returning anytime soon. With my eyes still closed, I pat Gillian on the head. Her crunchy hair clumps under my fingers. "Why do you even bother with this stuff?" I say with a yawn. "Y'know Mum's just gonna make you wash it out."

Gilly pulls her legs beneath her, sitting cross-legged on top of me. "Yeah, well, unless she's planning to use the garden hose, not much she can do about it, innit?" She crosses her arms. "Pretty sure forced showers aren't legal. It's in the Geneva Convention. Ratified by the United Nations and everything."

I can't help but laugh. "And somewhere, Mum is ruing the day she introduced you to TED talks."

Gilly gives me a grin, part sweet-fourteen-year-old, part obnoxious-demon-child. "She *did* say she wanted me to 'focus my intellect onto less destructive channels.' Knowledge is power, Joshie."

I chuckle and yawn again, scrubbing the sleep out of my eyes. I fumble behind me for the glasses on my shelf and blink myself properly awake before peering up at my sister. "Lemme guess. You and Mum have already gone three rounds, and now you want me to run interference?"

Her eyes slide sideways. "Nah. Not yet anyway." She fidgets with the hem of her skirt. Minuscule Sharpie writing, song lyrics chockful of curse words, weave between the tartan. "See, there's this party on Friday, and I know Mum's gonna freak if I ask..."

I shove my hands under my neck. "*Our* mum? The person who's been trying to get you to socialize since you made your last playdate cry so hard he vomited?" I narrow my eyes suspiciously. "Why would she freak, Gillian? And since when have you even been interested in parties? I thought year eight was, and I quote, 'a soul-sucking vortex spewed from the depths of Hades,' unquote."

She shrugs sheepishly. "Right, but it's not one of the losers in my class having a party, is it?" She steels herself, jaw tightening. "Okay, so I might have made friends with some really cool people, these girls... who might be in year ten..."

I burst out laughing. Narda yowls indignantly and scampers up my bookshelves. "And there it is. Dude, there is no way I'm convincing Mum to let you party with—what—a bunch of sixteen-year-olds? You think I've developed powers of hypnosis overnight? Anyway, why is this even important?"

Gilly flops onto the bed beside me with an affected, world-weary sigh. "It would be important to you, too, if you went to my school," she says dejectedly. "Everyone *sucks*, Josh! And hello, did I mention that they're all *super* boring? These are, like, the only interesting people in the *entire school*."

I reach blindly over my head again, fingers scrambling for the lowest shelf behind my bed. Gillian flips onto her knees and grabs my hands. She is surprisingly strong for someone who could probably fit inside my satchel. "Joshua Bailey, if your solution to my problems is a fricking Hindu Shuffle, I swear to god I will shove that deck of cards up your—"

"Argh, okay, let me go, I need those hands," I say, laughing. Gillian sinks back on her heels, glaring viciously. I prop myself on one elbow and peer at my sister over the top of my glasses. "So, what exactly will this party involve, Gillian? Blood sacrifices and Japanese death metal? A bunch of drunken Bacchanalia with the entire soccer team? No, wait, the soccer team's *mascot*? Bumpy Tony was looking exceptionally fine last sports day—"

Gilly grabs my face and squeezes. "It's gonna be a bunch of people hanging out with Thai food and French movies. *Godard*, Josh, not even the dirty French ones!"

I snort. "Yeah, 'cause that doesn't sound pretentious—"

It speaks volumes about my sister's keenness that she doesn't deck me. "Look, it's going to be tame. Fun and cool, but tame. Help *meeee*!"

When it comes to my mum and my sister, I reckon I'd have better luck trying to negotiate, say, a peace accord between Stalin and Trotsky, or Queen Elizabeth and Mary Queen of Scots, *after* Lizzie had, you know, beheaded her. But Gilly is looking at me with her pleading baby blues, and I can feel my resolve crumbling. Still, since it's my job to mess with my little sister, I can't help but ask, "So whatcha going to do for me?"

Gillian narrows her eyes. "Oh, 'cause I do nothing for you? I'll remember that next time Dad starts up at dinner." She lowers her voice to her best impression of Dad's cheerful tenor. "Josh, how's that exam prep coming? Josh, you gone through that course info yet? Josh, you know we'll be proud whatever decision you make, but you gotta make a decision.

Tick-tock, tick-tock, yak yak yak." She snorts. "You think I mentioned getting kicked out of Italian 'cause I wanted Mum on my arse again? I am not *that* masochistic."

I sit up, suddenly feeling this urge to get out of bed and sprint down the road in my PJs. "You got kicked out? How come? And why is this the first I'm hearing about it?"

She shrugs, not even a tiny bit shamefaced. "Maybe 'cause you tend to drift off when Dad's on your case. And, you know, I got booted for the usual. Talking back, being a disruptive influence. Same crap. It's only for a week, unfortunately. It's freaking tedious, Joshie. Not my fault the morons in class need six months to learn how to ask where the toilets are."

Gillian gives me a look—pointed and way too wise. I find myself staring at her face, caught between baby softness and the sharp edges of looming adultness; it's weirdly, overpoweringly nostalgic. It's becoming almost impossible to recognize the little person who used to cry over *Frozen*, the kid who stuck to my side like a barnacle, spellbound by my dinosaur books and vintage *Horrible Histories* that never seemed to freak her out, even when I re-enacted the gross bits with props. I've always thought I'm a pretty awesome big brother. But I suppose I have to concede that maybe I'm a shitty influence when it comes to school stuff.

I flop onto my back. To be honest, my positive outlook has taken a *bit* of a battering lately. A shift at the magic shop and Camilla's gig on Saturday helped keep me out of the house, but, as a life strategy, avoidance is becoming a bit tricky to sustain. I spent most of the weekend dodging my dad and evading Damien Pagono, who refuses to tell me where he got my number and persists in texting me rude memes. I have, however, managed to avoid all my homework, apart from my History reading and essay, 'cause every time I look at the other stuff my brain melts into a puddle of disinterested goo.

I tug the blankets over my face again. But then the alarm on one of the few functioning clocks behind my head dings, and I'm reminded that it's Monday. My stomach does an insane bounce that propels me reflexively upward. I roll out of bed and land in a pile on my rug, Gillian and a tangle of blankets cascading on top of me.

"Ugh, Gilly, I gotta get up. And you gotta fix your hair before Mum sees you. I really don't want to deal with her brain exploding all over the walls this morning."

Gillian peeps over the top of my quilt. "So you'll talk to her?" She untangles herself and pulls me up. "Josh*ua*. Come on, man! I promise I will give you a week—no, one whole *month* of not making fun of your hair. I'll do flash cards for those chapters in your Bio textbook that I *know* you haven't looked at yet. I'll let you test out as many card tricks as you want on me, and I won't even threaten to smother you in your sleep. *Pleeease*. Mum'll listen to you. Mum always listens to you," she says matter-of-factly.

I run my hands through the tragedy that is my hair. I've worn it long enough to hide behind since I was ten, but since it's reached a length where my sister could manhandle it into a Marie Antoinette bouffant last time we watched the History Channel, I should probably sort it out. Right this instant, though, the only thing I can think about is a shower and school and a certain dark-eyed person who has, mind-bogglingly, not run a mile from my inane babbling. I've caught her a couple of times looking askance at me from a distance—confused, sure, and maybe a bit ambivalent. But as crazy as it is, she actually seems willing to meander down our weird conversational rabbit holes. And then my wandering mind puts *shower* and *Sophia* in the same sentence, and my face explodes in a fresco of heat.

I shove Gillian out of my room. "Okay, fine, I will stick my head on the chopping block for you, baby sister, but can I deal with it later?"

Gillian turns in my doorway and gives me a smile edged with shyness. "Thanks, Josh. I know I sound all *High School Musical* or whatever..." She shrugs. "Not that I care. But, you know, it's nice being around people who don't think I'm a giant freak."

I pause. Gillian scuffs her feet on the floorboards, and for a fleeting moment my sister—formidable, fiery, with the recently developed ability to transform our unflappable mum into a frazzled rage-monster—looks vulnerable and miles younger than her age.

I reach through my doorway and pull her back, trapping her in a bear hug. Gilly, worryingly, hugs me back, not even attempting to squirm away. I find myself frowning into her crunchy hair. "Gillian Anna Bailey, you are a smart, interesting, awesome freak, stuck in a prison of blandness and mediocrity. If you're surrounded by people who can't see you, well, then they don't deserve your awesomeness."

"Yeah, whatevs. Thanks, Josh," she mumbles. Then she shakes herself out of her slushy mood and pulls away, evil grin back in place. "So you reckon Mum'll have a stroke if I tell her Emma's boyfriend just dropped out of college? He's got a neck tattoo. Mum *does* like to say we're not classist."

"Weigh up your priorities, baby sister," I say with a laugh. "I know getting Mum riled is your reason for existing these days, but want some advice? Choose where you direct your energy. If you want something badly enough, it's worth letting all the other stuff go."

I don't think too hard about the uncomfortable jolt I feel as the words tumble out. I don't think it's bad advice. Focusing on a singular goal is fine. I maneuver Gilly down the corridor, then focus all my energy into not falling over the cat as I haul arse to get ready for school.

First period kicks off with Mr. Grayson tripping into my Math classroom, looking every bit like an enemy of the revolution being led to the guillotine. He's obviously been drafted into the substitute roster, and pretty unwillingly, judging by the depressed pong that wafts in his wake. He tries to call the class to attention and immediately drops his coffee all over the stack of practice exams. Everyone pisses themselves laughing. I sink deeper into my seat. I feel a bit sorry for Mr. Grayson, with his Eeyore eyes, and his novelty mug that looks homemade. Its slogan: *Some people choose to be happy. I chose to be a Biology teacher*. I mean, dude, really?

Needless to say, this morning's gonna be a write-off. I crack open my new Robin Hobb novel, ignoring the rattle of furniture as the class rearranges itself. I'm tucked behind my desk at the back of the room; no one's gonna pay me any attention.

My eyes shimmy to my Math folder, which holds my half-finished homework. The conversation with my sister is still fresh—at least, I reckon that's the reason for the uncomfortableness in my chest that feels a whole lot like guilt.

I shove the folder into my satchel, and then I shove the satchel under my desk. I bury my head in *City of Dragons* again, half of my brain tumbling over this new Coin and Fishbowl trick I'm trying to hone. But I can't shake the uneasiness that's been haunting me for ages, like a shadowy creature from an H. P. Lovecraft story, dampening even the brilliance of a bonus, double free period.

See, despite my sister's pronouncements to the contrary, I am actually not a total dumb arse. When crap hits the fan, I can usually pull a finger out long enough to keep me afloat. I actually have, like, an infinite amount of energy for the things I love—stick me in a History class or in front of a Penn and Teller special or give me a stack of books about Arthurian Britain, and I'm all eyes and ears. I dunno. I've just never found the mental endurance to focus on stuff that doesn't automatically hold my attention. If I thought about it—at this particular juncture—it *might* be cause for alarm. 'Cause sticking the History Channel, card tricks, a ceiling-high shelf of fantasy tomes, hanging with my sister, and a fascination with the inner workings of old clocks into a vocational blender has—strangely enough—yet to spit out a workable career option.

I kick my legs up onto my desk. Best not to think about it.

"Yo, dude! Thought we were gonna be stuck listening to Finkler cream himself over derivatives again. Freedom, man! How awesome is this?"

Damien Pagono appears beside me, dragging his desk from the other side of the room till it bumps against mine. The legs scrape the linoleum, sharp and piercing. Shaun Khouri and his brainless friends turn around and unleash a barrage of pretty uninventive insults.

Damien seems unfazed. He sits, coolly, till Shaun and his mates lose interest, then kicks a foot up beside mine. "So. What are we doing with this glorious ninety minutes of freedom?"

I focus on my novel. When all else fails, denial is my friend.

"I could use the time to catch up on some writing. You ever read fanfic? I'm well into it. Been working on this *Harry Potter* story since we moved here. But, like, in my version, McGonagall and Tonks are totally doing it."

I angle myself away from him. I don't know what Damien's game is, but if he thinks he can smoke me out by talking till I cave, he really doesn't know who he's dealing with. Once I went almost a full year without speaking. Not even the combo of my parents and some very expensive therapists could sway me. This melon-faced douchenut has no chance.

"You know McGonagall? Wicked hot, for an old chick. I reckon it's the Animagus thing. And maybe the hat. She's well into some nasty business, too, in my story. Sex stuff," he adds helpfully.

I focus on my book. Black ink blurs on the page.

"Y'know Professor McG can turn herself into any animal? Talk about kinky."

Something about the lost city of Kelsingra...

"Tonks is totally up for the dolphin stuff."

My head snaps up. "Bloody hell, that's...*really* inappropriate."

A triumphant, crap-eating grin blooms across his face. "Whoa, he speaks! Thought I was gonna have to start signing next." He waves demented fingers in my face, forming no words but still managing to look offensive.

I slam my book shut. "Look, what do you want? Why are you hassling me? Do I look like I'm up for a chat about dolphin sex?"

Damien snorts. "Like it's ever the wrong time to talk about dolphin sex. And hello—you're calling *me* inappropriate? 'Cause staring at the back of that chick's head in Bio for the last, oh I dunno, ninety bajillion years is all kinds of kosher?"

I spin around toward him, face flushing. "That's...I don't know what...it's none of your business!"

He rests his hands behind his neck and swings his chair backward. "S'okay. She's hot. Got issues the size of Everest, but she seems cool for a smart chick. She can't act for shit, though. And her friend looks at me like she wants to roast my wang on a Bunsen burner," he says cheerfully.

Despite my better judgment, my ears prick up. "Right. You take Drama too, don't you?"

"Aw, see, you have noticed me!" He flutters his stubby lashes. "Always the quiet ones who'll be stealing an eyeful of your arse when they think you're not looking."

I cross my arms. "Trust me, your arse is the last place my eyes want to venture."

He laughs, an unselfconscious hyena-bark. "Fair enough. I'm counting it as a win that you're looking at my face."

"Okay, fine, I'll bite. Why are you so keen on being buddies? Did you lose a bet?"

He kicks his other foot up onto my desk. "Whoa, someone has self-esteem issues. Paranoid much?" His eyes flitter away awkwardly. "I just figure us losers and loners should stick together. You know. No one can be bothered with the new guy. And you don't seem fussed that everyone here thinks you're hoarding human hair in your lunchbox or some shit."

I snort. "I couldn't care less what people think."

"See? My mum always told me to make friends with the weird kids."

"I have friends," I say automatically.

He rolls his eyes. "Fantasy girl and your right hand don't count."

I nudge Damien's feet off my desk and take another look at him. The dude's sat next to me in Bio since he showed up at school earlier this year, and with a personality like his, he's kinda hard to miss. He's shorter than me, and broader, with one of those spongy, round faces that's destined to head straight into middle age without losing the pudge. He always seems oblivious to the fact that he's the grown-up equivalent of that smelly kid in kindergarten no one wanted to sit beside. Come to think of it, I don't think I've ever seen him hanging out with anyone at school.

Crap on a stick. I run my hands through my hair. "Yeah,

okay," I find myself saying. "But don't think this means I'm inviting you for sleepovers."

Damien grins. He digs a squashed granola bar out of his bag and tears off half, holding it out to me. I decline with a vague headshake.

"So, you and 'The Genius,' huh?" He whistles under his breath. "What are your intentions there?"

Despite everything, I find myself choking on a laugh. "What are you, her dad?"

"Just a concerned observer," he says through a mouthful of choc chips. "You haven't picked an easy target there, bro."

I sigh. "Don't call her a 'target.' And I really don't want to talk about this..." I sneak another hesitant glance at him. "She's really struggling in Drama, huh?"

He tips his chair onto its back legs again. "Yeah. I mean, shouldn't she be, like, off working for some secret think tank in the Netherlands? What the shit is she doing slogging through Heller's crappy improv games?"

I drum my fingers on my desk. I'm worried too. And not just about her morale in Drama. Though she lets slip only slivers of personal stuff, I've noticed some troubling signs lately, little jolts that've been building for months. And aside from my piss-poor efforts, I feel totally powerless to help.

So I may have spent the greater part of Bio this year trying to work out a variation on a Dove Pan trick in my notebook, and staring at the back of Sophia's head while constructing some pretty lame fantasies featuring her sitting next to me and sharing my eraser. But leaving aside my own intentions, or whatever, it's blindingly obvious that things aren't right in her world. It hasn't escaped my notice that Elsie's started angling her stool very slightly away. Sophia never really talks much in class, but she usually has at least a few quiet conversations with her bestie, heads bent close-but-not-too-close together. But lately, Elsie's been responding with only nods and brief, strained replies. Nothing like her usual self, full of hand gestures and warmth.

I've seen it coming for months, this friction between them. It's palpable, even from the outside, and it makes my heart break a little.

Beside me, Damien is still talking.

"Sorry, what?"

He ferrets out a packet of BBQ chips. "I was saying, chicks dig flowers and shit. You tried flowers?" His eyes dart sideways, grin still in place, but there's something kinda perceptive there too. "Or maybe you could just ask her what her problem is?" He packs his gob full of chips and shrugs. "Girl looks like she could use a friendly face."

I add a column in my mental notebook headed: *The Elsie/ Sophia Conundrum: More Possible Assists and/or Solutions*. I ignore the fact that Damien Pagono, with his shirt buttons askew and a whole pack of Lay's shoved in his mouth, is offering *me* romantic advice. If I were prone to self-pity, I'd be feeling just a bit pathetic right about now.

At the front of the classroom, Mr. Grayson has given up trying to salvage any authority and appears to be watching Netflix on his phone. "But what would I know," Damien says blithely. "My mum says I'm as useful as a one-legged guy in an arse-kicking contest. I'm holding out for college, man—maybe older chicks will be into weird dudes?" He shoves the empty chip packet into his pocket and nudges my foot—somehow his rank size nines have ended up back on my desk. "So. You gonna keep ignoring me?"

I'm tempted to happily forget this conversation ever took place, but then I catch another glimpse of Pagono's face. Beneath the bravado and chip crumbs, he looks bashful, and maybe a bit hopeful. Damn it to hell. My karmic juju better be skyrocketing.

I close my eyes. "Okay, fine. But dude, you gotta stop texting me dodgy memes. It's not endearing. How did you even get my number?"

Damien taps the side of his nose. "Internet's a magical place. Phone numbers, weird-as-shit fan art—I'll send you a link for this site that's nothing but pictures of the Hulk on the toilet."

"Fantastic," I say dryly. But Damien is looking at me like he's pulled off his first Acrobatic Aces, and I can't bring myself to sound completely sarcastic.

Mondays are usually pretty chill—Math, which I normally snooze through, double English, which is tolerable, and History, which is really the only school-related reason for getting out of bed. But this Monday seems determined to chuck a whole box of metaphorical spanners right into the eyeball of my day.

In my rush to leave the house, I forgot to bring my brûlée torch and snow-in-a-can, which means my Sophia plan will be behind by a whole day. Halfway through break I get a message from my sister that reads: *Today has turned into a Joy Division song* (which is Gilly-code for: *I will need Cartoon Network and tons of ice cream when I get home*). I text back a couple of poo emojis, 'cause I know not even my most charming patter will convince Mum to let Gillian loose with a bunch of strangers, and I can't think of anything else helpful to say.

But yeah, my head is a bit elsewhere, and my lack of attention serves to bite me gigantically in the arse. I forget to take the long way past the Careers office as I head to my lunch hideout, and I'm promptly pounced upon by Ms. Mehmet, the Careers counselor, who appears from out of nowhere like she's materialized from a Houdini box. I've managed to sidestep her all semester, but she's clearly been on a mission to track me down. The upshot is I get stuck in her office doing some inventive, evasive talking to avoid her questions, my stomach growling.

Damien finds me as I'm rushing to my locker and helpfully chucks a mini-bag of cookies at me before he scampers to Business Management. Judging by his expression when I accept them, I think this pretty much means we're engaged.

I'm kinda bummed that my careful plans have fallen in a heap. I'm trying my best to stay optimistic, but it feels just a bit unfair, the way the real world keeps worming, inescapably, into my life. And to top it off, I barely catch a glimpse of Sophia all day.

I'm operating on Teddy Grahams and hope as I escape

study group the second Mr. Kilby closes his laptop. My contact lenses are itching like crazy from the overheated classrooms, and my stomach is pitching. I burst out of the building, casting a glance at my watch as I scramble across the parking lot.

I know I've done nothing worthy of her attention today. Maybe the smidgen of curiosity I thought I sensed was just a figment of my imagination. Maybe she's already bored? I'm not so delusional as to think our little conversations would set her world on fire. I need to think bigger. Way bigger. Or maybe...maybe I'm already disappointing.

I skid across the soggy lot, tugging on my jacket and cap, and there she is.

She's sitting right on the corner of the bench near the gate. Her long fingers are clasped in her lap, her eyes trained on the darkening street.

I force myself to slow, though my heart seems to be trying its best to climb up my esophagus. I stop, for just a sec, behind Mr. Kilby's ancient MINI Cooper, and I call upon every internal resource, every public speaking tool and technique that I've forced myself to master over the years. I breathe, and then I walk.

"Hello," I say brightly.

Sophia glances up, no surprise showing on her face.

"Hello."

"Missed your bus?"

"Yes. That's happened a bit lately."

She's bundled within her coat but shows no reaction to the gusting bitter wind. In this light, her irises have a hue around them that's not noticeable during the day, circles of russet lighter than the almost-black of her eyes.

She gestures, a little stiffly, to the seat beside her. "Are you going to sit?"

I'm kinda proud of the fact that I don't bust out a happy dance. Instead, I pull myself up onto the backrest of the bench and plant my feet on the seat a safe, few lengths away from her.

When I lean forward with my forearms on my knees, I can just about see her profile. I wish I could sit close enough to see all of the subtle expressions that pass across her face, but I know she's not comfortable with anyone in her space. She turns toward me, narrow-eyed and contemplative.

We sit in silence. Before I can muster up some patter, Sophia's cheeks flush, the soft brown dusted with pink. She looks away quickly.

"Sorry," she mumbles.

"For what?"

"I'm staring. It's not polite. I've been told I can be a bit creepy."

I laugh, pleased that even through the nerves it sounds almost normal. "And I've been told I could pass for the wooden-spoon winner of an Edward Cullen look-alike contest."

She gapes up at me, her resolve to stop staring apparently forgotten. "Someone actually said that to you?"

I shrug. "Yeah, but to be fair, a giant dude in rollerblades had just kneed her in the head. I had to sit with her in the emergency room. I might have been dressed in a Kaonashi costume at the time. It's a long story," I say sheepishly.

Sophia still looks mortified. I scramble for something else to say, 'cause I can't stand the thought that *that* is how she sees herself. "And, y'know, as someone who spent most of his childhood impersonating a horror movie extra from a German silent film—and yes, that is also something someone recently said to me—I can say with authority that you are *not* creepy."

She waves a dismissive hand. "Right. And the fact that you're sitting way over there like I'm going to implode if you get closer?"

I balk. I drop onto the seat beside her, careful to not let our shoulders bump. "You don't like people in your space. That isn't a crime."

She shakes her head with a sigh. "So it's obvious even to a casual observer? Excellent." She peeks hesitantly at me. "It's not that I don't *like* it. It's just... I'm not good with people. I'm hopeless at figuring out what they want or expect. Sometimes it's just too much to unravel, and it's not always...comfortable. The not knowing, I mean. Other people can be very...intense." She shakes her head, like she's being thwarted by the words themselves.

I stare out over the road. The last of the school pick-ups is pulling out of the gate, red taillights bouncing off the drizzled asphalt. It's not like I hadn't guessed that she has some—well, issues with social stuff. But even though my observations have been slightly more concerted than casual, I'm starting to wonder just how much I've actually been allowed to see.

"Then I really don't understand why they stuck you in Drama," I blurt. "It's not completely bizarre to want to keep to yourself, to *not* want other people in your face. It seems kind of mean that they'd put you through that."

"It's my own fault," she says with a shrug. "It was just a suggestion. For a moment there, I actually thought it might not be a totally bad idea." She shrugs again. "It's not like I protested."

I swallow down my words, caught by the blank tone in her voice. "Your parents must have, like, crazy high expectations?" I say carefully.

She looks at me incredulously. "What? No, not at all. I mean, it's not like they wanted me to get a PhD at twelve. They didn't even want me to skip grades, no matter how many times it was suggested." She looks out over the gray road. "I don't think my mum and dad ever really knew what to do with me," she says, almost as if she's talking to herself. "I remember lots of closed-door conversations when I was a kid, always right before I ended up enrolled in junior softball or Girl Guides or something."

"Really? You were a Girl Guide?" I say, ferreting this new information away in my ever-expanding Sophia file.

"Briefly. When I was seven." The corners of her lips turn up as she peers at me again. I'm startled by this new smile, enigmatic and verging on cheeky. "I might have used some ping-pong balls and, ah, unsupervised cleaning supplies to build a few...concussion grenades at Winter Jamboree. It's not like I blew anything up. Well, a couple of sleeping bags, but that was an accident. I wasn't invited back, though."

I burst out laughing. "Wow. I may have a totally wrong picture of you in my head."

"Oh?"

"Yeah, I have this image of little you, y'know, sketching formulas on your windows with crayons—I never pictured you taking inspiration from the *Anarchist Cookbook*."

She crosses her arms but doesn't look displeased. "Any idiot can make napalm in a toilet. It doesn't exactly qualify you for a Nobel."

Bloody hell, what was I doing at seven? Probably trying to master a shoddy Overhand Shuffle and stockpiling my words for what would soon become an ambitious bout of silence.

I'm treated to another one of those brief, shrewd glances. "It's not that impressive. And… I believe I'm talking to the guy who can make his own spontaneously igniting flash paper. Right?"

It's my turn to blush. For some reason it's not something we've talked about, not directly, anyway. I dunno why. Suddenly, I'm struck with this awful realization—like I've dangled my heart on a parlor rope, and she hasn't even noticed that it's out there swinging. Why won't she acknowledge it? Maybe 'cause she sees my stupid feats for what they are: harebrained and insignificant.

Luckily it's almost fully dark now, and I doubt she can see my flaming skin. The dark makes it harder to see what her face is doing too, though she's still pondering me closely.

Sophia averts her eyes. "Anyway. The other kids seemed

to think it was cool. And my Den Mother said I wasn't going to win friends with my 'sparkling personality,' so I worked with what I had." She seems to shake herself out of nostalgia-mode. "After that, my parents stopped trying to enforce the social stuff as much. But I still think they wish I'd just try and be normal."

"Normal?"

She shrugs. "Sure—a regular paste-eating, Drama-class-attending, party-going kid. You know. Normal."

"No. I don't know what that means," I say flatly.

She looks at me quizzically. And then she chuckles. "Well if that's true, you're the only person I know who doesn't have a definition for it."

She stands up. The drizzle has started again, so light I can barely feel it, but I can see it tumbling in the streetlights behind her. The damp has made her hair look impossibly thicker, raven pieces curling around her face. Sophia pulls her jacket hood over her head. "I have to go. Sorry for...sorry." She gives me a wave and walks away before I can unglue my stupid, worthless tongue.

I shove my hands into my jacket pockets, realizing through my clearing brain-haze that I've been drumming them like crazy on my thighs.

I wonder if she can feel my eyes on her as she disappears into the dark, if my longing is transmitting in waves through the dank parking lot. It's an effort to keep my legs still, but I force myself to lock every muscle and sinew in place to avoid running after her. It wouldn't do any good. I've got nothing useful to do or say. I need to think. I need to plan. I need to do…something. But I can still see her face, gloomy and defeated, and nothing, no matter how big, feels like it could possibly be enough.

♥

Chapter Ten

The Causality Principle

I think I'm coming down with something. I seem to have amassed a collection of physiological symptoms, which some frantic googling indicates could be either a mitral valve prolapse or the early stages of dysentery. My skin is clammy all the time, my stomach permanently in knots. The glimpses I catch of my brother as he skulks around our house send my insides plummeting. Being stuck in the Biology lab beside a silent Elsie makes my chest constrict. And even approaching the Visual and Performing Arts Center is enough to make swallowing difficult. Maybe I have developed an ulcer? Trust my body to inflict some old-man ailment upon me on top of everything else.

Nothing out of the ordinary happens this week. There are no surprises, no disruptions, nothing other than a brief flurry when Mr. Grayson rear-ends the principal's car on parent-teacher night.

Joshua smiles when he sees me, but it seems oddly unnatural on him. It's like he's constantly on the verge of saying something but keeps changing his mind at the last moment. I don't know what I was thinking. Why *wouldn't* he think that I'm a huge, intractable freak? Obviously, whatever brief...whatever it was has passed now. It's fine. Though I do feel like a bit of a dipshit, because I *still* haven't been able to discuss any of this with Elsie. It's like part of me is holding back, hoping that...well, hoping. It's an uncomfortable, alien feeling.

I don't think my lack of focus is apparent in class, though. Elsie does give me a few odd looks, but it wouldn't cross her mind to wonder what I've been up to. Her school diary is filled with flyers about America, and once, when I tracked her down at break, I found her sitting with Marcus and Nina and their friends, poring over the Atlanta *Lonely Planet* on Marcus's iPad.

I want to talk to her. I feel guilty, like I am responsible for this growing distance between us. But every time I open my mouth, something in the back of my brain tells me to stop.

After intense analysis, I conclude that I am either experiencing the world's slowest stroke or that some part of me is reassured by the fact that the person who knows me best doesn't know about this one thing. And though I poke and prod at this mystery, throwing multiple theories against my mental walls, I have no idea why that might be.

I clock with interest that Joshua and Damien appear to have become friends. I see them in Biology, Damien nattering in Joshua's ear. I have no idea what's happened there. But on Friday they seem to be having a heated discussion, Damien whispering animatedly while Joshua shakes his head, a flush staining his cheeks. When Damien waves his hand in my direction, I decide to stop snooping and focus hastily on my books.

Elsie cancels our Friday night study session, telling me that she has a “family thing” as she rushes off to band practice. She doesn’t look me in the eye. I have no clue how to process her evasiveness.

Turns out, I don’t have much of a chance to try. Because on Friday evening, another first happens.

A boy calls me on the phone.

I answer the unknown number after pondering my screen uncertainly. There is a pause on the other end. I hear distant music and the sound of someone clearing their throat. My heartbeat seems to amplify in the quiet.

“Sophia? Um, hi. It’s Josh. Joshua Bailey? I hope you don’t mind me calling? I just wanted to...check in and...say hey.” He clears his throat again. That hitch in his speech is more apparent over the phone, the muffling of his Ss and Ts that is, in an inexplicable way, interesting. “Are you busy?” he says.

I sit down on the edge of my bed. “No. I’m trying to learn Russian,” I say, and immediately feel ridiculous. I don’t know what normal people do with their Friday nights, but flicking through the online *Transactions of the Moscow Mathematical Society* probably isn’t it.

“Russian? Whoa, that’s cool. Ivan the Terrible, Rasputin, the Revolution—although, you know, probably not so cool if you were a Romanov. The whole execution by firing squad thing would’ve tanked. So how many other languages do you speak?”

And even though this week has seriously sucked, I can't help but smile a little as he launches into conversation as if no time has passed since the last time we spoke. "Three. Well, sort of. My French and German are okay. The Russian is adequate. For now."

He whistles. "I never had the patience for languages. Only thing I remember from year-seven Chinese is how to ask for directions to the mausoleum of Chairman Mao."

"Really? Strange, since you've obviously spent hours perfecting, what—disappearing a pencil into your ear?"

I feel like I can hear him grinning. "What can I say? My focus has always been pretty specific. So why Russian?"

I glance at my desk. My last email to the Steklov Institute remains unanswered; the picture of Perelman is curling at the edges now. I realize that my obsession is bordering on unhealthy, but I can't stop thinking about him. Lately I've been wondering when exactly his downward spiral began. Was it one thing, one event, one catastrophe that tipped him over the cliff edge he'd been teetering on? Who was he when he was young? Was he optimistic, confident in the limitlessness of own abilities, or did he already feel the panic of impending disappointments pressing down on him? Christ—was he hiding out in his bedroom on a Friday night while reading obscure geometrical theories in Latvian or something? Probably. This thought does not make me feel any cheerier.

I think I've been silent for a few beats too long. I think about the parameters of the standard conversational topics that I know. But when I open my mouth, I find myself launching into a diatribe about Grigori Perelman, about the Poincaré proof and topological spaces and his mystifying vanishing act. My hands are shaky when I finish, and as soon as I fall silent, the heat rises, blistering, in my face. I can't believe I have just unloaded all of that, without so much as a pause for breath. What must be going through his mind—

"Whoa. That's intense. He turned down a *million* bucks? Dude must've really wanted to stick it to the establishment. But bloody hell, what a grand finale." The sound of genial tapping echoes through the line. I can just imagine him drumming his ceaseless hands on his desk or something. "Though I suppose it would suck to have the highlight of your life happen when you've still got tons of it left to live," he says thoughtfully. "You think he maxed out too soon?"

My hands are trembling. "Maybe. Something like that."

"Maybe…I think that's also the most I've ever heard you say in one go," he says quietly.

I rub my gritty eyes. "I used to talk more, I think," I hear myself say.

I used to talk a *lot* more when I was a kid. Before I figured out what the shared side-eyes and giggles of my classmates meant, before I learned that they could be avoided if I just kept quiet. I think I used to get so excited that I lost myself, not realizing that normal people just didn't care about the things I found exciting. I'd forget that my voice was supposed to stay at a certain level, not too loud or too high, that my hands were allowed to gesture, but only so emphatically. But there always seemed to be someone around to point out what I was doing wrong. In those fleeting moments when I forgot to be cautious, and vigilant, there always seemed to be someone who was happy to put me back in my place.

The sound of the rain is loud in the quiet house. “Sorry. All that is probably pretty uninteresting.”

He is quiet for a long moment. “You know, Sophia, you don’t have to be so careful about what you say,” he says softly. “You don’t always have to… pretend.”

I snort, a pathetic puff of air that has no energy behind it. “Ask anyone in my Drama class if I have any skills in pretending. Check with your friend Damien. I can’t even successfully fake being a normal human.”

“That’s not what I meant. It’s just, I know what it feels like,” he says slowly. I hear the sound of a door closing in the background. “Triple-checking everything in your head before it comes out of your mouth.”

“How do you have time to check anything before it comes out of your mouth?” I blurt.

He laughs. “Okay, whatever. I know I talk too much.”

His tone is light, but I’m struck by a wave of panic. “I’m sorry! I didn’t mean to be insulting. Sometimes I say something, and in my head it sounds perfectly logical, but somehow it ends up sounding rude when it comes out of my mouth.”

“Hey, I’m not that easily offended. Don’t stress.”

I exhale. “I’ve been told I’m not always a nice person,” I mumble.

“Who told you that? Wait—first of all—I think you’re nice.” His voice brightens, as if he’s discovered the answer to a tricky problem. "You're, like, the most honest person I've ever met. You want people to like you, but you don't pretend to be something you're not to make it happen. I know you'd never do anything to deliberately hurt anyone—I've seen how you are with Elsie." He clears his throat, an unasked question hovering between us. "But, Sophia, for whatever it's worth—you don't always have to be nice for me to like you."

I look up, somehow surprised to find that he is not sitting right there beside me. It's the oddest thing, this disembodied conversation. In real life, I can never seem to figure out the appropriate amount of time to devote to eye contact, especially in those moments when I'm focused on what a person's saying and not, you know, on what my face is doing. It's the reason I find myself talking to my feet or staring at a person until they get all awkward.

But I remember him holding my gaze, neither put-off nor discomfited by my blinkless stare. Waiting, patiently, for me to speak.

"I've been told I make people uncomfortable," I say, experimentally. "It doesn't seem to matter that I don't do it on purpose. The rules with people aren't always logical. Everyone I know keeps trying to fix me. Everyone seems to think I'd be happier if I could just be the way everyone else is and, you know. Smile when I'm supposed to, I guess."

"Oh, I call bullshit," he snaps. I startle at the harsh tone in his voice. "And no, I'm not annoyed with you, not at all, but I'm pissed that people've made you feel that way. It isn't your job to make them comfortable. Maybe it's not you who needs to keep pretzeling yourself to make everyone else happy? Maybe who you are is perfect, and everyone else just needs better glasses."

I get up and pace a circle from my bed to my desk. I don't know what to do with this strange, squashed feeling in my chest. I sit heavily on my bed again. "Joshua. Can we talk about something else?"

He exhales, his breath heavy through the phone. Then he chuckles. "Sure. All right. Small talk. Amazing weather, isn't it?"

I look out my window at the bleak, dark sky, not a single star visible. "Melbourne weather sucks balls. Next."

He laughs again. "Okay, no weather. Did you catch the game on the weekend?" He bursts into guffaws before I can respond. "Nope, I can't even. Come on, your turn."

"Okay." I think about something I've heard my dad ask our neighbors when he fails to avoid them while collecting the mail. "Got plans for the weekend?"

"Weekend plans, how mundane! Let's see—my sister needs help building this HMS *Endeavour* model for her Australian History class, which means I'm going to end up neck-deep in craft glue and popsicle sticks while she listens to podcasts. I'm working at the shop on Sunday... oh, some friends are having a party Saturday night."

"You're going to a party?"

"Yeah, probably. I bunked on the last one, and I never heard the end of it."

"Oh," I say. I'm not sure what I expected. Of course he's a normal person, with friends and normal friend-things like parties and movies and whatever else normal people do. He's not some freak who gets stressed in a crowd, who hasn't been to a pool since he was eight because the thought of a stranger brushing against his skin makes him feel all prickly. Of course he'd be fine at a party. He's a normal guy with a normal life—

"Sophia?" he says quietly. "Um, there's going to be heaps of people there, and the place can get kind of crazy—"

I head back to my desk and my Russian and my Perelman. "It's okay. Have fun."

"Hey, see, I'd really like you to meet my friends, but I'd never ask you to do anything that you didn't want to do—"

"I get it. Don't worry, I wouldn't want to be stuck at a party with me, either."

I hear him take a deep breath. "Sophia, would you like to come with me?" he says in a rush.

I look around my room. The answer is no, of course I don't want to go to a party. I want to spend Saturday night in my bedroom, in my pajamas, with vintage Hartnell *Doctor Who*. The "no" is gathered behind my breath, but somehow it refuses to release. I don't know what's possessing me; it's like a book that I haven't read, a Schrödinger's box with an unknown paradox inside. And then I think about Elsie's stubborn insistence that I "learn to be fine on my own," and I feel my resolve harden.

"Sure," I hear myself say, distantly. "I'll come. If it's okay? Will your friends mind? Are you sure you want me to—"

"I want you to," he replies.

My eyes skirt around my room. I'm struck by the alarming thought that I'm behaving just like Sandra Bullock from Elsie's crappy movie: preoccupied with the color of the leaves in autumn, when I should probably be investigating the time hole in my mailbox that has the potential to suck the universe into oblivion.

"But, ah, Sophia, there's something I should say first. I just need to get this out of the way, before...well, before. I need to say this in advance."

"What?" My voice sounds kind of hoarse.

On the other end of the line, I think he might be smiling. "I'm *really* sorry about Adrian."

♠

Chapter Eleven

The Multiverse Conjecture

I am sitting in the kitchen, staring at the blinking microwave clock. Dad made a giant lasagna before he and Mum headed to the movies with Auntie Rema and Uncle Wes, but my stomach is tumbling and there's no way I can eat. I'm wondering if it's too late to run to Elsie and beg for her advice. I'm also *really* wishing I'd managed to absorb even the rudiments of Method Acting theory—maybe I could have developed a completely new personality between now and 8 P.M.

I don't do parties. Generally, yes, because I can't deal with crowds, but also because I just know I'm not *fun*. I'm not loud or enthusiastic, and I don't get small talk and never, not even when Ms. Heller has threatened me with detention, have I been able to master a breezy, carefree laugh. How am I supposed to keep this boy entertained? Is that even what's supposed to happen? And what if—

Toby wanders into the kitchen, his glasses tucked into the collar of his pajama shirt. His hair is standing up like a lopsided black mohawk, as if he's been continuously running his hands through it. He recoils in the doorway when he sees me.

"What are you doing?"

I glance at the clock again. Less than two minutes have passed since I last checked. "I'm going out. To a party. With a friend," I say, testing the words. They feel foreign in my mouth. It's cold in here, but beads of sweat are forming on my forehead.

Toby frowns. "A party? You? With who?" He crosses his arms.

My fingers curl where I have clasped them on the table. I stare at my brother, at his stupid pinched face and his ridiculous Kmart pajamas, and all the anger and annoyance and anxiety I've been fighting seems to coalesce into a tight, focused ball. "What is it, Toby?" I snap. "Am I stealing your air molecules? Ruining your view of the fridge? Or is it just my face that makes you mad?"

Toby takes a step backward. For a moment, I think he will just back out of the room in a huff, but he runs his hands through his fauxhawk, and his laugh is sharp and short. It sounds like he's been sucking on a lemon, the laugh forced out through vocal cords shrunk tight with acid.

I think the bitterness in Toby's laugh surprises even him. His face collapses in on itself. It's almost fascinating, like witnessing a Tetris game of tumbling, mystifying emotions. My words have dried up, but clearly, Toby has found his.

"Yeah, your face makes me mad. You and your helpless, life-is-so-tough act. You...you know, the rest of us have to actually work for stuff. That doesn't mean anything to you, does it? You're selfish. And the shitty thing is, you're not even capable of recognizing it. You don't *feel* anything."

Toby takes a deep breath. For a moment, I think he has something else to say; for the briefest second, I almost imagine that he hesitates. But then he squares his shoulders and marches out of the kitchen without another word.

I stare at the microwave clock. Four minutes have now passed. Distantly, I'm aware that was probably the longest sentence Toby has directed at me since his voice broke. I'm also aware, in this odd, detached way, that at least I can now confirm my hypothesis. My brother hates me.

I get up and carefully smooth down my dress. I suppose it should be comforting, in a way, to know where I stand. Mystery solved. Elsie will be delighted.

I try to rouse some righteous indignation, but all I feel is tired, and unaccountably empty.

I feel things. I *do*. I just don't share myself with the world in the way I'm supposed to. But maybe none of that matters. Maybe all the work that my teachers and my parents have put into making me a whole, functioning human is not for me at all, but so the rest of the world can feel comfortable with who I am. And clearly, I am sucking zebra balls at it.

I understand that spontaneous human combustion is a myth, but I fear I might take out the kitchen with a nuclear blast of frustration if I don't get out of the house right this second.

Twenty minutes and a taxi ride later, and I am standing on a corner block surrounded by tall hedges, wondering what part of my cerebral cortex is responsible for this ridiculous mission. A small iron gate springs midway along the hedge border. I pause and peer through the bars. Joshua's house lies beyond.

Though, really, I'm not sure that "house" is the correct moniker. It's not exactly a mansion, but I am guessing there is probably a mansion-adjacent descriptor for it. His front yard could comfortably hold my entire house.

Perpendicular rosebushes line a path that leads from the side gate to the porch. The yard is pristine, all clean edges and giant trees. But my eyes are drawn to the inconsistencies; a kid's bike dumped on the driveway, a pile of shoes on the wide porch. It's like real people have been dropped into the middle of a fantasy landscape.

The gate closes behind me with a *snick* as I walk down the bluestone path. My body is doing its water-kneed, fight-or-flight shuffle, reminiscent of every trip across the lawn to the Arts building. I shouldn't be here. I should have stayed home with George Boole and Tom Baker. But whatever has drawn me here doggedly refuses to march my feet backward.

The porch lights brighten as I approach the house. My eyes drift upward, taking in the second story and the gabled windows of the rooms above it. A warm glow emanates from the window of what looks to be a turret.

Fact: Joshua Bailey is loaded.

I stop at the bottom of the porch stairs, my phone clutched in my sweaty palm. I'm not sure what to do, so I send an impulsive text.

Hey. I'm at the front of your place.

I peer nervously up at the house again. It remains silent, and yet I can practically feel his energy barreling toward me.

He throws open the door, eyes darting. When they land on me, his face morphs into a big, shy smile.

I try to return it, but all I manage is a grimace. "Um, I know I'm early but I needed to...I mean, I wanted to..."

Joshua trips lightly to the edge of the porch and looks at me over the railing. "No, no, it's fine. You just surprised me is all. Hey!" he says, grinning wildly. "You're at my house!"

I don't bother commenting on the obviousness. He's wearing a black-and-gray checkered shirt, his hair curling over the collar, and jeans but no shoes, his bare feet poking out of frayed cuffs. The warmth radiating from inside the house battles with the arctic bluster of the wind through the yard. Joshua wraps his arms around his body and tucks his hands into his armpits.

I wait for a few heartbeats, but none of Joshua's usual verbal calisthenics are forthcoming. So I blurt out the first thing that comes to mind.

"I didn't know you wore glasses?"

He adjusts the black frames. "Ah, yeah. Busted. You didn't give me time to put my contacts in."

"Oh. Sorry. They don't look bad or anything. The glasses. They look good," I say, before my brain finally slams on the brakes.

He runs a hand through his hair. "My sister says I look like, and I quote, 'an anemic Clark Kent if he were the nerdy one in a hipster boy band.' I don't think it's meant to be flattering."

I shiver as I'm hit by another gust of frigid wind. Joshua takes a few hurried steps backward. "God, I'm an idiot. You must be freezing! Come inside."

I take the porch steps till I'm standing beside him. He pauses in the doorway, head tilted. From somewhere, loud music blares, punctuated by angry shouted lyrics.

Joshua looks over his shoulder at me. He places a finger on his lips, eyes twinkling, and whispers, "On my signal, make a run for it."

I hesitate. "Joshua, I don't want to get you in trouble—"

He reaches behind him, fingers closing lightly on the edge of my sleeve. "Nah," he says in a stage whisper as he tugs me into the house. "It's fine, it's just, I'd rather my sister didn't know you were here. Trust me, an interrogation from a Viet Cong proctologist would be way less invasive." He hustles us into a spacious foyer. I take in impossibly high ceiling, polished floorboards that extend down a long corridor, and a curved staircase off-center, with another, narrower corridor running behind it. To the left are wide double doors that open into a library, plush armchairs nestled in a circle and heavy shelves overflowing with books.

I glance at Joshua, only just now processing that his fingers are still looped loosely around my wrist. He seems to be staring at the spot where our hands meet. Behind his glasses, his eyes are a little wide. He lets go of me quickly at the same time that I, reflexively, pull away. He sticks his hands in his pockets.

"So this is home," he says.

Granted, I don't have the keenest judgment when it

comes to other humans, but the inside of Joshua's house isn't what I imagined from the imposing exterior. There's artwork on the walls that looks fancy and expensive, but it's fighting for space among framed kids' drawings and finger-painted canvases. The furniture that I can see is mismatched and well-worn but still manages to look coordinated. And it smells *warm* inside, like baked fruit and wood smoke.

"Huh," I mutter. Joshua looks at me quizzically, but there's no way I'm going to voice what I'm thinking—that his house is a little like Joshua himself. Contradictory and anachronistic and improbably comfortable.

There's a sudden crash somewhere, and a shriek, followed by a chorus of yelling. Joshua makes this little *yeep* sound and hurries us toward the narrow corridor behind the staircase.

"Shouldn't you, um, check on that?" I say.

He listens for a few seconds. "Nah. My sister broke something or flushed something down the toilet." He grins, his bare feet carrying him onward. "Don't worry—there's a particular sound you learn to recognize if someone's bleeding."

I tiptoe behind him. We pass a few more closed doors, and I can only hypothesize at the contents within. Servants' quarters? Rooms filled with nothing but ancient funerary urns? The heart of the TARDIS?

Joshua pauses in front of a solid door at the end of the seemingly endless hallway. He nudges it with his hip and holds it open with his back.

I gather the splintering bits of my psyche and step over the threshold.

"Holy…wow. This is your room?"

"Ah, yeah. Sorry, it's a little cozy."

Joshua's room is minuscule, no bigger than a walk-in closet. There's barely enough room for the double bed pushed against the wall and the small chest of drawers that faces it. There's just enough floor space for a thin rug, faded blue and covered with stars. The sliver of space between the drawers and the bed contains a leather chair and a tiny desk scattered with pens. Like the rest of the house, the ceiling is high, but painted a deep, dark blue, giving the impression of a night sky far above. But the thing that draws my eye, that makes me turn slowly in place like a mystified rotisserie chicken, are his walls.

All four walls, from just above my head to the distant blue ceiling, are lined with mounted shelves, row upon row that encircle the small space. They're filled with double-stacked books and knickknacks, weird stuff made of wood that I can't identify. Placed in between, scattered over the shelves, are multiple ancient-looking clocks, all of which seem to be set to different times, and none of which appear to be working. There are a few dusty framed photos of Joshua with a dark-haired girl half his size, and along the very top shelf, rows of boxes and old stuffed toys. It's like being cocooned inside a very tiny, ancient library. Or the cell of a well-read lunatic.

"Um, the clocks are mostly presents from my folks," Joshua says from behind me. "It's kind of been a running joke since I was a kid, I guess." He grins sheepishly. "I've been half-arsedly trying to learn how to fix them, but it's harder than I thought. Clock-making used to actually be a master craft, you know, before they all became manufactured on assembly lines." He shrugs. "One day I might actually get around to learning."

He takes a single step from the doorway and ducks his head under the shelves to smooth down his comforter. He flicks on the banker's lamp mounted upside-down beneath the lowest shelf and nudges the door closed behind him, all in one balletic move.

His hands are still, which is somehow more disconcerting than his ever-present tapping. I don't know exactly what information makes me draw this inference, but I think he might be nervous. "It's a bit much, I know. I was really into *Harry Potter* when we moved in here," he says with a crooked smile.

I look at him blankly.

"The cupboard under the stairs?" His eyes follow mine around the cluttered room. "Mum's been trying to get me to move to a proper bedroom for years, but I dunno. I like it in here."

I sit gingerly in his desk chair. "It's...cozy," I echo.

Joshua takes a seat on the edge of his bed. "What can I say? I'm comfortable with small."

We contemplate his space. With the door closed and the room lit only by a lamp, I should be right on cue for a momentous freak-out. I barely have the wherewithal to register that no schoolbooks of any kind are visible, and there are no study charts or timetables stuck to his walls, when from beneath the desk something soft brushes my leg. I yelp as a fat, gray tabby launches itself into my lap and immediately proceeds to knead my legs with razor-sharp claws.

"Ah, that's Narda. Sorry. She has no boundaries." He reaches for the cat, but I shoo his hands away.

"No, it's fine. I like cats." I run my hands across the scruff of her neck. Narda flops into my lap with a huff.

The weight of the tabby settles the edges of my nerves a bit. "Joshua, considering the available evidence, I'm going to hypothesize that your parents aren't exactly poor."

Joshua makes a face. "They've done okay. So?"

"Well, so, I guess then, a reasonable question would be, what the hell are you doing at St. Augustine's? It's not exactly the type of school you guys go to—"

"'You guys'?" he says, sounding amused, I think, and maybe a little annoyed.

"Yes, *you guys*. People with money. Aren't there special schools with secret handshakes?" I wave my hand at his room. "Places where you can live out your Hogwarts fantasies for real?"

Joshua stares at me for a long moment. Then he bursts out laughing. "After all this time, I still can't tell when you're serious and when you're giving me shit."

I don't know what's come over me, but I think I may be a little drunk on my own daring. "I am both serious and giving you shit," I say silkily.

Joshua flops backward on the bed, bare feet dangling over the end. He's still chuckling. "You make us sound like the Lannisters."

"Well, your house does have more than two stories. And a turret. You are one incest-cousin away from being a *Game of Thrones* character."

Joshua laughs. "I would so be the moron who gets beheaded in the first season."

"Turns out, far too much has been written about great men and not nearly enough about morons," I say distractedly. Narda leaps off my lap and pounces on Joshua's dancing fingers.

He sits up again and shakes his head. "And she quotes *GoT*," he says under his breath. "I don't think I'll ever not be surprised by you, Sophia."

I let my eyes wander again. One of his bottom shelves is stocked with old biographies, ancient-looking books bound with leather and gold. I reach above my head and slide out a random volume. The cover is a turn-of-the-century poster of a white guy in a turban, sepia-tinted, like the kind I've seen in his locker.

"So what is it with you and these historical guys? Why don't you have any biographies of Criss Angel or Cyril Takayama or David Copperfield—"

"Um, excuse me?" he says, swinging his legs over the side of the bed. His eyebrows are making a valiant effort to climb into his hair. "Since when are you interested in magicians?"

Even though I feel my face get warm, I refuse to be embarrassed for conducting an elementary investigation. "I met you. I googled things. You talk a lot, and I don't always understand everything you say. So. Research."

He shakes his head, smiling. "Wow. I'm flattered?"

I turn the book over, my eyes skimming the photo on the back. "Don't be. I'm curious. What is it about these classic guys that you like? Or maybe I should ask what it is about the newer guys that annoys you so much?"

He takes the biography from my hands. “It’s hard to explain. I guess it’s because I like the stuff from a time when the thing was skill alone? Like, when there was still all this awesome stuff to discover, stuff that people had never seen done before. Those TV guys, the big Vegas dudes with all the expensive sets and tigers and stuff? No ordinary person can do that. It’s too…big. And they just keep making it bigger and more and more flashy and professional—you know, you get run over by a steamroller or make the Statue of Liberty disappear live on television—”

“Hey, I saw that on YouTube. That was sort of impressive.”

“I know, right?” he says with a sigh. “But, like, where do you go from there? What kid who’s learning how to execute a perfect Double Lift card trick or something would even bother…” He tucks his legs beneath him, sitting cross-legged on his bed. “I sound like a tool,” he says, drumming his hands on his feet. “I just mean, once something’s been done, bigger and better than you could ever hope to pull off, why would you even try…why would you bother starting if you knew you were always gonna fall short…”

I stare at him. “Okay.”

He looks up, his fingers stilling. “That’s it? No counter-point? No pep talk?”

I shrug, my hands suddenly prickly. “No. I just…no.”

Joshua reaches distractedly for a worn deck of cards. He flutters them through his fingers, his eyes focused on nothing I can see.

I watch his hands. “You’re ambidextrous?”

He looks down. “Sort of. I was mostly left-handed when

I was a kid, but then I trained myself to use my right, so I guess…" He grins, faintly. "Well, mostly, I think I had too much time on my hands."

I rotate, slowly, in his chair. When I turn back to face him, he seems to be observing me extra closely. I plant my feet and stop myself spinning.

"Sophia Reyhart. You're in my bedroom," he says quietly.

"Stellar observation," I mumble. More unexpected heat warms my cheeks.

He unwinds his legs and leaps up. "We should get going," he says, slipping a black vest over his shirt and his feet into socks and gray Chucks. He reaches for the trench coat and hat that are hanging behind his door. He pauses, a frown creasing his forehead. "Are you sure you're ready?"

I straighten out my dress and zip up my jacket. I'm almost tempted to say no—there's something nice about being in this space, something calming and almost flannel-pajama comfortable.

"Sure thing," I say brightly.

Joshua holds his door open, and I reluctantly step out—and almost barrel into a scowling girl in black tights and an oversized T-shirt. Her face is set in that fierce look of undirected annoyance I've seen pubescent kids brandish so well.

"Damn. Busted," Joshua says under his breath.

The girl's makeup-heavy eyes travel over me. Her mouth curves into a slow grin.

"Joshie," she purrs, leaning against the wall and giving me a once-over that feels like it's scouring my skin off. "Look who's being a sneaky little alley cat. Are Mum and Dad aware you're entertaining lady-guests in your boudoir? You do know those condoms they gave you with the puberty talk have probably expired, yeah?"

An indignant flush creeps up my face. This girl can't be more than thirteen, and she looks like a tiny, depressed elf, only with the measured voice of our middle-aged Latin teacher.

Joshua angles himself in front of me. "She emerges from her cavern, spreading sunshine and cheer," he says dryly. "Do we need to have a talk about appropriate guest-conversation again, Gillian?"

She brightens in a way that makes her seem infinitely younger. "The secret is not having bad manners or good manners, but having the same manner for all human souls," she says, in an accent that I think is supposed to be British. She also, bafflingly, does a little jig.

Joshua looks like he's trying really hard not to laugh. "Okay, Eliza Doolittle. Stay real. Is it too much to ask that you, I dunno—don't talk about condoms in front of my friend?"

"What can I say? I'm precocious," she says, deadpan.

Joshua turns his back on her and gives me a pained smile. "I would apologize, but I should probably save the proper groveling until I see how much damage she does," he says in a mock whisper.

"And speaking of manners, are you going to introduce me to your 'friend'?" she demands, fingers forming air quotes and all.

He turns around and clasps her lightly across the back of the neck. "Gillian, this is Sophia. Sophia, my sister, who may or may not be the love child of Robert Smith and Nosferatu, Gillian."

I suspect it's a bad idea to point out that I have no idea who those people are. I'm crap with kids, and worse with sarcasm. "Hi. Um, nice to meet you, Gillian."

Gillian wriggles out from Joshua's grip. She looks me up and down again. I force my eyes to remain on hers. "Cute T-shirt," I say, which is something I've heard girls say to each other on TV. Gillian merely raises an eyebrow. "I mean," I babble, "Le Tigre. My friend's brother used to be obsessed with them. I wouldn't think someone your age would be into them?"

"Yeah, I'm a paradox," she snaps.

"*Okay*, that'll do," Joshua says, straightening to his full height. He's giving his sister a look that makes her steely gaze drop.

"Sorry..."

Joshua raises an eyebrow. "And...?"

"Nice to meet you too," she says sullenly.

Joshua wraps her in a one-armed hug. "Okay, we're leaving. Don't conjure any demons from the netherworld. And, you know—maybe you could make a start on that homework, or whatever? Love you."

She rolls her eyes. "Yeah, whatever. Love you too," she mumbles.

We don't speak as we walk outside. I'm still reeling from my encounter with his sister—especially after Joshua's brief detour to find his contact lenses left Gillian and me alone in their foyer, somehow discussing the French botanist Monique Keraudren and the flora of Madagascar.

I'm filled with an odd sensation of melancholy as we walk down the giant driveway. It seems so easy for them, so *normal*. Even Elsie's brothers, who once trekked en masse to our primary school to confront a kid who'd stolen Elsie's lunchbox, don't use the "L" word. I have about as much chance of hearing those words in my house as I do of proving the existence of dark matter.

"So, I'm sorry about Gillian," Joshua says, snapping me from my thoughts. "She's a tiny rage-monster, true, but if you scrape away the attitude, she's actually a really decent person." We reach the main road, huddling beneath the lights of the tram stop. "Gilly is just a hell of a lot smarter than most people, and it's kinda like this weapon she doesn't know how to wield—" He pauses, looking at me strangely.

"What?"

He shakes his head as the lights of an approaching tram crest the hill. "Nothing. Nothing at all."

♥

Chapter Twelve

The Mechanics of Being Joined at the Face

The tram is so packed that Joshua and I don't even bother trying to speak over the noise. I avoid public transport whenever I can. This giant cylinder, reminiscent of the stomach of a steel whale, is exactly the reason why. Up at the front is a big group of drunk girls decked out in pink bridal gear, whose voices carry octaves above the crowd. There are a few guys sitting on the floor blasting music through a phone, their hair in various unnatural hues, clothes covered in bolts and spiky metal things. A man across the aisle is yelling loudly into his mobile. He seems to be having an urgent conversation about a garden hose he just purchased. There are five giant older guys in soccer uniforms, voices fierce and booming. I can't tell if they're angry, excited, or about to start a riot, and I'm more than a little relieved when they jump off after a few stops.

In front of us is a couple who have gone four stops without breaking their kiss; the activity on the tram seems irrelevant to them. Partly I find it remarkable that two people can be so absorbed in each other that they're able to ignore the chaos surrounding them, but I'm also concerned that someone is going to lose a chunk of tongue as the tram jolts in fits and starts.

I huddle in a back corner near the door that doesn't open. Joshua stands in front of me, one hand braced on the overhead rail. He doesn't seem put-off by the fact that he is being bombarded by bodies, sweaty arms and hands brushing against him. He plants his feet shoulder-width apart, and though he keeps getting jostled, he moves neither closer to me nor further away. It takes me six stops to realize that he has installed himself as an immovable wall, keeping marauding tram-people away from my corner.

He stares out the window into the dark, looking lost in thought, and it leaves me free to examine him up close. He has a small cluster of freckles on the right side of his neck, the only features on his otherwise unmarked skin. His hair is longer than I noticed when we first met, curling in tendrils around the collar of his jacket. His contacts seem to make his irises ever so slightly darker; behind his glasses his eyes had a lighter, bronzy tone. Intriguing. So many features that make up a normal face, no more or less extraordinary than any other face in the world. Yet it draws my focus, strangely beguiling.

Joshua turns his attention back to me when the tram makes a left down a busy street in Fitzroy. We push our way off at the next stop, and I take a second to catch my breath.

He watches me as I steady my breathing. He looks torn. "Sophia, we don't have to go. We can turn around or do something else even—"

"No." I straighten my shoulders. If I have learned anything from Ms. Heller, it's the way sham confidence can be suggested by the right posture. "It's fine. I'm fine. Lead the way."

I follow him down an alleyway, the walls on either side covered with graffiti. It looks like someone has tried to cover up a sketch of a rodent with a giant dong, using a poster of the Channel Seven weatherman—only someone has ripped off half the poster and drawn a penis on his head. I don't understand why graffiti seems to be so predominately phallic-themed. I think it is a question to ponder another day.

Joshua keeps shooting looks at me. I'm starting to feel a little light-headed, slightly disconnected from my body. Though maybe this is a good thing? Perhaps if I can't invoke a new personality in the next thirty seconds, I can leave my old one out on the street, like a gecko shedding a useless skin.

In front of a peeling blue door is a small group of people sitting on milk crates. The place looks like the back end of a dilapidated bar.

A scruffy guy in a beanie, about our age, is sitting on a deck chair, holding a guitar. He's playing a song that everyone else seems to know. Another guy, clean-shaven and wearing glasses and a matching beanie, is leaning lazily against his legs. Guitar-guy finishes playing to a smattering of applause. Glasses-guy gazes up at him all moo-eyed. Someone else grabs the guitar, and the two guys mash their lips together.

Joshua waves at the people lingering near the door, and then he leads us inside.

"Um. Oh," is all I'm capable of saying.

Beside me, Joshua grimaces. "Yeah. I know."

The inside is something of a cross between a country pub my family visited once and the house of a hoarder with eighteen cats that I saw on TV at Elsie's. It's jammed with ill-assorted furniture and giant speakers that are vibrating with the force of the music. It's also wall-to-wall with yelling, laughing, gesticulating people, who all look like they dressed haphazardly in the dark. There seems to be a preponderance of tattoos, unnaturally colored hair, and beards.

I hug my jacket around me, unaccountably glad I picked my knee-length coat, even though it's as humid as a greenhouse in here. Fashion is confusing, but the plain green dress I'm wearing is unmistakably out of place. It's like that time I showed up at the Nayers' wedding anniversary wearing jeans and a sweatshirt Raj gave me for my birthday. The sweatshirt featured the slogan "fractions speak louder than nerds." For a long time I didn't know what I had done wrong, only that I suffered through the night fielding brutal looks from various Indian aunts, with that horrible lingering feeling of having made a faux pas that I could have avoided by staying at home.

People wave at Joshua. He says hello to a few guys, who do that backslap thing I've seen boys do. I've never pictured Joshua as a back-slapping, fist-bumping *guy* guy. It's a little bit troubling that I've managed to miss this component of his character.

He steers me through the whirlwind of people and smoke, the fingertips of one hand lightly on my back. I feel predictably queasy, like my insides are stretched too tight beneath my skin. It's taking every stress-response technique in my book to keep me from fleeing.

Joshua stops every few moments to shake hands or kiss someone on the cheek, but I can see in my peripheral vision that he is keeping one eye on me. He introduces me to everyone but doesn't linger, always keeping us moving, that hand never straying from my back. Inadvertently, I find myself storing names and faces alongside random bits of trivia, but mostly I can't tear my eyes away from Joshua.

The silent, ghost-like boy from St. Augustine's is totally in his element here, swarming in a sea of goodwill and friends. He smiles warmly at everyone, and people smile warmly at him. He never looks lost for something to say. This person could never be invisible in the back of a classroom. *This* Joshua stands out, like a cosmic spotlight is following him. I wonder how I ever saw otherwise.

He touches my elbow and points across the room to a messy-haired boy who's attempting to maneuver another huge speaker out from behind the bar. "That's Jasper. This is his place," he says near my ear. "He's pretty cool, though he can come across a bit more...aggressive than he actually is. I should warn you, if this is gonna end up being one of his all-nighters, he will be throwing furniture off the second story at some point." I look up at Joshua in alarm, but his face just looks amused. "Just don't bring up anything to do with Leonard Cohen. Or Bill Callahan or Nick Cave," he says. "Actually, maybe just avoid talking music with him if you want to escape with your sanity intact."

"I'll keep that in mind. Joshua, how the hell do you know all these people?"

He shrugs. "Around. Here and there. Work, and, you know...places." He grins.

A giant with more arm tattoos than I have ever seen grabs Joshua around the neck in a choke hold and plants a noisy, wet kiss on his cheek. I'm guessing this is an example of beer-fueled party affection and probably not unusual for this group. Though I really want to hand him a tissue for the shiny spot of lipstick that she has left on his face.

"Hello, Amy," he says through gritted teeth. "Um, Sophia, this is Amy, my boss." He extricates himself and wipes the back of his hand pointedly across his cheek.

"Well hey there," she says. She looks back and forth between Joshua and me, blue hair bouncing across the shoulders of a hairy fur coat. Then she smiles at me. It's a kinder sort of smile than I expected from someone so blustery. I smile back tentatively.

"So how goes it, Ames?" Joshua says. He straightens out his shirt and angles his body a little in front of me.

"Just dandy," she replies. "Oh, hey, I almost forgot to tell you, I sold that Walt Sheppard box today—that's this crazy-expensive collectable piece that's been gathering dust in the display cabinet," she says to me. "Yeah, some chick with a Sheppard obsession actually paid the whole fifteen hundred for it—"

She freezes, her beer bottle dangling over Joshua's shoulder. It takes me a second to register that the music has changed from something with crashing cymbals and wailing guy vocals to soft violins and wailing girl vocals.

"What?" Joshua says as he attempts to remove himself, again, from her arms.

"Nothing. I just...like this song. Jesus, I think I told him that."

She stares, stone-faced, across the room. Messy-haired guy, the future furniture-thrower, gives her a wave before turning back to a wall of records. "Like, what's Jasper's problem?" Amy growls.

Joshua gives me a pained look. "I dunno, Amy," he says. "It's a mystery. But you know what? You could always just cross this little ol' room and ask him."

Amy all but bares her teeth. "I'm gonna get drunk," she mutters. "Nice meeting you, chick," she says before vanishing into the dark.

"Do I want to ask what that was about?"

Joshua shakes his head. "It's complicated. Actually, you know what? It really isn't." He gestures to Jasper and then nods his head at Amy's retreating back. "Those two? They're stubborn idiots."

Before I can ask any follow-up questions, something catches his eye across the room. He straightens, tucking his hair back and doing that wiggly shoulder-move that I have come to recognize means he is bracing himself.

"Hey, hey!" a melodic voice calls out. "You're here!"

A girl shoves her way toward us, waving madly. She's wearing a silky red dress with a billowy skirt and a pair of heavy, purple boots that everything in my limited fashion vocabulary tells me should not be worn with a dress.

"Hey, Camilla," Joshua says. He gives her a hug. "Yeah, we made it."

I can tell right away that she's one of those bubbly, confident girls, the ones who instantly make my skin feel all clumsy and askew. The type of girls I have gone out of my way to avoid since I was old enough to realize how they see me, the ones who give each other smug side-eyes when I say something weird, or call me "cute" in a way that even I know is supposed to be patronizing. I can only imagine the things Elsie would have to say about this shiny, smiley girl.

I try not to shrink, instead transferring my attention over her shoulder. She's dragging a guy behind her, a tall boy with blond hair and a small, nice smile. He leans around her and shakes Joshua's hand, then peers curiously at me.

"Hey, guys," Joshua says casually. He looks at me. "These are my friends, Sam and Camilla. Sam, Camilla, this is my... friend. From school." He pauses, and something in the pause makes me inexplicably nervous. "This is Sophia," he finishes.

I'm not sure of the catalyst for the events that follow. There are too many people in my vicinity, and all of them seem to suddenly engage in a series of rapid, senseless actions.

The girl in the red dress—Camilla—snaps her eyes to me. For a brief moment she stares, agape. Then she lunges forward, as if she's going to hug me, but stops at the last moment. She gives me another huge smile and an enthusiastic wave instead. "Hey! Ah, welcome! It's really nice to meet you, Sophia."

The blond guy behind her—Sam—and Joshua seem to be engaging in some obtuse, silent communication above my head, mainly consisting of eyebrow quirks. Then Camilla turns to Sam, her eyes widening, then narrowing, before flicking to somewhere over his shoulder. He clears his throat.

"Ah, yeah. I'll be over there," Sam says, before bolting in the direction of the bar.

I turn my back on them so only Joshua fills my view. "Have you been saying stuff about me?"

Joshua's cheeks turn crimson. "Um. I may have mentioned you. Once or twice. It's nothing more ominous than that, I promise."

"Bollocks," Camilla mutters.

My whole body tenses, but when I turn around, it's not us that she is looking at.

Sam is at the bar, next to a short guy who appears to be wearing one of those curly novelty clown wigs. Sam leans down, gesturing frantically as he talks in the short guy's ear.

Camilla shoots Joshua a look. His face seems, I think, pained yet resigned. Sam and the other guy walk back toward us.

The short guy stops in front of me. "Hello," he says solemnly. "My name is Adrian. I've heard nothing about you at all. Can I ask, what is your name?"

Behind him, Sam clears his throat. And I could swear he surreptitiously pokes curly-haired guy in the back of the head with an elbow.

"Hey, man," Joshua says, shaking the guy's hand. "How's it going, Adrian?"

Adrian's eyes are zeroed in on me, his round face alive with a thousand expressions. He's standing way inside the zone of my personal space, and I can't tell if he has been dancing or running, but he is also sweating profusely.

Then I notice the picture on his T-shirt.

I point at it. "*Doctor Who*?"

He beams, a wide smile that makes him sort of cute-ish. "Hell yeah," he says, stepping even closer. "Did you watch the last behind-the-scenes special? Man, did you wanna give Moffat a slap in the nads too?"

I let out a small chuckle, even as I move backward. "Um, okay—yes, and, well, maybe, a few times."

Adrian looks like he's about to explode, but then Sam grabs him by the neck of his T-shirt and hauls him away.

"Sorry. He's not housebroken. We're trying, but it's like wrangling a puppy with ADHD."

Camilla jabs Sam in the ribs. "Don't be mean. We're just all really excited to meet you, Sophia," she says.

Three smiling faces stare at me with various levels of intensity. And I am struck with a sudden blinding insight into the possible fate of Grigori Perelman. Perhaps it was simply this—one ill-advised foray into the world, one Smirnoff-soaked Steklov Institute bash, one excruciatingly awkward, inept exchange with other humans—that broke his peculiar brain.

Fact: Three perfectly nice, normal-ish people are waiting for me to speak, and the prospect of retiring to a Russian hovel with the cockroaches seems increasingly appealing.

I back up a few paces, having rapidly reached the end of my small-talk reserves, only to discover that Joshua has disappeared. I cast my eyes around frantically and see him moving hurriedly back through the crowd.

He is carrying two plastic cups and hands one to me as he reaches my side. "Just Sprite," he says. "I assumed you wouldn't want booze, although maybe that was a crappy assumption. I mean, I don't drink, but I'm not judgy, and there's plenty of other stuff if you want, beer or—"

"It's fine," I say, taking a long sip as Joshua's friends drift into their own huddle. I use the soda and conversational reprieve to attempt to pull myself together. "I'm not sure either of us wants to see the effect alcohol has on me. Have you seen that YouTube clip of Mr. Grayson? I'm assuming I would be something like that. But with less splitting the crotch of my pants, hopefully."

He gapes at me. "Ms. Reyhart! Was that a joke at your own expense?" He grins. "I don't see you being a sloppy drunk. Or a crying drunk. Oh, clearly you stopped watching that vid way too soon," he says with a laugh at my no-doubt quizzical expression. "Just wait till he drops his kebab."

The music changes to something that sounds like it was made in an atomic testing ground, rendering further conversation impossible. Joshua and I lean against the back of a couch and watch the melee in strangely companionable silence. For the first time all night, I feel the sharp tension in my shoulders begin to ebb.

Joshua drifts into conversation with his friend Sam. His eyes keep floating back to me, so I do my best to give him a reassuring smile. But then I am cornered by Camilla, who lands beside me in a pouf of red skirt and looks at me expectantly.

I fidget with the zip on my jacket. It's hot in here, and sweat is starting to pool at the base of my spine. I slip the coat off, but immediately regret it. I feel exposed, uninteresting and pedestrian in my plain dress. I hug the jacket to my chest and hope that Camilla will take pity on me and find someone else to talk to.

"So. Joshua said they've made you take Drama? Man, that must be all kinds of sucky."

I blink at her suspiciously. "No one forced me. But it's not my favorite thing in the world, no."

Camilla doesn't seem fazed by my abruptness. She sips her beer. "I've tried it," she says, her plummy accent carrying over the noise. "People kept telling me the only cure for stage fright was to just get up and do it. As if fear can be cast out, like Merrin casting the demon—" She giggles. "Sorry. My boyfriend's a bad influence. But yeah, I made myself do this play—I was Molly the orphan in *Annie*, Marylebone Primary's end-of-year extravaganza." She shudders. "Seriously, all it did was guarantee that stage lights now give me PTSD. And proved that the best use for an Annie wig is as an improvised puke bucket."

I take a moment to evaluate this person, who seems a thousand miles away from introverted. "So what you're saying is, you should have just stayed in your comfort zone?" I say cautiously.

Camilla shrugs. "Not exactly. But jeez, I've never understood how being forced into a situation where you're possibly going to pee your pants is supposed to make you less freaked. Do things when you're good and goddamned ready, I say."

I sigh. "What's so wrong with living in a bubble?"

Camilla is watching me closely. "I know, right? Like, everyone should want to be front and center, belting out a song at the Grammys or collecting their Oscar or Nobel—"

"Well, maybe a Nobel wouldn't be the *worst* thing—"

"But maybe not everyone is supposed to be a superstar!" she says, spilling some beer as she gestures emphatically. "Maybe some of us are perfectly happy writing music for superstars to sing."

I stare at her curiously. "Then again—what's the point in doing anything extraordinary unless other people can see it?"

She laughs. It's light, I think, not belittling. "Ah, is that the whole does-a-tree-falling-in-the-woods-make-a-sound-if-no-one's-around-to-hear-it thing? Or, like, that dude with the dead cat in a box? I never understood his whole deal. Something isn't really a thing unless someone's observing?"

I smile. "That's... kind of accurate, actually."

I look across the room again. Joshua is laughing at something Adrian is saying. Sam's hands are covering his face, but he seems to be laughing too.

Joshua looks happy. Comfortable, safe in his own skin, some other, better version of himself. His hand is wrapped casually around his cup, not tapping or fidgeting or any of his other anxious tells. And even though I can't hear him, somehow I know that there isn't a hint of a lisp in his voice. He fits in here. The realization makes me feel inexplicably dejected.

"Hey," Camilla says softly. "It's quieter out back. You know, if you need... space?"

I clutch my jacket. "Does everyone here know that I'm a giant freak?"

She rolls her eyes, but her smile is gentle. “Trust me, Sophia. There isn’t a single person here who I’d classify as normal.”

Joshua drifts back. Camilla touches my arm briefly before she walks away.

“Okay?” he asks.

I look around. Adrian now appears to be demonstrating some kind of Sontaran battle maneuver to a tiny blonde girl. The two beanie-guys from outside, now hand in hand, have joined them.

“Your friends are nice, Joshua. But, maybe I could use some air…”

Joshua shouts across the space almost before I have finished speaking. “Hey, we’ll see you guys later, okay?” Then he steers me toward the rear of the bar-house.

It’s darker here, the music muffled. The huddles are smaller, the conversation more subdued.

Joshua makes a beeline for an orange sofa. Beer boxes are stacked in front of it, forming a wonky partition.

“Are you really okay?” he asks as we sink into the soft couch, side-by-side.

I’m fleetingly waylaid by a vision of the damp park bench on the edge of the school grounds. I can’t explain why, but this parallel universe situation makes me feel even more unmoored.

“I’m fine. This is…fun?”

Joshua nods. “Sure. Now tell me how you really feel.”

Suspicious-smelling smoke hangs above us, so thick that if I stand, I suspect my face would be obscured by the cloud.

"Your friends are great, Joshua. But I don't think I make a very good first impression. Or second impression." I sneak a glance at him, but his face is infuriatingly indecipherable. "You make it look so easy. You're good with people. I didn't think...I don't know why you don't use that skill set at school."

Joshua seems nonplussed. "You go there with the same people I do, right? Okay, maybe our entire year level isn't made up of douchebags, but most of them aren't interested in people like us." He shrugs. "Why would I waste my time?"

My brain flickers over the "people like us" comment, but I'm not sure what to do with it. Instead, I lean backward, the couch doing its best to swallow me whole. Joshua mirrors my posture, long legs stretched out. He is doing that thing he does, watching me without expectation, waiting for me to reply.

"How had I been at school with you for so long and never heard you speak?" I blurt. "Clearly you've mastered the whole talking-to-strangers thing. You don't ever seem to run out of words."

Joshua laughs. "Most of the time that's just patter."

"What?"

"Patter. You know." He turns on the couch and crosses his legs. I lean against the smelly cushions, tucking my feet sideways. A crisp deck of cards materializes in his hand. He taps it against his knee, then proceeds to shuffle it in an elaborate move that I recognize from my research as a Riffle Shuffle.

"Okay, so, it's like this," he says as the cards flutter through his fingers. "The most difficult part of close-up magic is managing your audience's attention. Unless you're one of those stage dudes who relies on a half-naked assistant or some doped-up tigers or whatever—and I think you know how I feel about them—well, you only have a couple of options."

He holds the deck flat in his left palm and cuts it cleanly in half with the fingers of the same hand. The two halves pivot around each other, expertly guided by just his fingertips. Then he uses his index finger to flick one half of the deck up. The Queen of Hearts' severe face peers out at me. "One—you can use your hands and movements to direct the eye where you want it to go." He cuts the deck again, using a finger to spin the two halves over themselves a couple of times. He flutters the cards from his left hand to his right, a rapid waterfall that lands in a perfect deck. He turns the bottom of the deck up toward me. The Queen of Hearts gazes out at me again.

Joshua ignores my eye roll as he shuffles the cards again. "And two," he says, so quietly that I have to lean forward to hear, "you can tell a story. It's about guiding your audience's focus. Which part of the trick they're paying attention to, which bits slip under their radar. You can do all that, if you're good enough, just with words; with the tone of your voice, inflection, volume—"

"So you're saying that the fundamental key to all magic is the ability to bullshit?"

Joshua gives me a sharp side-eye. "Not bullshit. That's no fun. Besides, most people can read insincerity a mile off.

It's more like...well, the most important thing is that your audience knows you're on their side, that you're part of the same game. You're sharing something, not pulling a con.

I read this thing once that said that really good magicians possess an instinct for how people perceive the world. It's about the ability to get a read on strangers, to know what makes them tick. How you're gonna bamboozle them while making them glad you did." He shrugs. "I dunno. I kinda like that."

He shuffles the deck again, a simple Dovetail Shuffle, before fanning the cards out and then folding the pack in the opposite direction. He holds the deck out to me.

"Okay, just because I can't follow your hands doesn't mean I don't know how you're doing this. Obviously you're keeping tabs on the card somehow, either by your finger placement or some sort of counting I can't see—"

He grins as I take the card from the top of the deck. I have a sneaky suspicion that, were she in possession of a consciousness, the Queen of Hearts would be smirking too.

"Bammo," Joshua says with a smile.

I hand him the Queen, and he nestles her into the pack again. "But, you know, I wasn't always awesome at it," he says, tapping the pack distractedly on his leg. "The talking, I mean."

"No? Why do I find that hard to believe?"

"Really," he says, laughing. "I was...awkward when I was a kid. I was pretty much a hermit and, like, horrendously shy. I was convinced the entire world was one big confusing trick that I was never gonna figure out. And, you know, I had the speech thing."

"You mean the lisp?" I cross my legs, realizing too late that I am mirroring his pose again.

He stops tapping the cards. "Noticed that, huh?"

"Oh. Only a little. Most of the time it's barely there, but sometimes, I think when you're nervous or stressed?"

He leans his head against the couch. The fingers of his hand flutter over the deck. I can see him resisting the urge to shuffle. "Sometimes I slip when I'm not concentrating," he says with a quick glance at me. "It was pretty bad when I was little. For a while I just gave up and stopped talking altogether." He closes his eyes. "'Selective mutism' my therapist called it. Dunno why it needed a name. I wasn't unhappy, I just...preferred my own company."

"But let me guess, that wasn't acceptable?"

He smiles wryly. "Nope. Got to learn to play with others. Thanks to a couple of years of speech therapy and a billion hours copying close-up magicians on YouTube, I don't sound like Daffy Duck's clumsy twin anymore. It still comes back though, sometimes. Sometimes it's hard to focus." He twirls the cards half-heartedly.

"It's just a tiny flaw—no, forget that, it's not even a flaw," I say as spots of color appear on his cheeks. "You know Isaac Newton had a speech impediment? Charles Darwin could barely talk, he stuttered so bad. But *no one* remembers that. Your thing, it's irrelevant. It would have been irrelevant even when it was at its worst. It's such a wasted effort, this need to be flawless—"

I look away with a sharp breath. For the briefest moment he managed to spin a spell that hushed the noise in the room and the clamor in my head. But when I look up, into the suddenly loaded silence between us, it hits me: there are too many people here, too much laughter, too many bodies pressed together like amoebae bumping in an alcohol-infused swamp.

I wrap my hands around my knees. And I try, desperately, to focus on my breathing. But I feel it coming, fluttering behind my belly button, building behind my lungs. When I dare to glance up, Joshua is looking at me, and I know, somehow, that he knows.

He stands up in one motion. "Come on," he says softly. I follow him blindly. Joshua touches my elbow and points to the staircase that leads up behind the bar.

I move past him and take the stairs two at a time. It's just a little quieter here, the party blocked from view. The stairwell is dark and blissfully empty.

My feet stop a few steps above him. "Can I ask you something?" I say.

I turn around. He has paused behind me, his face in shadow. "Of course."

"When we first met—that day at the college—you said you weren't surprised that I didn't know what I wanted. You said that it made sense. What did you mean by that?"

Joshua takes a single step upward. His face looks thoughtful and torn. "I don't know if I can explain it," he says eventually.

"Well, I'll just add it to my list of nonsensical things." My breathing is shallow, my stomach whirring.

"This is going to come out all wrong," he says. "But when I first saw you—way back at the beginning of high school—

you were excited about *everything*. While everyone else was, you know, pasting their butt cheeks together or whatever, you were trying to..." He shakes his head. "You were trying to figure out, like, the mysteries of the universe." He buries his hands in his pockets. Maybe it's the lighting in the stairwell, but his eyes seem to glow, more light than dark.

"I guess I wasn't surprised that you would struggle to find somewhere to place all that...potential. I kept seeing you trying to shape yourself, Sophia, to squeeze yourself into everyone else's boxes, and all I kept thinking was: what you're searching for *can't* be in any of them. They're just way too small."

"Mysteries of the universe. That's a nice thought. But I'm not sure it was ever true. Are you disappointed I'm not like that anymore?"

He looks at me quickly. "No! How could I *possibly* be disappointed getting to know you? And, you're not *not* like that anymore! You have no idea—when you're absorbed in something, your face has about a billion different expressions... maybe no one else can see them, but I can. It's something to witness, you know, you working through a problem... and you always look so calm when you're with Elsie, like the tornado that follows you around just settles when you're near her. You get all glowy when you talk about *Doctor Who*, which I don't quite get, but I've never met anyone who sees the world the way you do. It was always the thing I liked most about you. It's the thing I like most about you now."

I feel for the banister with one hand. I move forward, down one stair and then another, until we are just about at the same height. I am still a hand-width away, but I can look him directly in those weird, changeable eyes now.

He's looking at me with so many things I can't read, like I hold the answer to a puzzle that's been plaguing him. I want to bolt home to my bedroom. I want to punch him in his ridiculous, open face and tell him to *stop looking at me like that* because I have no freaking clue what I'm doing. And most of all, I want to stop everything around me, just for a few seconds, so I don't have to evaluate or analyze or think.

He's not blinking. I'm not even sure that he is breathing. I can't help but think that it's going to be inconvenient if both of us pass out on these stairs.

He reaches out and places a hand on my hip. It's almost weightless, barely a touch, but his hand is big and warm, and it envelops the space from my hip bone to the small of my back. His fingers are tentative, moving almost imperceptibly. It doesn't do anything to help my ragged breathing. It's not like an accidental brush from a stranger. It's undisputable and deliberate and it makes my entire consciousness feel like it is tunneling down to the spot that he is touching.

"Sophia," he says. He swallows a couple of times. "Is this okay? Do you...want me to take you home?"

I reach through the swirling vortex of rubble and noise that is my brain, but nothing of any logic is forthcoming. So I lean forward, over the space between the steps, and I kiss him.

The beat from the music thumps through the stairwell, and for all of five seconds, Joshua's lips don't move. One of my hands is still holding the railing, and the other is resting on his chest because I don't know where else to put it. His body freezes beneath my hand.

And just when I'm thinking I've caused some sort of psychosomatic paralysis, his body shudders, and he takes the remaining steps between us in a single bound. His hands curve around the nape of my neck, and he is kissing me back.

And dammit—my stupid, traitorous heart splutters like it's forgotten how to beat a sensible rhythm. My hands find their way to his face, pulling it down to mine because he is far too tall to kiss when we're standing on the same level. His hands curve over my face as he kisses me, like he's trying to touch every part of it at once.

It is a good kiss.

If there were some sort of kissing barometer or altimeter, Joshua's kisses would be, like, instrument-imploding level.

Fact: Joshua Bailey kisses me like he's been waiting to kiss me his whole life.

My lips move against his. But I can't get my brain to stop spinning. I'm hyper-aware of our bodies pressed together, and I can feel every place where we are touching—my hands on his chest and his palms on my face. It's so much heat and contact, so much of another human being in my untraversed space, and it's this, more than anything, that makes me falter.

I pull away with a sharp intake of breath. He looks like he's struggling just as badly for air.

My hands are operating on autopilot. I disconnect his gentle hold on my face and clasp my hands into his.

His entire expression is a question mark, full of expectations that I have no chance of meeting.

Say something say something say something, my brain chants. *Say anything at all* to make this less terrifying.

"Sophia," he says breathlessly. His eyes are so full and hopeful. "I think I might be in love with you."

Yep. That should do it.

I feel it coming, like the rumble of a train across a faraway track, the compression of my chest and lungs. My face is instantly sweaty, but my hands are freezing, so icy that my knuckles lock in place. I can't breathe. I know that what I am experiencing is just a misplaced fight-or-flight response. But knowing that doesn't make the visceral response any less real. All I know is that I am going to die, right now, on this beer-stained stairwell, if I don't get away this instant.

I shove past him and all but tumble down the stairs. I push through the crowd, past the startled face of Joshua's friend, Sam, before bolting out the blue door. Distantly, I register that it is drizzling again, my feet skidding on the cobblestones before I stumble onto the road. There are people everywhere, so many people, all loud and happy and so freaking normal. I dash across the street and somehow find my way into a mercifully passing taxi. I recognize, distantly, that my actions are so theatrical they would probably gain me a resounding A in Drama, if Ms. Heller had the misfortune of observing me.

I give the driver an address, hearing my robot-voice as if through a vast void.

I can still feel the lingering press of Joshua's lips. I could swear, though I know it is impossible, that the warmth of them still lingers.

I can't kiss a boy who looks at me like I'm the only thing that matters in the world. I know, for a fact, that nothing I am or will become could be momentous enough to warrant that.

I can't kiss a boy who makes my heart stutter; my heart should know what the hell it is doing. I cannot sort out my flawed, failing brain if my basic autonomic functions start letting me down too.

I can't. I am not that girl.

Surely he has to know that? If this continued, sooner or later, I know he would figure out that the person he thinks he wants is only theoretical.

I can't do this.

Even if part of me wants to rewind time and replay that kiss over and over and over again.

♠

Chapter Thirteen

The Exclusion Principle

Colin opens the door to the Nayers' house. Warmth radiates from inside, almost painful against my skin. I left my jacket on the bar-house stairwell, and the icy drizzle feels like needles on my bare arms.

Colin uses his feet to corral Chuck behind us as I squeeze inside. A one-eyed ginger tabby I haven't seen before also tries to make a break for freedom. The cat sniffs my foot suspiciously as Colin manages to shut the door.

Colin leads me into the living room, where he, Ryan, and Rajesh are playing Trivial Pursuit. Raj looks up at me, yelps, and immediately covers his head. Elsie and I haven't been allowed to play Trivial Pursuit since we were eleven, when I won because I knew that a pluviometer measures rainfall. Ryan accused me of cheating, and Elsie got so mad she chucked one of her mum's dog figurines at him, fracturing his nose with a porcelain Irish setter. I had nothing to do with the nose-breaking incident, but the Nayer brothers seem to find it infinitely more amusing to feign fear of me instead of their sister.

Ryan gives me a curt "hey." Colin flops onto the couch, Chuck jumping into his lap.

"Whatup, Pinky?" Raj calls. "Hey, excellent timing—where are a snail's reproductive organs?"

"On its head," I answer on autopilot. My voice sounds strange, like my ears are filled with water. Raj *whoops* amid a chorus of protests from Colin and Ryan.

"Nice one, thanks," Raj says, dropping a green wedge into his wheel with a megalomaniac's chuckle. He glances at me standing there, dripping on their foyer carpet, and does a bit of a double take.

"Hey there, Pinky. Everything okay?"

I pick up the random ginger cat. "No. I don't think so. Is Elsie home?"

The three Nayer brothers point, wordlessly, up the stairs. I cuddle the protesting tabby and float up to Elsie's room.

Elsie's bedroom hasn't changed much since we were kids, except for the new posters that keep appearing on her walls. She never bothers removing the old ones, just tapes new pictures on top of one another. By now the layer of paper is so thick, I think it has actually reduced the space inside, like an embodiment of a Gabriel's Horn paradox. Peeling away Elsie's posters would be like excavating layers of sediment, or the heartwood of a tree trunk—her *Powerpuff Girls* buried layers beneath the shirtless guys from *Magic Mike*, the Rihanna-in-an-orange-bra hidden deep under an Emory

University poster her uncle sent all the way from Atlanta.

Her collection of popular science books has doubled over the years, as has the range of multicolored bras that lie permanently scattered over her floor. Felipe, Elsie's life-sized human skeleton, is propped in a chair near her window. He's wearing a knitted bobble hat and has one of Colin's Hawthorn soccer scarves draped around his clavicle. Elsie's bedroom is probably my second most comfortable place on Earth, always familiar despite the ever-changing ephemera.

"There are seventy sextillion stars in the known universe," I say after hovering unnoticed in the doorway. "If intelligent life exists elsewhere, why do we think it'd bother to buzz us here on Earth?" Elsie practically falls out of her chair as she spins around from her computer. "We are a small, ridiculous species, Elsie. Forget about the probability of aliens in the universe. *Why* would anyone bother to come looking for us?"

Elsie clutches her heart. "Jesus, Sophia. Give a person some warning!" She pushes her chair backward. "What are you doing here? I thought you had family stuff."

I tear my eyes away from her screen. The extra reading for Physics—an article on Fermi's paradox, with Mrs. Angstrom's little green alien drawing—is open on Elsie's monitor. Another window in the corner of her screen is playing a clip from what I think is *Sleepless in Seattle*.

I nudge a basket of shoes out of the way and sit ungracefully on the floor, the purring lump of ginger cat still in my arms.

"Colin let me in," I answer. My stomach is starting to feel a little less like it's being wrung from the inside. But I have no idea what I want to say.

Elsie follows my gaze to Felipe's scarf. "Yeah, Colin's crashing for a couple of days. Apparently 'my hot water is on the blink' is boy code for 'my housemates have spent this month's gas money on gourmet pizza.' I mean, I love my brother. But when it comes to money, Colin can be a real dickbag."

"Right. Poor Colin."

Elsie sits on the floor beside me. She is in her plaid pajama pants and an ancient *Doc McStuffins* T-shirt that I think belonged to one of her cousins. She takes the cat from my hands, then gathers a towel from a pile on her floor and hands it to me.

"This is Pumpkin, by the way. Number four or five—no one can remember how many gingers we've had." Elsie chuckles, her eyes trained on Pumpkin's head. "So. What's going on, Rey? If I had to guess, judging by the look on your face, I'd assume Toby has finally snapped and Express-Posted Viljami's decapitated head home to Finland?"

Elsie smiles, but it's small and strange. She deposits the cat on her bed and sweeps an armful of clothes off before dragging herself up to sit on her quilt. Her hair is just washed, flowing in fat, loose waves. Her eyes flash yellow and purple from the string of butterfly lights on the wall above her bed.

I lean my cold face against her covers and close my eyes. Alarmingly, they feel a little damp behind my eyelids, but of course, nothing resembling tears is forthcoming.

Elsie drums her fingers lightly on my head, just hard enough to coerce my eyes open. Reflexively, I shift away, then feel yet another swoop of guilt and shame.

"Okay. So you're upset?" She fidgets with her blankets. "Sophia...are you going to tell me what's been going on? Because for the last few weeks it's sort of felt like you've been visiting another planet." She clears her throat. "Maybe I'm just paranoid, but it feels like lately...like you haven't wanted me around as much or something?"

I sit up straight. I've been so busy trying to sort through the tangle in my head that I haven't given much thought to how this must seem to her. I haven't been pushing Elsie away. Not on purpose. Have I?

Elsie swings her legs off her bed and walks around to face me. "Sophia, you're taking a really long time to answer that question." She crosses her arms. "Do you...have you not wanted me around?"

"Maybe," I say slowly. "I'm not sure. I don't think it's that simple, Elsie." Elsie's mouth drops open. She snaps it shut again, blinking way too rapidly. But when she speaks, her voice is eerily calm.

"Sophia, you're going to have to explain that. Hey, I know, how 'bout you just pretend I'm an idiot?" she says with a sharp smile. "Pretend I'm a moron whose brain moves a couple of clicks behind yours, okay?"

I twist the damp towel, knuckles white. I have been trying for so long now to find the words to explain to my best friend why my future feels so terrifying, why I can't face talking about college or the prospect of her not being around for it. But I know I'm not capable of articulating the things I feel.

Instead, I decide to focus on my most pressing dilemma. "See, Elsie, there's this thing I've been trying to manage. Or understand, I suppose is a better word. Something that I didn't factor on having to deal with...this thing that I'm having, or was having, or, I don't even know. With this boy..."

I'm pretty sure my syntax is hopelessly jumbled. I can't say his name out loud. I feel, once again, the failure of my own vernacular, the inadequacy of stupid, stupid words. I have this brief notion that perhaps I could express everything more clearly in a chart or a Hasse diagram, but I think I'd have as much luck trying to quantify the events of the past month using the marionette puppets that starred in the year-seven production of *The Sound of Music*.

I glance at Elsie. She has been pacing back and forth in the free space between her clothes. The look on her face is one I've never seen before.

"It's all been a bit confusing, to be honest," I mumble. "He's strange, but I think good-strange, and then tonight there was this party...I mean, you know me and crowds, but I thought I could handle it. And I did. I was handling it fine. But then it got...well. I don't know. There was this thing..."

I take a deep breath, regrouping my thoughts into orderly rows and columns, and I give her a rundown, in bullet points, of everything that's happened over the last month. I even manage to dispassionately report everything that's transpired since I landed on Joshua's doorstep tonight.

I don't know how to explain the kiss. I could describe it with anatomical precision, since my eidetic brain remembers every nuance. I know that the scientific study of kissing is known as philematology, and that the scientists who study kissing are known as osculologists. It sounds like a cool profession. Useful. Enlightening.

But out of all the things I lack the language for, I especially can't articulate that kiss.

I'm lost in the memory, so it takes me a moment to notice that Elsie has stopped pacing, and that she still hasn't said a word. She's blinking quickly again, her head tilted like she's trying to hear something in the distance.

She looks me square in the eye, and my heart makes an uncomfortable stumble because it is the first time she has made eye contact since I started speaking.

"Elsie?"

Elsie sits down heavily right in front of me. "You went to a party?"

I can't tell if it's the rain on the roof or the blood in my ears that makes me suddenly claustrophobic. "Yes. But it wasn't a big deal. It was a last-minute thing—"

Elsie holds up a hand. I search her face for any clue as to what is happening, but all I can tell is that her brain is whirring.

"Sophia. When we got invited to Harriet Lohman's sixth birthday party with the rest of our class, what did you tell me?"

I swallow. "I said that Harriet Lohman was having a jumping castle, which, on average, are responsible for thirty people a day being hospitalized. And I think I said that I wanted to finish some Geometry homework—"

"And when we got asked to the year-seven formal by

those guys from the debate team, what did you say?"

I think for a moment. "I said that I didn't want to hang out with Ben Bartlett because he didn't understand fractional exponents—but to be fair, Elsie, he always spent the class reading comics on his phone, then asked me for help later. And, um, I said there was a Fermat's Last Theorem documentary on TV that would be more fun."

"And what did I do?" she says in a voice that sounds too full.

"You stayed with me, Elsie. You always stay with me."

She stands up, a shirt from her floor-pile clutched in her hand. "Rey," she says softly. "Tell me why you've been keeping things from me?"

Without any idea what I should be doing, I stand as well. My skin is still cold, like the warmth of Elsie's house can't unfreeze it. Elsie backs away.

Elsie has only a couple of photographs among the clutter on her desk—a picture of her with her brothers on a trip to India a few years ago and two photos of her and me. In one, we're at Sizzler for her thirteenth birthday. We're a few years older in the other, both wearing surgical masks and her mum's scrubs. It was taken the last time we dressed up for Halloween, even though I talked Elsie into skipping trick-or-treating that year, which pretty much signaled the end of our Halloween tradition. Elsie is all broad smiles in both photos. I look like I'm made of marble. I've always hated photos of myself. No matter what I'm thinking or feeling when the picture is snapped, my face always manages to look blank and vacant. I always look insubstantial, diffused around the edges. I think it's because I'm built of numbers, of data and facts and peculiarly firing synapses. Maybe, in the real world, I am simply more faded, less *there* than everyone else.

"Elsie, are you mad?" I whisper, my eyes on the Halloween picture. "Please, I'm sorry, but I don't know what I've done and I've had a really bad night and I can't focus on you right now—"

"You can't *focus* on me?" she yells. I jump, dropping the sock I didn't realize I'd been grasping. The chatter from downstairs ceases. "When have you ever focused on me, Sophia? You think I don't know that you barely even register I'm here?"

"That's ridiculous, Elsie. Of course I notice you—"

"Oh really? Then why don't you ever ask about *anything to do with me*? You never ask about my plans for next year—you're not even a bit curious about what I want or how I feel about anything! You have no idea what's going on with me. Has it ever even crossed your mind?"

"But, Elsie, you told me you didn't want to talk about it—"

She bundles the shirt in her hand and flings it at the wall. "God, that's just something people say! Of *course* I want to talk to you—" She laughs, but I have no idea why. "Who else do I have? Who else am I supposed to talk to?"

I think back over this past year, running frantically over every conversation we've had. I know I have asked her about things. School and homework. Her opinion on *Doctor Who* and Keanu Reeves and Maryam Mirzakhani. We spent three hours one Friday in June debating the relative merits of Mr. Grayson's thinning comb-over versus Mr. Peterson's fire-hazard toupee. Maybe I haven't said much about the future. But I don't know how to talk about something that makes me feel stressed and sad.

I feel myself tunneling into my center, shrinking inside my skin in a way that I do when I'm overwhelmed, but never, ever with Elsie. She seems to take my silence as a statement, because her face becomes redder and her voice so much angrier.

"I'm *scared*, Sophia—I can't coast the way you can. And I've been busting my arse with band practice, which you never even *acknowledge*! When was the last time you came to a recital? When was the last time you asked me how it's going?"

"But you play the *xylophone*!" I blurt. "It's not a key part of the orchestra. Zimmy Taylor plays the cowbell, and her friends never come to anything—"

Elsie's eyes widen. Horrifyingly, they also brim with tears. The last time I saw Elsie cry was when Ryan accidentally deleted *Harold and Maude* from their DVR. I can't speak. I can't process anything else tonight; the emotive centers of my brain are shutting down, underneath this awful, stomach-ripping sensation that something unrecoverable is spiraling out of my control.

"That's what you think of me," Elsie says, her dull tone more frightening than anything else. I can't reconcile her inflection with the tears that are careening down her face, and all I want to do is crawl under her blankets and have her explain everything to me, like she always did when we were kids.

"Elsie, please, just tell me—"

"No," she whispers. "I'm done being your interpreter. I have made so many sacrifices for you. I've missed out on *so* much, all because my best friend has a breakdown every time anyone even *suggests* she interact with other humans. But the moment you find someone worth making the effort for, all that becomes meaningless—"

"But Elsie—"

"No. Stop," she says, sobbing now, heedless of my shaking hands and frozen face. "You've been holding me back all these years, Sophia," she chokes out. "You have no idea how lonely being your friend is."

And though I know it's a physiological impossibility, somehow my heart feels like it has cracked into a million pieces.

This time I don't flee. I simply turn and walk back down the stairs. Pumpkin, the ginger tabby, weaves between my legs as if to see me out, or possibly to hasten my departure by tripping me on the staircase. I have a vague impression of Colin, Raj, and Ryan, silent in their warm living room, their game of Trivial Pursuit abandoned. Distantly, I think I hear one of them call out after me.

The street is damp and dark. I walk, my focus absorbed by the uneven footpath. I count in a Fibonacci sequence, always my go-to pattern when I was little, as comforting as the sheep Mum told me other kids count to help them sleep.

The drizzle has turned into a downpour, which soaks my green dress through. I realize, as I stumble over my count, that somehow in this crap-storm of a night I have lost my copy of *Six Easy Pieces*, which, yes, I was carrying to a party inside my jacket pocket.

I think it's the loss of the book that finally breaks whatever spell was holding me together. Breathing is rapidly becoming problematic.

I lie down on the nature strip between the road and sidewalk, my forehead in the grass. It smells of dirt and wet green, but I breathe it in as if this earthly connection can resynchronize my body and disconnected brain. My entire world is reduced to filling my lungs. I wonder if this is what Houdini felt, right before he burst free from his water torture cell. The fact that this knowledge is now embedded in my brain is unutterably distressing.

I don't know how long I remain horizontal. Eventually I am so numb and cold that something in my hindbrain sparks to life, reminding me that a wretched evening is still no justification for hypothermia. I sit up and realize I've been lying in a murky puddle of brown water, which has left two boob-shaped circles on the front of my dress.

I pull out my mobile, blurring my eyes against the multiple "missed call" notifications, all from the same number. I fumble for my contacts, and I call the only person I can safely assume is also friendless and alone on a Saturday night. Though my throat is still locked, I manage to croak out my location. Then I bury my face in my knees and totally fail to cry.

Toby's Corolla pulls up to the curb with a very un-Toby-like tire squeal. I drag my face up to see his bespectacled eyes scanning frantically through the windshield. He's out the door and across the road, only checking both ways twice, which is how I *know* this is a crisis.

Toby skids to a stop. He drops onto one knee, right there on the roadside. I stare at his kneecaps, the damp already soaking his pajama bottoms.

"Sophia, are you hurt?" he barks. "What happened?"

I open my mouth. Strangely, all I have been able to think about for the fifteen minutes since I called Toby is Richard Feynman. How he hated studying English, detested the rules of language. He knew it was nothing but imprecise human conventions, arbitrary, made-up vagaries that had nothing to do with anything real. This phrase keeps floating through my head in Feynman's twangy voice: there is a difference between knowing the name of something and knowing something. I suppose he meant that not having the words for a thing doesn't make it any less true or real.

"Did you not think to put on pants?" I ask out loud.

Toby's face furrows. "No. I didn't."

He stumbles as he stands, then reaches down and pulls me up, his hand briefly under my arm, though he lets go quickly as I wobble to my feet. Whatever he sees as his gaze runs over me renders his face less frantic. It sinks slowly back into its usual mask of blankness and irritation.

"If this is one of your episodes or whatever, you should've called Mum or Dad. I've got half a dozen assignments that aren't becoming un-terrible by themselves." He looks around the street as if only now realizing that he is outside.

"Toby, do you think I'm a horrible person? It's okay if you say yes. I'd just really like to stop trying to guess what's in your head."

Toby slicks a hunk of dripping hair from his eyes. He shakes off his parka and all but throws it over my shoulders. "God, I don't have time for this," he mutters.

Warm fabric wraps around my torso, enveloping me in a faint cloud of home-smells. "You don't have time for me?" For a second, I think my voice almost manages to break free of its monotone.

And for just the briefest moment, I think I see something pass over my brother's face. It's gone too quickly for me to identify. "I don't have time for teenage dramatics or whatever this is," he says uncertainly. "If, well—did something happen that I should know about?"

Facts form an orderly line inside my head. It's almost welcome, this ability of mine to systematize and classify, even now, when I am so bone-tired that the bed of damp grass at my feet looks appealing. I seem to have lost my will to speak though. I shake my head.

Toby gathers my discarded bag and thrusts it into my hands. "Right. Then let's go. Get in the car, Sophia."

I figure I might as well follow a directive. Perhaps this is where my future lies—blindly observing orders, using my skills for whatever I am told to do with them. Like those mathematicians who cracked the Enigma code, but the underlings with names nobody remembers.

I huddle in the passenger seat. Toby fiddles with the heating, cranking the temperature and aiming a vent my way.

"Put your seat belt on," he growls.

I look over at him as I click my belt into place. Disheveled and damp, he flicks on his wipers, but he doesn't pull out into the traffic until he has slicked back his hair and untucked an errant bit of his pajama shirt collar. It's like he can't move forward until he has smoothed and straightened himself into place.

I wonder if a hug from my brother would trigger my anxious touch response. Most likely, all higher brain functions would cease, rendered catatonic from shock. I don't think I have ever giggled in my life, but I have this sudden flash of Toby attempting to hug me with those spindly arms that he once sprained trying to hang fairy lights on our Christmas tree, and it almost sends me into hysterics.

I face the road, deciding to focus solely on the windshield wipers. I am unable to process anything more tonight.

I rub a hand over my chest. Somewhere beyond the pounding palpitations, it hurts. Fact: My heart is only the size of a fist, but it is capable of pumping blood through the one hundred thousand miles of vessels that cascade through my body. I know it is still doing its job. If I were prone to hyperbole, though, I could almost imagine that my heart has given up on me too.

♦

Chapter Fourteen

The Observation of Black Holes

Suffice to say, everything sucks. Everything sucks diseased monkey balls, on the body of a vivisected lab monkey, in the lab of a scientist plagued by chlamydia.

If my life were following the path indicated by a dozen Hollywood films, then this would be the moment when I should be making my great, life's-work breakthrough. I think I'm meant to be sketching the solution for the Riemann hypothesis on my windows with magic markers, un-showered and disheveled. Sometimes I wish I were a character in a movie. Christ, I'd even settle for being a character in one of Ms. Heller's plays, safe in the knowledge that even though I am behaving absurdly, I am still following someone's script.

I shower, because I really don't see the point of wallowing in my own dead skin cells. And I avoid writing on walls or windows. It doesn't seem all that conducive to good work, and anyway, there are plenty of crisp pages in my perfectly functional notebooks. They feel like just about the only place where I can park my disquieted brain.

He has called me on the hour, every hour, since I left him standing on that stairwell. I know this because I have spent most of Sunday working through the Vector Calculus syllabus from my college course, my heart palpitating every time the *Doctor Who* theme sings from my phone. Needless to say, I have not solved the Riemann hypothesis. I *have* made a total of three really obvious errors in my Lagrange multipliers homework, which is disturbing enough to send me back to bed for almost an hour.

In between, I have watched two documentaries on the frogs of Costa Rica and invented a new flavor of iced chocolate by accidentally mixing Milo with Mum's antacid medication instead of soy milk. My stomach already felt horrible. Mylanta-Milo did not help.

I have visited the IMDb page of every romance movie Elsie has ever given me and created a table in my notebook listing relevant themes and plot points. It's the only non-mathematical study I can think of that could possibly be of use. My research methodology may be flawed, but I do manage to draw some broad conclusions: that the adult women in these movies read nothing but Jane Austen and are required to spend all their waking moments discussing their feelings. And that all resolutions must involve emotional speechifying, extended soliloquies that I am convinced no person could construct on the spot, no matter how many improv classes they'd taken.

I even made myself re-watch *The Lake House*. It persists in being awful and offensive. The thing that bothers me most? The fact that not one person is curious enough to investigate a miraculous time-traveling mailbox, instead using a staggering anomaly of physics to exchange letters about the smell of flowers in the rain. Despite knowing how it ends, I remain disappointed that Keanu does not get hit by that bus a second time. Even on repeat viewing, Elsie's adoration still makes no sense. The fact that I can't see what I'm missing, no matter how hard I try, makes my stomach hurt even more.

Elsie always did tell me that I willfully miss the point. She never explained how to fix that, though. What if my problem isn't determination or willpower, but some innate defect there's no fix for?

I have sent half a dozen emails to the St. Petersburg Steklov Institute of Mathematics, and one letter to *Playboy*, after I stumbled on an article about Grigori Perelman in an online magazine. A hand-drawn portrait sits alongside the feature: Perelman's face sketched in scribble like some cheap penciled Picasso, the pieces warped and disjointed. I guess that's how most people would see him—the broken genius with the crazy eyes, a quirky aside in a magazine primarily devoted to half-naked women. I'm not sure what my mum concluded when she walked into my room with a sandwich only to find my screen filled with breasts. I wasn't exactly operating on full capacity and had zero means of interpreting her malleable expression or the hand that lingered for a moment too long on my hair.

I'm plagued by this urgency to talk to Perelman. What made him retreat from the world? What happened to his work? Did the one thing he was passionate about let him down in the end? Did he ever find someplace where he belonged, other than inside an equation? Or did his messy, ill-fitting pieces prove impossible for anyone else to understand? Did he discover, finally, that there was nowhere at all in the world where he fit?

Is he happy? Does it even matter if he is?

If nothing else, my Cyrillic improves a lot. But no one responds. I do receive an automated response from *Playboy*, however, telling me that an autographed print of Miss August has been sent to me in the mail.

I sit at my desk, surrounded by books. A cup of tea materializes beside me, delivered by my father, I think. It's in a novelty mug that Dad bought me a couple of years ago. It has a picture of a guy and a girl on it, vector graphics like the ones on public toilets, and underneath is the caption: *Statistics. The discipline that helpfully proves the average human has one testicle*. I think it's supposed to be funny. At least, Dad has a good chuckle whenever he's making his Milo.

I catch my parents exchanging a few furrowed glances as they rush from work to family events and back again, but neither of them asks me anything but the most perfunctory questions. I don't know; I think maybe they see what they want to see. I've always suspected that they gave up trying to decode the inner workings of my brain a long time ago. Or perhaps they truly do think that I'll be okay? Maybe I'm a much better actor than I've been giving myself credit for.

At some point, I pick up my Drama homework. I'm meant to be working through some exercises aimed at "demechanizing physical and emotional behavior." From what I understand, this primarily involves me spending an hour trying to pick up a shoe. The thought of attempting to untangle it all makes my insides feel scraped. I don't think I can cope with any more uncertainty, not one more fragment of failure.

So I curl up in bed with my books, and I stick to math. That—at least for now—I understand.

And then, just like that, the calls stop.

Of course. It makes sense. Given time to weigh up the evidence, what else could he conclude? It's what I wanted—space, and time, to unscramble and reset. It doesn't explain why I keep staring at my screen, though, thankful for its silence and dismayed by it too.

This is why I avoid people. There are too many things I should be focusing on. Staring at my phone, unable to decide whether or not I want it to ring, should not be one of them. Christ, maybe I *am* Sandra Bullock. Constantly frazzled, unable to manage the simplest of life decisions—disregarding the mailbox that transcends space and time, while being obsessed by shitty love letters and a dog.

But the fact is, outside of my family, there are only two people who matter to me, just two people who have ever bothered trying to see the me that I am afraid of. And somehow, I have failed them both.

Maybe Perelman had the right idea.

Maybe retreat is the only option.

♥

Chapter Fifteen

Good timing is invisible. Bad timing sticks out a mile.

—Tony Corinda

I stopped calling her only when Camilla threatened to flush my phone.

I probably should've stuck to my guns and stayed under my blanket in the dark till my decomposing flesh became too tempting for Narda. But *nah*, I had to be the sucker who gets browbeaten into going to a gig at a craphole bar called—I'm not even kidding—the Heartbreak Hotel. Why I agreed to inflict myself on the world, in a fat-Elvis themed cafe, is anyone's guess. I think, subconsciously, I just can't handle letting anyone else down this weekend. But I plan on sitting in silence for half an hour and then vanishing back to my cave.

Camilla takes one look at my face as I slouch in and uses whatever magic she possesses to extract the whole story. I don't even know where my verbal spewage comes from, 'cause it feels wrong, and sort of disloyal, invoking Sophia's name in this place of beer and hipster shirts. But I'm worried about her, and freaking out that I've done everything wrong. And I *really* need someone smarter than I am to tell me what to do.

Camilla, I notice, is carefully quiet. At some point the chick on stage launches into a ukulele solo of the crappiest, saddest Shins song ever, and I bury my face in the couch cushions and groan. The couch stinks like arse. In fact, the entire bar stinks like arse. Maybe everything stinks, and I just haven't noticed before. That'd be about right—the whole world reeks, and I'm the one git walking around with his face buried in a fantasy bouquet. Bloody hell, am I really that big a dick?

"Jesus, Joshua, morbid much?" Camilla says, bashing me on the arm. "Get your face out of the cushions. Adrian found half a ham sandwich and a condom in there a few months back. Seriously, do you even want to imagine what someone was doing with both of those things at once?"

I sit up. I adjust my glasses, then throw them onto the coffee table. Right now, there is nothing in the world I need to see clearly. Funnily enough, though Sam is still perched on an armrest, the rest of the group have made themselves scarce.

"Camilla, I just want to know what I did wrong. Why won't she answer the phone? Do you think...should I go find her?" I peer at my now-blurry mobile, but it is snatched out of my grasp before I can dial.

"Joshua Bailey," Camilla says, managing to sound both gentle and unyielding. "Give her some space and time. She's not testing your persistence. She needs to *not* talk to you, at least for a while. Just back off. For your own good. And hers. *Trust* me on this. Do not be that guy."

Bammo. And there it is. Have I really become *that* guy?

But, see—aren't you supposed to *want* to make someone's life better when you care about them? Was I being too pushy? Where is the rule book that explains how that works? And without it, how am I supposed to figure this out?

Houdini would've just teleported a thousand roses or, like, a gazillion doves into her bedroom.

But I am not Houdini. Or Dai Vernon or Thurston the Great, or even stupid douchehead Copperfield. Copperfield wouldn't find himself sinking into a whirlpool of failed expectations. Copperfield would've just sawed himself in half with his stupid oversized buzzsaw, or, you know, made the Statue of Liberty disappear just for her.

What I am is some lanky doofus who can pull a coin out of his nose, a sad party magician with a lingering speech impediment, the lamest non-person in the universe. I am a loser with no ambition and no goals, whose greatest achievement so far is learning how to pull off a One-handed Faro Shuffle. While I wait, desperately, for any sort of inspiration, my prospects are fast reducing to being a sad street busker or Damien's underling at the crappy pizzeria he's bound to end up working at.

Of course I'd never be enough for her. I'm barely enough for myself, and hey, I'm not even that picky.

"Joshua," Camilla says, clasping my hand in hers. She retrieves my glasses and sticks them crookedly on my face. Sam looks on with sympathy. "You are so great. And Sophia seems pretty great too. But have you ever thought that maybe it's just not supposed to be...your time?"

I close my eyes. Suddenly, all I feel is tired. "Maybe, Camilla. Maybe you're right. Can I please have my phone? I'll back off. I promise."

Since I am out of options, I will do as I am told.

I won't call her. I'll leave her be, if that's what she needs. I just need to know that she is okay.

And there's one place I can go to find that out.

I've prepared a speech, but I don't think it's gonna help. There's a snag in my voice that I can already sense, my tongue thick in my mouth, sibilants lying ready to be misarticulated all over the place. Stuff it. It's not like she can think I'm any more of a giant loser.

It's a nice house. The lawn's a bit overgrown and has a whole bunch of chew toys strewn across it. The front door has a cool brass knocker in the shape of a Great Dane's head. I step over and around a giant pile of guys' shoes, mostly Chucks and New Balance sneakers.

I give the dog head a few raps, shoving my other fist deep into my jacket pocket.

Elsie Nayer throws open the door. She is wearing an unzipped Hawthorn hoodie over a thin, pink nightie. The silk slip just about conceals her torso, and she's, um—well, she's not exactly unendowed, and the expanse of brown skin and curves that fills my vision is, well, momentarily startling. But then I notice that her eyes are puffy, and her hair is bunched up into a tangled bird's-nesty bun. She looks me up and down. Her eyes narrow.

I adjust my glasses, wishing I'd found the energy to put my contacts in. "Hey, hi, Elsie. Ah, sorry to just show up at your house. Look, I know you don't know me, but my name's Josh. Joshua Bailey. We're in Mr. Grayson's Bio class together? I, ah, wanted to talk to you because—"

"It's you," she says softly. She steps onto the porch, heedless of the wet tiles beneath her shoeless feet. She's a little shorter than Sophia, but she walks right up to me and stares me down, and I find myself shrinking beneath her glower. "You're the guy. The magical mystery boy." There's a vague tinge of sarcasm in her voice, but I'm more concerned that her chin is all wobbly, her red eyes filled with unhappiness. She zips the hoodie up to her neck, somehow making the gesture look pissed and sad too.

I swallow. "So I guess she told you about me? I kinda had the feeling that she maybe hadn't mentioned me before?"

Elsie snorts. "Yeah. Seems like I don't know jack lately. How fricking unobservant can one person be. Man, and I want to be a doctor. Oh yeah, dude, sorry about the face cancer, guess I missed that giant, oozing tumor growing out of your forehead. My bad."

My brain must have become used to playing catch up from all the time I've spent with Sophia. I put two and two together, and the answer I come up with makes me cold. "Elsie, I'm really sorry if I've done something to upset you too—"

"What do you have to be sorry about? You're not my friend," she says matter-of-factly.

The misery chorus that's been following me cranks up a couple of bars, like it's added in a few depressed backup singers and a moaning sax solo from one of those eighties hair-ballads Camilla likes so much.

Elsie stares at me, radiating fire and something else, something raw and hurt. My hands are drumming frantically inside my jacket pockets. I take a breath and force my eyes to center on Elsie. I clench my fists to stop my fingers moving.

"I know we're not friends," I say slowly, hearing the catch in my voice, which is flying of its own accord now. "You have no reason to trust me. But I think I've upset her, Elsie. I don't know what's happened between you guys, but you're her best friend and I just thought—"

"You just thought I'd be up for playing matchmaker? Sorry. Out of the three of us, I'm now apparently the least qualified to offer romantic advice."

I take a step back and consider Elsie. Sophia's guardedness is more cautious than cynical; despite all her reservations, there's always been something kind of candid about her and open. But Elsie wears her caution like a shield, thick with wariness and suspicion, an invisible coat of barbed wire wrapped around her. And right now, Elsie Nayer is looking at me like she'd love nothing more than to string my nuts on a necklace.

"You're mad at Sophia?" I say.

She crosses her arms. "Good observation, Criss Angel."

I sigh. "God, I hate that guy," I mumble. "I mean, eye makeup doesn't make you a badarse. And put a shirt on, man. No one's coming to your show for the nipples."

Elsie blinks. She looks like she can't decide whether to snicker or deck me. Her eyes are still damp, but her clenchyness seems to have unlocked a bit. Despite the elephantine weight on my shoulders, I feel myself relaxing just a little bit too.

A skinny dude sticks his head around the door. "Heya—everything okay out here?" he asks warily. He tries to give me a hardarse stare, but it's kinda diminished by the mint-green *Adventure Time* Beemo T-shirt he's wearing, and the fact that he is sucking strawberry Yoo-hoo through a straw.

I think back over a conversation Sophia and I had once about Elsie's family. "Hey—it's Raj, right?"

Both the skinny kid and Elsie look at me incredulously.

He steps out onto the porch. "Ah, yeah. And you would be?"

Elsie waves a hand. "So apparently Joshua here and Sophia are—what phrase did she use? Oh, right, having a thing that might be a something."

Raj looks back and forth between us. "No way! Our Pinky and this guy?" he says, gesturing at me with his thumb. "*Ohhh*," he adds, his face lighting up. "So is *that* what's going on with you and Sophia? You jealous?" Raj looks me up and down, an uncanny echo of his sister. I'm starting to feel irrelevant, like a sideshow exhibit under review. "Elsie, seriously? This loser? Wouldn't have pegged your thing as the reject-from-Slytherin type. No offense, dude."

Elsie groans. "God, can you piss off, Rajesh!" she says, but there's no real animosity behind it.

Her brother rolls his eyes at me. "Yeah, good luck with that," he says, before scampering back inside as a shoe flies in his direction.

Elsie sits with a thud on the wet concrete steps. I hesitate, till she gestures at the spot beside her. I sit, cautiously. She hugs her legs to her chest and tugs her hoodie over her knees.

I stare out at the expanse of heavy gray sky. It's started drizzling again—not enough to need an umbrella, but a light mist coats my skin. It couldn't be any more appropriate for my mood; not unless it started raining tiny bleeding hearts or a shower of dead doves.

I sigh, then give Elsie a weak grin. "So. You're not, are you?" I say, picking up a random black Converse from her doorstep. "I mean, jealous, or whatever? 'Cause really, I'm not that awesome."

Elsie rests her chin on her knees. She gives me a vicious side-eye. "Yeah. I doubt you're my type. I prefer my guys to be a little less lamppost-shaped."

"Oh, I get it. Because I'm tall. And really, not hot. Definitely neither awesome, nor hot, and yes, way too tall. You dodged a bullet there, Elsie Nayer."

Elsie snorts. "Settle down, funny guy." She rocks lightly, chewing fitfully at a hoodie string. "So. Sophia. You like her?" she says eventually.

I let out a sad laugh. "Yeah. I like her, Elsie. I like her a lot."

She looks at me for what feels like an age. "Huh. How did I not notice that?" she says, almost to herself. She nudges my shoulder, an unexpectedly genial gesture that almost sends me flying off the step. "You got that look in your eye that I should've seen a mile away."

"What look?" I ask, even though I'm pretty sure I don't want to know.

"That look that says you're halfway to picking out cat names and matching dinnerware. It's obvious." Her eyes flicker across my face. "I mean, now that I know what to look for."

The disordered pile of shoes behind me is screaming my name. I half-turn and grab a few from the pile, setting them side by side in their proper ordered pairs. "Doesn't matter. She doesn't want me." Elsie is watching me, her chin resting on her knee. I should probably leave this pile of grubby shoes alone, but I don't think I can sit here for much longer unless I do something with my hands, put right at least one thing that's out of whack. She doesn't look bothered. She just watches me, shrewd, dark eyes containing a dash of sympathy.

"Listen, Joshua? Lemme tell you something. Sophia doesn't need us. She doesn't need anybody." She waves a hand in the air, a defensive swat against imaginary flies. Her face crumples, then rights itself, then crumples again. I don't think I've ever seen anyone work so hard to fight off tears. My instinct is to throw a comforting arm around her, but everything I've observed about Elsie Nayer suggests it wouldn't end well for me. "Sophia Reyhart just humors regular people. She's sure as shit just been tolerating me."

"Elsie, you don't really believe that. Do you?"

She shrugs. "Why not? Most of our lives, I've just been flailing around behind her while she does her thing. She's never needed friends. I always thought I was different, you know? But I'm not. Rey doesn't want anybody."

"And, but...d'you think she prefers it that way?"

Elsie lets out a laugh-choked sob. "How should I know? I have, like, five minutes left before I leave here, maybe forever, and my best friend has spent the last bit of it lying and...and *excluding* me. She needed me just as long as she didn't have anyone else, but now I'm discardable."

I place the last pair of lime-green Chucks beside the now-neat row. It's only vaguely satisfying; there are untied, uneven shoelaces to deal with and mismatched red and blue laces in one set of runners that make my eyes hurt. I rub my hands over my face, wondering if the Nayers would mind if I just curled up on their doorstep and slept for the next century.

"I don't know what to say, Elsie. The last thing I wanted was to mess up stuff between you two. Maybe you have a right to be mad, or hurt, or whatever, but just don't leave her alone. Please. Whatever you think, she needs you. Maybe... you're the only person she needs."

Elsie tugs angrily at her bird's-nest bun. She gives me that sack-shriveling glare again. "There's nothing she needs that you or I can give her. The sooner we both accept that, the better." She swallows convulsively. "Anyway, I'm not the one who made the decision. Sophia left me behind a long time ago."

I stand. My fingers are jiggling, trying to take flight. I am making nothing better by being here, and I'm suddenly convinced that every second I stay is somehow making things worse.

"Elsie, I'm really, really sorry. But I know you guys can fix this."

Elsie's tears spill without warning. I stare at her, frozen and useless. I dig through my pockets and hand her a crumpled piece of silk from my Vanishing Thumb kit. The plastic thumb is still attached. She takes it from me with a snicker.

"Yeah. She said you were weird." She stands and peers at me, full in the face, the evaluating look so similar to her best friend's it makes my knees wobbly. "But I dunno," she says softly. "I think maybe normal is overrated. Something tells me you might be okay."

I heave a sigh. "Thanks. Elsie, I...don't think it's a good idea if I call her, but please don't give up on her. You and Sophia, you'll work it out. You have to."

With no better options, I go home. I lie under my shelves with an old deck of cards, but I can't find the drive for anything but the most basic shuffle. I ignore the school books still safe in my bag, my dry, pointless homework, and the crumpled pages of a practice exam wedged in the bottom of my satchel. I reckon today is not the day to face the growing roil in my guts, the feeling that might seem a lot like panic if I acknowledge how far behind I've probably fallen. And I ignore my phone—the only person who wants to talk to me is Damien Pagono, and I'm really not in the mood for another extended chat about boobs. I'm struck with the god-sucky realization that this sensation of floating in the world with no purpose or meaning might be all I have to look forward to.

I have no idea what to do with myself.

So I YouTube some music.

I stick on my headphones. I hunker down in bed. And I pray real hard that my cat finds some sympathy for me and eats my spleen while I'm asleep.

Chapter Sixteen

The Proof of Dark Matter

Monday. My nights have been almost sleepless. I briefly consider skipping school but quickly decide that avoidance is illogical. There are only weeks left till graduation, but barring an asteroid collision or an invite from a secret-genius division of the CIA, I cannot miss all of them.

This morning, Ms. Heller decides that we need to work on "grounding ourselves in our physicality," so our exam rehearsals will be replaced by a special class on *Baal*. It's a play about a guy who sleeps with lots of women, murders someone, and then dies alone in a forest—so it's both relevant and appropriate.

I should be relieved that she's giving us a brief reprieve from exam preparation, but I am so exhausted I'm not sure I even care anymore. I go through the motions, reciting my lines, until my character thankfully drowns herself. Ms. Heller scowls—clearly my monotone and stiff, misplaced hand gestures are not Tony Award-worthy—but regardless, my work is done. I retire to the darkness at the back of the room where I can, hopefully, take a nap.

There is nothing in my locker this morning but books. Nothing in my bag but my TARDIS pencil case and Specialist textbook and a crisp green apple, courtesy of Dad. My pockets contain nothing but lint and old tissues. There is nothing on my homeroom desk but new graffiti that reads *Stefano Kendrick is a giant bag of dicks*. Elsie is absent. I see no sign of Joshua.

"Hey, ah, Ms. Reyhart?"

I jump. Damien Pagono has materialized beside me. He is not sporting his usual smug face, but actually looks a little uncomfortable, I think.

He pulls a chair in front of me and straddles it backward.

"Can I help you?" I say tiredly.

He shrugs. "Nah. Can I help you?"

"Pardon?"

Damien squirms. He searches through his bag and pulls out a squashed chocolate bar, which he immediately proceeds to devour.

"Look," he says through a mouthful of Snickers. "I dunno what happened with you and my boy Josh, but—he's a good guy. Like, really decent. So maybe you could, I dunno, cut him a bit of slack? Or at least, undo whatever made his face look like someone's napalmed his play house with his cat or some shit in it?"

I want to have this conversation with Damien Pagono about as much as I want to get up on that stage and perform an improvised rap battle. But I parse Damien's garbled sentences, and I'm arrested by one thought.

"I've upset him?"

For a moment, something foreign flashes across his face. I think he actually looks a bit mad. He shrugs again, his expression settling back into neutral. "Look, I ain't judging. I don't know what went down—the boy's a vault, and it's not like we're sharing BFF bracelets—but yeah. He's pretty blue."

I glance at the front of the room. Romy Hopwood and her friends are parked on the stage steps while Ms. Heller potters around Jeremy, who can't seem to figure out how to work his wig.

The girls are laughing, doubled over, that kind of gasping, tear-filled laughter where no one can catch their breath. Every now and then they get quiet, amid gulping breaths and lots of *shush*ing. But then one escaped giggle or snort sets the whole group off again.

I wonder what particular psychological phenomena is responsible for collective laughter. Romy is hugging her friend Amber, her arms seemingly the only thing stopping the smaller girl from tumbling off the stairs in glee. What is it that makes this laughter ostensibly real and genuine? Why do I recognize it as true laughter, as opposed to, say, the staccato guffaw that is the only thing I am able to produce when the spotlight shines on me?

I close my eyes. "Listen, Damien? I...I'll talk to him, okay? I'll talk to him, but I really don't want to talk about this with you."

Damien stands. "Okay. That's cool. But, hey, ah, Sophia? You know, I've always thought you were pretty okay." He clears his throat. "If you ever wanna, you know, practice your monologue, or whatever, I'm down. I'm less shit in this class than in everything else and, well, maybe I can help. Or whatever."

I stare at him. His cheeks are a little red, small eyes downcast. I wait for the punchline, but nothing is forthcoming. I can't imagine what he could want, but for some unknown reason, I am suddenly sure that he is not messing with me.

"Maybe. Thank you, Damien."

He grins. "And don't tell Josh I talked to you, okay? 'Cause he's a nice guy and all, but I reckon he might, you know, conjure one of my nuts off if he knew."

I may have learned nothing in this class. I can only hope that by some miracle of thespian osmosis, my subconscious has absorbed a few rudiments, some tiny fragments of acting skill.

I think perhaps I'm about to find out.

It's cold in the main building as people head outside for morning break. The wide doors snap back and forth, icy air careening through the corridors.

I concentrate on keeping my breathing even. The ceaseless churn that I've been experiencing since Saturday is something beyond my usual anxiety—something beyond fight or flight.

But when I round the corner and see Joshua leaning with his forehead against a row of lockers, my heart seems to shift into something heavy and disquieting. The line of his back is slumped, and his hair is covering his face. I see his fingers fluttering almost indiscernibly against the door.

All I want to do is turn and run. But something in his defeated posture calls me forward. It's magnetic, this thing between us, the thing that got me into this mess. It makes my feet move of their own accord, despite the nerves and nausea.

"Hello," I say.

He opens his eyes and turns around.

"Hello, Sophia."

I stop a few steps away. The grates on his locker door have left an impression on his forehead, three horizontal lines pressed into his skin. It makes him look sort of confused, or quizzical. I have this insane urge to smile. I don't think it would be helpful.

I plunge my hand deep into my blazer pocket. "I'm sorry about the weekend. It was a mistake," I blurt. Heat immediately floods my cheeks.

Joshua's face contorts. He swallows, his jaw working back and forth. "I didn't mean for that to happen," he says slowly. "Or to tell you those things. I swear, I never planned to—"

"No, you didn't do anything wrong." My right hand forms a fist in my pocket. "It's not you—"

Joshua laughs wearily. He runs a hand through his hair. "Really? That's the line you're going with?"

I can't meet his eye. "I suck at this. You know my information on these things comes from questionable sources," I mumble.

My eyes flicker back to his. He smiles, briefly. "Elsie's crappy movies. I remember. Did I ever tell you Gilly and I watched *Sleepless in Seattle*? I liked it. I mean, when my sister wasn't pretending to vomit in her mouth. That kinda ruined the ambiance. Her verdict, and I quote, was that 'old-people love is sick and wrong.' I think maybe she missed the point."

His words bounce over each other at a steady clip, though his speech is beset by more tics and hitches than I have heard from him in a long time. "Oh, and by the way, you do not *suck*, Sophia."

My brain tumbles back to the darkened stairwell, the things he said to me, the misguided, wonderful, terrifying way he sees me. I try, for an instant, to find the words and the will to push past my fear. But then Joshua takes a step toward me, his dark eyes solemn.

"Sophia, I'll do whatever you need. If you need me to leave you alone, I will. I just want...wanted...to help. That's all."

The corridor has almost emptied. My hand in my pocket is clenched so hard it's hurting, nails biting into my palm. But what can I tell him? That it's not his help that I need? My brain just doesn't work this way. I don't know how to be a normal girl, the sort of girl he needs, and it's no use pretending otherwise. As much as I wish it could be different, my brain is a giant arsehole. I can't live in his bubble. I need to burst it, once and for all.

I back up a few steps and shake my head. "I'm sorry, Joshua," I say softly.

If I had to put a label to his expression, I think it would be resigned. He nods. "Yeah. Me too."

I turn and walk away. I need to go back to my life, to the moment before all my messes became tangled up in some boy with kind eyes and a hopeless ambition to fix all my problems.

I withdraw my hand from my pocket as I stumble outside, releasing the coin that I've been clutching. I don't know what's more disturbing—the fact that I have Abraham Lincoln's face imprinted on my palm, or the fact that I had every intention of returning his lucky talisman and have no reasonable explanation for why I didn't.

♥

Chapter Seventeen

For those who believe, no explanation is necessary.
For those who do not, none will suffice.

—Joseph Dunninger

So I made it through the week. Well—endured it. I showed up to class. I even wrote some stuff. I didn't grab one of the multiple granola bars Damien kept shoving at me and beat him over the head with it. I'm counting that as a win.

I'm not working till this afternoon, which means I get to spend Saturday morning flat on my back, shifting my gaze between the underside of my lowest bookshelf and the stack of practice exams on my desk. Beneath the shelf, a tiny spider is cocooning an insect in a web. Her legs, like fine eyelashes, dance merrily around the body of the hapless bug that's soon to be her dinner.

"Oh how I envy you, little bug guy," I moan.

The clomp of size five Doc Martens turns my head. Gillian's scowling face pokes around my door. "For god's sake, Josh, could you be more wretched? Last time I saw something this pathetic, it was smeared over the highway on that Christmas trip to Wollongong."

"Gilly, go away. I need to be alone."

The door flies open with a thump. "Yeah, I don't think so.

This room is starting to smell like someone took a dump in a hazmat bin. And do you know you have a Dorito in your hair?"

She sinks onto my bed and yanks the chip out of my hair. Then she grabs my face and squeezes. "Joshie, come on. Snap out of it, man. There's only room for one depressed a-hole in this house."

I force a laugh through mashed fish-lips. "I'd never peg you as depressed, Ms. G. Infuriated, sure. Obstinate and uncooperative…" I sigh. "What've you got to be sad about?"

My sister pats my cheek, a sting bordering on a slap. "Turns out I've got another emergency parent-teacher meeting-thingy this week. I dunno, you call the head of Humanities a 'reject from the Mr. Bean teaching academy' one time, and suddenly your 'attitude is in need of adjustment.' Teach me something worth learning and maybe you'll see my attitude improve. Right?"

And there it is again. The sharp wrench of guilt and responsibility, wrapped in a neat bow of self-loathing and shame.

I close my eyes, covering my foggy glasses with a forearm. "Gillian…I'm sorry. I am the worst. I'm a piss-poor excuse for a brother. Man, the only way you could have a worse influence is if you had one of the Manson family, or, like, Caligula for a sibling—"

"Joshua—are you *kidding* me?" she squeals. She shoves me over with her hip and flops onto the bed beside me. Her hair smells of baby shampoo and the chemical tint of new green dye. When she looks at me with her giant cobalt eyes, I find myself, mortifyingly, misting up a bit.

"Josh—you're the only reason I bother showing up to school at all. Ever since I was little...anything worth knowing, I know from you."

Gillian's face scrunches. Her eyes are confused, innocent, and yet anything but. I remember all the nights she spent right here when she was little, scared of shadows and storms. But now, as Gilly watches me uncertainly, I'm struck by this awful feeling of inevitability, like I'm fast-forwarding into a future that I'm not ready to see. Who is this turbulent person going to become? How will she shape herself into a real person with a place in the world? What if she can't? The thought makes me feel shitty and dog-tired.

Gillian rests her head on my shoulder. "Josh, listen up, because I am never going to say this again. You are a doofus and, like, freakishly tall—seriously, dude, you look like a llama—and the magic thing is so dorky I can't actually believe we were spawned from the same people." She drums black-inked fingernails on my arm. "But you're also a good guy. You can be funny, and smart, when you're not trying to pull a chicken out of my ear or something. You know a lot of really random stuff, and, okay, a lot of it's about old, dead people, but still, you've got this weird knack of making it all seem kind of cool and interesting. You're nice. You deserve someone nice. And if this chick doesn't get that, well then, screw her." She narrows her eyes. "You want me to run her over with the car? I know where Mum keeps the spare keys."

I rest my cheek against her head. "No homicide, Gilly. It's not Sophia's fault. None of this is her fault. It's just...crap timing. But, you know, thanks for the offer. Please don't murder anyone on my behalf." I kiss the top of her hair.

"You are a bit awesome, you know that? Scary and unhinged. But awesome."

I can all but feel Gilly rolling her eyes, even as she snuggles closer. "Tell me something I don't know."

I laugh, rubbing my eyes beneath my glasses. "I kinda hate myself a little bit right now."

Gilly shrugs, her shoulder jostling my head. "You wanna help me design a tattoo? I've been reading up on how those guys give themselves prison tatts, and reckon I could do a decent job with a ballpoint pen and a safety pin."

I smack the back of her hand. "Pass."

"Well then...do you wanna watch *Frozen*? There's left-over apple turnover in the fridge. Dad made it. It's not, like, totally vile."

"*Frozen*? Do we even still have that? I thought Mum gave it to the Salvation Army. Unless someone rescued it from the trash...?"

She sits up, her cheeks a charming shade of red. "So?" she snaps.

I sit up beside her. "Gillian Anna Bailey. If you wanna watch *Frozen*, just say so."

She punches me in the arm. "Hey! I'm trying to be nice, you jackhole."

I stare at her. She drops her eyes.

"Yeah," she mumbles. "I wanna watch *Frozen*."

The suckfest continues on Sunday, though I have made the heroic decision to remain in bed, semi-comatose, rather than confront the real world.

I'm trying to drown out my life with YouTube, headphones in my ears, my head shoved under a pillow, when I sense someone standing in my room. I'm hoping they'll either go away, or maybe, if I'm lucky, they'll beat me to death with one of my broken clocks. I keep my eyes resolutely shut until an impatient hand swats me in the foot.

I reluctantly extract my head to see Sam standing at the end of my bed. He buries his hands in his hoodie pockets and rocks back on his heels, looking as uncomfortable as if he'd walked in on me splayed out naked, performing a Midas Touch.

I close my eyes. Music swells through my earbuds. I may have been listening to the same song on repeat, possibly for the last few hours, possibly longer. It's torturous, but probably the karmic juju I deserve.

I feel Sam shuffling around to the side of my bed. He tugs out one of the buds and leans down, pressing it to his ear. And then, the giant tool-faced git bursts out laughing.

"Jesus. Are you serious?" he says through demented cackling.

"Leave me alone," I mumble. "I'm busy. I am *grieving*."

"No, you're not," he says between snorts. "What you are doing is lying on your bed, in the dark, listening to Air Supply and feeling sorry for yourself. You are being a twelve-year-old emo. From 1982."

I yank the headphones out, music still blaring. A sudden fury whooshes through me as I bolt upright, smacking my head on the bottom shelf. Sam takes a hurried step backward. He looks like he's trying not to piss himself laughing.

"What are you doing here, Sam? Shouldn't you and Camilla be, like, brushing each other's hair or, I dunno, picking out names for your future babies or something?"

He blinks a couple of times, then shrugs. "She's put her foot down about Leia. I'm still working on it. As for what I'm doing here—Camilla made me come. Apparently, this is a guy situation. Although I'm not sure what sort of situation calls for two guys to hang out in the dark listening to eighties ballads, so Josh, please, can you turn off the music? I think some of my testosterone just evaporated, and dude, I'm not sure I have that much to spare."

And despite everything—despite the fact that my heart feels like it's been blowtorched—I laugh. It comes out as a painful croak. I flick off the music and toss my phone onto the floor. Sam clicks on a lamp, and dazzling light floods the room. I flop onto my back and peer at him through splayed fingers.

He sits at my desk and glances around. "Hey, cool poster," he says, pointing at my Mandrake the Magician frame.

I shrug. "It's stupid. It's a stupid bloody thing for a grown guy to have on his wall. Take it if you want."

"Yeah, nah," he says dryly.

"How did you even get here? How d'you know where I live?"

"Bus, train, tram," he says evenly. "Your sister let me in. And Camilla tracked you down. Actually, Camilla dragged me into the city and railroaded Amy." He smiles wryly. "When she's in the right mood, I think my girlfriend might be the only person on the planet who's scarier than your boss."

I grunt. "You shouldn't have bothered. Anyway, I can pretty much guarantee you've got no advice that's gonna be of any use to me."

"Yeah, advice isn't exactly my thing. I'm not the most useful guy when it comes to this stuff. But believe it or not, I think I know what you're feeling."

"You have no idea—"

"Like getting kicked in the nuts, repeatedly, by a giant with a steel foot would be less painful?"

"Nice metaphor."

"Accurate?"

I sigh. "Yeah. I suppose."

Sam hoists his arse onto my desk. His eyes follow mine to the distant blue ceiling. "Josh, Camilla is..." He shrugs with a sheepish smile. "Camilla is my *person*. But not because I think she fell out of the sky or anything asinine. We got *really* lucky. And, if circumstances were different—if her dad moved somewhere else, or if I was a bit stupider—we might never have happened. Circumstances, dude. Like, statistically, how many people are likely to end up hanging in an abandoned campsite that doubles as a serial killer's lair, or building their house on an Indian burial ground—"

I groan. "Please, I'm begging you, no horror movies—"

He holds his hands up. "All I'm saying is, there are a thousand scenarios in which Millie and I could be passing each other as strangers on the street. And yeah, occasionally I wake up in a sweat thinking about that, but my point is—I don't think it was fate. I think it was luck. Luck, and that bizarro chemical thing, and not being a complete arsehat. And timing."

"Right. Timing," I echo. I bury my face under my pillow again. I think I can safely say that my timing isn't stupendous. Who am I kidding? If it were to rely on its current brilliance, my timing would probably see me strangled in my own straitjacket, drowning in an underwater torture cell, my face eaten off by tigers.

I sit up. "God, you're right, Sam. I mean, seriously, what the hell am I doing? I can't make a decision beyond the next five minutes. I can't think about anything after this year without my brain melting. I have shit hair. I live in a bloody cupboard. I am a loser, a joke, the tail end of a failing trick that's gonna fizzle into nothing—"

Sam rolls his eyes. "Josh, do you think you could maybe focus on one crisis at a time?"

"Where do I start? Sophia was the one thing I was certain of." I hear the words come out of my mouth. They sound pathetic even to my ears.

Sam grimaces. "Right. Well, maybe then—there's your problem?"

I blink at him. Without my glasses on, everything is blurry, yet something hovering on the edge of my vision seems to suddenly become clear.

I know that what I'm feeling for Sophia is real. That thing, the sad crush I had before I knew her properly, has been replaced by something solid and true, and the thought of letting it go makes me feel like I'm sinking. But while I've been pouring all my energy into thinking about her, I have successfully managed to ignore the fact that it is now September, and I still have no plan, no ambition. I have written off the rising terror that I have totally crapped all over this school year, because as long as my attention was misdirected, nothing else needed to matter. I remember Camilla's irritated words from what seems like a lifetime ago. Maybe I have been unfair. And not just to Sophia.

I dig my palms into my eyes. "Sam...maybe you're right," I whisper.

Sam dusts his hands. "And she says I suck at this stuff," he mutters under his breath.

I look around my room. It looks like a tomb and smells like a tomb's dirty sock basket. It's so small in here, my little cave, made smaller by my blockade of books and broken clocks, which I always meant to learn how to fix but somehow have still never gotten around to.

I reach for my glasses. "Sam, man, I think something might have died in here. I mean, something other than my pride and heart and all hope for the future."

Sam rolls his eyes. "Dude, the theatrics? I don't think I've included anything that melodramatic in any of my scripts. And I have one where a staffroom of teachers gets eaten by a horde of mechanical slugs. But yeah, it reeks in here. Can we go somewhere else? Your sister said I looked like a Yaoi character. I don't even know what that means. But I'm not sure it's supposed to be flattering."

I swing myself off my bed. The room sways; whether from days of inertia or the shock of an epiphany, I can't say. I grab my mobile, noting approximately eighty-five thousand messages from Damien, and not all of them featuring *Harry Potter* gifs.

"Yeah. Think I need some air. And, ah, I have this mate, I guess, who I should say hey to." I send Damien a text and am immediately spammed with replies. I sigh, but I can't help but chuckle too. "You should meet him. Picture Adrian's taller, more disgusting cousin."

Sam's eyes widen. "Jesus. This I need to see."

He hands me my jacket. Stepping out of this room feels dangerous, a confident statement I'm not sure I'm ready to make.

I take a deep breath and crack open my door. "All right. So plunged the Bolsheviki ahead, irresistible, overriding hesitation and opposition—"

Sam wrinkles his nose. "Dude, do you ever get the feeling that we might not be the coolest people in the universe?"

I laugh. "Yeah. I reckon that's pretty much a given."

Chapter Eighteen

The Illusion of Space-time

Time, as it is annoyingly prone to do, passes. I manage to kill a whole swathe of it with *Doctor Who* and even a bit on the vague pretext of studying for the upcoming Drama exam. But mostly, it's math that saves me.

Perelman is an arsehole. I mean, how hard is it to return an email? I briefly consider tearing down his photo, but after some reflection, I draw a pink Sharpie mustache on his beardy face instead, and leave it where it is—right next to the two of hearts that seems to mock me, but which I can't find the will to discard.

I ignore my brother, and my brother ignores me. It's like we have slid inexorably into parallel dimensions, passing each other with just the barest suspicion that the other exists. It's fine. I bury my head in my work, powering through the extended reading in my college syllabus, which actually proves interesting enough to distract me from everything, including Elsie, who refuses to make eye contact when I see her at school. I don't know what to do. I find myself frozen next to her in Bio, walking toward her in the corridor and then, at the last moment, fleeing in the opposite direction. I just can't face her telling me again how badly I have let her down. But more than anything, I know how selfish I am being; the solid foundation I have propped my back against is suddenly absent, and its loss is more than I can grasp. It's my problem to deal with alone though. I may not fully understand why, but I do know that I have hurt Elsie enough.

And then there is Joshua. My unsolvable problem, my messy-haired mystery. I see him in the corridors and in the back of the Biology lab and after school, walking across the parking lot that feels like it will be wet for the rest of eternity. Occasionally our eyes will meet accidentally, or at least, I think accidentally. Sometimes he gives me a tiny half-smile. Most of the time he looks away. Sometimes I think he looks sad. Sometimes, when Damien is yammering in his ear, he laughs and the sound never fails to turn my head. But there's something in his demeanor that's different too, something more serious, like his focus has turned elsewhere. I have no idea where his head is at. I guess I wasn't prepared for how strangely...amputated that would feel.

Of course, the entire mess that is my life can be summarized by one irrefutable fact: I am still stuck in the hell that is Drama. I'm muddling my way through, still stumbling toward my exam, still convinced that my imminent failure will be the thing that sends my life spiraling from its dysfunctional state to full hermit-living-in-the-storeroom-of-the-Math-faculty phase.

Ms. Heller is unrelenting. She captures me one day after class, just as the lunch bell rings, a firm hand on my arm. I pull away, glaring, but she doesn't seem to notice. Ms. Heller looks, if anything, like she has reached the end of her tether too.

"Sophia, stick around. Let's chat."

Damien pauses in the doorway. He gives me a look that I think might be sympathetic before Ms. Heller shoos him away.

"Sure. Whatever," I say, slumping into a chair. I don't think I was ever a petulant kid, but I'm feeling decidedly irritable and not in the mood for another futile pep talk.

"Okay," she says, taking a deep breath. She stands in front of me, hands on her hips, multiple bracelets jingling. "We are running out of time. I know you weren't exactly thrilled to be in this class, Sophia, but I honestly thought I could help you. But now I'm starting to think that you're so resistant—I'm starting to wonder if this was the best move."

Oh, you're only realizing that *now*? And I thought *I* was bad at reading people.

I cross my arms. "So what do you want me to do?"

She twists her hair up on top of her head, squaring her shoulders like she's preparing for war.

"I want you to trust me. And I want you to try. Okay?"

She gestures for me to stand. I feel something brewing deep in my gut, something hard, something defiant. It's not panic. I don't know what this feeling is, but I stride up the stage stairs with a distinct frostiness gathering in my bones.

She makes me march from one end of the stage to the other, blowing air through my lips in noisy raspberries. She makes me hold an empty cup and saucer in my hands, pretending to sip invisible tea in various states of joy and suffering. I do it all, feeling further and further removed from myself. But then she hands me a monologue from *A Streetcar Named Desire*. ("I took the blows in my face and my body! All of those deaths! The long parade to the graveyard!") Seriously, what in ever-loving Christ does this have to do with my life?

I have had enough.

I come to a standstill at the edge of the stage, where a sole year eleven is practicing the flute in the orchestra pit.

"No."

Ms. Heller pauses. "Excuse me?"

I see her face, the growing confusion. It almost makes me backtrack, this awful sinking feeling that comes with the knowledge I am letting someone else down.

But then she takes my arm again, heedless of the tension it so clearly generates in my body, and she ushers me to the back of the stage, where a giant mirror sits propped against a wall. It's just me, my blank reflection, and Ms. Heller's earnest face over my shoulder.

"What do you see, Sophia?"

I cross my arms again. "I see myself. I see brown skin. Teeth. Lips. Zygomaticus muscle. Eyebrows that my cousins are always trying to get me to pluck. What am I supposed to be seeing?"

Ms. Heller closes her eyes. She exhales noisily. "Okay, let's try this again. I am trying to light your fire, Sophia! I'm trying to get you in touch with yourself—"

"Argh, stop! I've wasted enough time this year trying to touch myself!" I grimace. I turn away from the mirror, Ms. Heller narrow-eyed in front of me now. "Did you ever think that maybe I *am* in touch with myself? The things that make me happy—well, maybe they're not the things that you understand, but—do you get that I *never* felt inadequate until people started telling me I needed to be fixed?"

My hands are trembling. But I feel my brain cracking open, like it has discovered proof of an equation that's been eluding me.

I am not good at this. I am not supposed to be. The things that I am good at, the things that "light my fire," might be narrow and weird and mysterious to almost everyone else. And sometime, someday, maybe I will suck at those things too. But at least they're *mine*.

I am tired of hiding in my own shadow. I am tired of pushing aside the things that make me *me* for some shinier version of myself that ticks everyone else's boxes.

"Ms. Heller, I know you mean well, and I'm sorry I suck at this. But I don't think you have anything else to teach me here."

I push through the backstage curtain and descend the stage stairs. The flutist in the orchestra pit ignores me, lost in her own world as she blows a jaunty tune. I gather my things and walk outside. And then I keep walking, past the East Lawn and the old amphitheater, past the main building and the parking lot and the bench and the school gate and, heart hammering, I head home.

My house is, unsurprisingly, freezing. I dump my things in the kitchen and note, with senses on full alert, the furious clack of a keyboard in the living room, loud in the silence.

Maybe Ms. Heller has actually managed to unleash something in me, something primal, something itching for release; or maybe recent events have obliterated any instinct of self-preservation.

I march over to the thermostat on the kitchen wall and flick on the central heating. It roars to life, like some monstrous beast in the ceiling has awakened.

The angry typing in the next room stops. A moment later footsteps barrel toward the kitchen, and then my brother appears in all his frazzled glory.

He does a double take. "What are you doing here?" he snaps.

"I'm skipping school. What are you doing here?"

Toby strides over and flicks off the heating. "I'm working. Or trying to. And what do you mean you're 'skipping school'? Since when do you play hooky?"

I glare at him. Like my hands are operating independently of my brain, I reach out, slowly, and turn the heater back on.

Toby narrows his eyes. He paws at the controls again. The heater stops with a groan.

I hold my brother's eye and, very deliberately, I reach for the wall. "I. Am. Cold. I'm *sick* of being cold. Viljami is an idiot. If you think freezing your balls off is necessary, then go stick them in an ice bath. Other people live here too."

Toby's whole face puckers, his oh-so-familiar sour-lemon look. He tries to grab for the controls again.

I shriek, a foreign sound like an insane banshee, and slap his hand away.

Toby squeals. He holds his hand to his chest, eyes wide and wounded behind his glasses. I reach for the heating again. He yelps and slaps my hand back.

And then, like we're two toddlers fighting over the last Lego, my brother and I are slapping each other's hands in a frenzied, and frankly ineffectual, skirmish. Toby, five years older than me, glasses askew, hair flopping out of his side part, looks exactly like he did at his last primary-school sports carnival—face averted, eyes closed, hands floundering wildly in the vain hope of pitching a shot put ball anywhere but onto his teammates or his own foot.

"Toby! Stop it!" I yell as his watch connects with my wrist bone. "Why do you hate me so much?"

Toby physically recoils. It's such a definite movement that his glasses tilt even more precariously, hands frozen mid-strike. It would almost be comical, if it weren't for the fact that this is my brother, reeling from his aversion to me.

"I don't... I never said...you hit me first!" he splutters.

I stomp to the other side of the kitchen and drop heavily into a chair. "Yeah, well," I say sullenly as I rub my stinging hands. And then, because my brief *Fight Club* foray seems to have reduced my intellectual capacity to that of a moron, I finish, "you started it."

I bury my head in my hands and massage my temples, expecting him to be gone when I open my eyes again. But then I hear the scraping of a dining chair. I look up. Toby flops down across the table from me, breathing heavily.

"I never said I hated you," he says slowly. "I might not have an eidetic memory, but I'd remember if I'd ever used those words. And I haven't."

"Maybe you never said it out loud. I don't have to be a genius to draw some inferences."

Toby fidgets with the seams of his sweatshirt. "Why do you even care?" he says suddenly. "It's not like anything other people do bothers you. You don't yell. You don't cry," he adds, as if this is some sort of revelation. "You never cried, not even when you were little. You don't even really laugh."

I gape at him. "Say something funny, dipshit, and I might."

Toby blinks. "Did you just call me a *dipshit*?"

I glare. "Yes, I did. You obviously put a ton of weight into the fact that I don't throw my emotions around like Blanche DuBois—"

"Blanche who?"

"Oh, so *not* the point! But, if you're weighing up what you think of as evidence and drawing bogus conclusions, you are, quantifiably, a dipshit."

I don't know if it's the dusty, disused heater, but something tickles at my nose. I sneeze, feeling suddenly feverish. It'd be just my luck to come down with some exotic plague, on top of everything.

I rummage in my pockets for a tissue. "And to answer your question: yes, Toby. It bothers me."

Toby just stares. Suffice to say, I can't read his face. I think it's sort of appalled, and maybe sort of fascinated too.

"You don't ever say that though, do you? You're just always jammed inside your head. You don't behave like anyone around you matters."

I rest my forehead on the table, still sniffling. "I don't do a lot of things, apparently. I don't fight with my best friend, and I don't go to parties with nice people who I'm a total zero in front of, and I don't kiss boys. I definitely do not do that."

I raise my head a fraction. Toby's eyes widen. "Is that what this is about? A...a *guy*?" His jaw tightens. "What guy? Sophia, did he do something? Did he—"

I sneeze again. "Settle down, Captain Jack. He didn't do anything. It's all me. And this is not about a guy. It's about you and me and the fact that my presence seems to be as appealing to you as a uranium enema."

Toby seems to unclench a little. Sweat is darkening the hair around his temples, plastering strands to his face. He takes off his glasses and clears his throat. "Right. Well then."

For a moment, I think he's going to stand and mumble one of his customary, curt dismissals. But then he digs in his pockets and holds a dry handkerchief out across the table. Of course. Toby is the only person on the planet under ninety who still uses hankies. I take it and blow my nose, then look up at my big brother through slightly clearer eyes.

"Better?"

"No. Not really. But thanks."

Toby's jaw twitches. "I'm not as smart as you," he says, as if the words are being pulled from some distasteful corner of his brain. "I'm supposed to be smarter."

"Because you're a boy?"

"Psh, no! Because I'm older, and, and I've worked my arse off, and I should *not* be tanking fricking Business Taxation—"

I sit up straighter as my brother sinks, defeated, in his seat. "Wait, what? You're failing? How?" I think back over one of the rare moments when Toby actually talked about his life. "Last time Mum asked, Viljami said you guys were 'killing it.' Unless, you know, that means something else in Finnish—"

Toby slumps even further. "Yeah, well, turns out Viljami might actually be full of paska. I don't think he's handed in one assignment this semester..." Toby sighs, his chin finally hitting the edge of the table. Brown eyes peer at me through cockeyed glasses. "What do you want me to say? I'm just about managing to keep my head above water, but I almost don't care because I'm so bored studying superannuation. I sometimes fantasize about running up to the podium and pantsing my lecturer, just to break the monotony."

I shake my head, as if I can force this information to compute by jiggling it into the proper slot. "Toby, if you hate it so much, why are you still there?"

He struggles upright again. "What else am I going to do? Drop out? Start something new from scratch when I've got no idea what I'm even into anymore?" He glares at me defiantly. "It's a good course. It's the best option I have. Excuse me for giving a shit about my future."

I balk. "You think I don't?"

He throws up his hands. "How should I know? You never say. And you always look unhappy lately—how am I supposed to know what you're thinking?"

"Well, you didn't seem to have a problem taking a guess," I mutter. "What were your exact words? I'm *selfish*. I don't *feel anything*."

Toby exhales. He suddenly seems to find Dad's fridge magnets fascinating. "Sophia, those things I said... well, yeah. I shouldn't have."

I shrug. "Maybe I deserved it."

Toby looks like he'd rather be on the receiving end of that uranium enema than having this conversation, but he straightens his shoulders.

"So...you had a date?" he says uncertainly.

It's my turn to slouch into my chair. "I don't think it was a 'date.' It was a thing that I sucked at, because apparently I suck at all the things. Maybe you didn't mean it, Toby, but you were right. Mum and Dad should have shipped me off to one of those experimental labs when I was a kid. I might as well be just a brain in a jar. I shouldn't be allowed to interact with normal people."

"When did I say any of that?"

"Boxing Day, lunch. I was five. You were going through your *My Little Pony* phase. You used to wear sparkly gel in your hair and Princess Luna pajamas."

"Christ, you never forget anything, do you?" He folds his arms on the table. "You've really been holding onto that? I'd just seen *The Matrix*, and you'd eaten the last ice cream bar. I was mad. I didn't mean it."

I force myself to meet my brother's eye. "Why don't you just say what you mean, Toby? Don't equivocate. I'm really bad at figuring that out."

Toby's brow furrows. "I don't understand you," he says slowly. And then, curiously, like he's been holding onto the question, "Sophia, what are you afraid of?"

I unleash a snort of humorless laughter. "You want a list? I'm afraid of wasting my life. I'm afraid that I'm just synapses and neurotransmitters, but maybe there's nothing else there. Maybe that's all I am? I *know* that I'm not easy. I'm grouchy and strange, and there are *so* many people, Toby. So many people who can do the exact same things I can. Why would I be any different? What makes *anyone* think I have something special to add?"

Toby is gaping at me. "Sophia—is that—why would you think—" He shakes his head. "That is the most I think I've ever heard you say since puberty."

"Then I guess we can add brain farts to the list of things that suck about me," I mumble.

Toby glances at Mum's Elvis clock above the stove. "You know, Sophia, when you were, like, two years old, you were obsessed with this crappy stuffed pig toy. You'd carry that thing around with you everywhere."

"Mr. Pinkerton. I remember. I don't know what happened to him."

"He's in a box in the shed with all your primary school stuff. I put him there when we moved."

"You did?"

Toby shrugs. "Mum was going to give him to the Salvation Army, but I thought...maybe you'd want him again someday."

"Why would you do that?"

Toby takes off his glasses and rubs his eyes. "Because everyone thought you were too advanced for kid stuff, but you loved that pig. You were a contradiction, always." He gives me that pained look again. "I was really excited to have a sister. But I never... *got* you. You know?"

"I know," I say, hugging my arms around myself. "I'm not what you guys wanted—"

"No, stop. That's not what I meant. Don't be stupid."

And even though I'm shaky on the inside and out, I chuckle. "Toby, I don't think that's a word anyone's used on me before."

Toby's smile is small and wry. "You might be brilliant, Sophia. But yeah. Sometimes you are also pretty stupid."

We sit in silence as the house warms, balmy air from the vents sending bits of fridge detritus blowing around the kitchen. I contemplate my brother. His body language still screams tension: shoulders hunched, sharp chin tucked in. But his face is less pinched than I have seen it in ages. I remember, suddenly, the last time I saw him looking so sheepish.

For my fifth birthday my parents took us to the zoo. I was going through an insect phase, so the only thing I was interested in was observing *Ornithoptera richmondia* up close—the Richmond Birdwing Butterfly, the largest subtropical butterfly in the country. Toby stood in the middle of the butterfly house with this glassy look on his face, eyes fluttering like he couldn't decide where to look first. I remember him standing on the suspension bridge, mouth agape, until a Sapho Longwing flew into his eye, whereby he burst into tears, and we all got dragged to the otters instead.

And I think, in this moment, that I understand something about my brother. Dropped in the middle of a butterfly house, or, say, a lecture on *n*-dimensional Euclidean geometry, I understand exactly what's happening. There's a language that makes perfect sense to me. But for someone who was unfamiliar with advanced topology or the greater subdivisions of the order Lepidoptera, I suppose it might be a bit overwhelming. When I think about Toby's wide-open face, the moment of what even I could recognize as wonder before he was winged in the eyeball, I think I understand something else too. Toby lost in the butterfly house is me most of the time.

I may not understand the technicalities of people—their behaviors are a mystery, their mating habits confound the hell out of me, and yes, okay, I get a little freaked when they come too close to my face—but that doesn't mean I'm not fascinated. Occasionally I catch myself gaping at them, confused, but still mesmerized. And sometimes, I even think they're beautiful.

I take an unsteady breath. "Toby. You are a pain in the arse. You have terrible taste in music, and I really wish you would learn to part your hair in a way that doesn't make you look like a brown Friedrich from *The Sound of Music*. But…I love you."

Toby's face turns a shade of purple. "Aw, come on. You don't need me to say that *Brady Bunch* stuff. When has that ever been us?"

I stare at him.

"Right. Well then." He coughs. "Me too," he mumbles.

I push my chair back. "Toby—do you think we could... maybe go do something? I mean, something other than homework. Just for a little while? I think I really need pajamas and Matt Smith."

Toby stands and scrubs his palms on his jeans. "Is he the one with the scarf?"

I scowl. "Tobias, how is it that we both emerged from the same uterus, and yet you have not managed to glean even the vaguest *Doctor Who* knowledge?"

Toby rolls his eyes. "I've been busy retaining useful information. Or trying to. Not all of us have unlimited capacity to squander on angst and dudes—"

I shove him in the shoulder, and he stumbles sideways into the fridge. His face is neutral, but I *think* he might actually have been trying to crack a joke.

"Hey, Sophia?" he calls out. I pause in the kitchen doorway and turn around. Toby clears his throat again. "You'll be okay. You know that, right?"

Statistically, no, I don't know that at all. There is every possibility that I will graduate with sweeping aces like everyone expects, but then stumble into my adult life and meet a sliding series of failures and disappointments. There is more than a slim probability that everything that is exceptional about me now will turn out to be redundant. Fact: If you throw a group of geniuses in a room, *someone* has to be the dumb arse.

"Sure, Toby," I say with a conviction I'm not sure I'll ever truly feel. "I'll be fine."

♥

Chapter Nineteen

The Potential of Free Particles

I have never skipped school in my life. It's not that I've feared the wrath of my teachers; I've just always had this vague suspicion that some unknown catastrophe will befall me if I break the rules. The strange thing is, I return to school, and not one person comments. Life seems to have continued without me, and a week passes without any side-eyes or questions. I suppose I should feel insulted, but instead I'm oddly comforted. No one notices me or cares what I do, and the realization is strangely liberating.

Of course, no amount of epiphanies can assuage the fact that there are still six weeks of school to go, and my problems have not miraculously solved themselves.

I'm standing in the swirl of lunchtime chaos, trying to decide which way to go. I've been spending most of my lunch breaks in the new library, having discovered this really great documentary on Hilbert's Tenth Problem, which Mr. Simpson, our librarian, has been letting me watch in one of the AV rooms. Today, though, it's sunny outside, and I'm feeling particularly antsy.

I glance to my left, my eyes drawn through the crowds. Joshua is at the far end of the corridor, wrestling with his bag. Damien is beside him, as he always seems to be lately, nattering something that makes Joshua smile.

By now I should be used to the erratic heartbeat every time I catch a glimpse of him. I don't know why it hasn't gone away yet—logically, lack of proximity should have diminished it. But the ache is still there, novel and raw.

I turn away. There's some sort of commotion happening near me, but I register only the hum of it. Way down the other end of the corridor, on my right, is Elsie. She's looking at one of the hallway bulletin boards, her black topknot neat and severe. Elsie has still not spoken to me. I have not worked up the courage to speak to her either. The few times I have ventured to the old library at lunch, she hasn't been there, but I have seen her a couple of times near the basketball courts with Nina and Marcus and their friends, looking blank and bored. Once, when the rain let up, I saw her sitting alone on her blazer on the edge of the East Lawn, her head buried in a textbook.

My feet are locked in place between these two people, as essential as charged electrons circling around me. But no, that's not accurate or fair. I am not the center here. And I want no one's energy to revolve around me.

I glance at Elsie again. She's still staring at the bulletin board, but even from here, I can tell she's not really reading it. I square my shoulders. I need to step up to the plate, to grab the bull by the horns, to... well, I'm sure there are a thousand sports metaphors. I need to do something. I need Elsie to be my friend again. Anything else is unthinkable.

Someone jostles me, snapping me out of my fugue. The year-eleven boys' soccer team is hurtling through the corridors on the way to practice, pushing through the crowd in a blue-and-white, Bengay-scented herd. They're trying to maneuver some giant mesh bags of equipment and apparently lack both coordination and spatial awareness. They seem unaware that there are other people here, and the entire team seems to be trying to fit through at once.

It's too crowded for me to move anywhere. A booted foot steps on my toe, and my face becomes jammed in a fragrant armpit. I try to stumble backward, but the owner of the armpit grabs my arm and yanks me to one side. I find myself shoved against the corridor wall, eighty-odd kilos of soccer-guy pressed against me.

"Let me go," I yelp.

"Yeah, hang on," he says distractedly, his eyes on his teammates and their ineffectual activity. His bare thigh in barely-there shorts is pressed against mine, and his hand is clammy, and he smells like Gatorade. My lungs are trapped behind him, squashed against his back. I try to move, but my legs have become liquid. Panic, blind and choking, rises from the depths of my belly. I can't breathe. I can't move.

Oh Christ, this is how I'm going to die. In the shitty school hallway, with a squashed egg sandwich in my pocket, asphyxiated by armpit sweat and without even a Cole Prize to my name—

"Oi! Dude, did you not hear her? Or have too many kicks to the head turned your temporal lobe to mush?"

I force open an eye. Elsie is standing just beyond the

wall of boys, her hands on her hips. She scowls, gesturing impatiently. "Come on, dickhead. Move."

The guy turns, and almost seems startled when he sees me behind him. He lets go of my arm quickly. I stumble toward Elsie, my breathing ragged, my heart pounding like it's about to burst through my skin. Elsie all but scoops me behind her.

"Get some peripheral vision, arsehole," she snaps.

Soccer guy—who I now see is also one of the clarinet players in the school band—looks briefly sheepish, before he is caught in the tide of the rest of the team and swept down the corridor.

I suck in a few desperate mouthfuls of air. A sheen of sweat covers my skin, slick and cold, but I keep breathing until the panic ebbs into a quiet, woozy murmur.

Eventually I look up. But Elsie's eyes aren't on me. Joshua has materialized just a few feet away, his school bag discarded at the other end of the corridor. He glances at me, and at Elsie, and then back at me, his expression all twisted and torn. But then he looks at Elsie again, and something passes between them. Whatever it is makes his face relax. He smiles, just the slightest lift at the corners of his mouth. Then he turns and walks away.

My voice seems to have lost all volume. "Elsie," I croak.

Elsie shakes her head. "You need air. Come on."

She walks ahead, sneaking looks over her shoulder as I follow behind. I inhale giant mouthfuls of the fresh, cool breeze as we push through the double doors.

Elsie turns with a flourish. "Are you okay?"

I close my eyes. "Yes. I think so. Thanks, Elsie."

She shrugs. "You looked like you were going to vomit right there on the floor. No one needed to see that. Although, if you *did* spew all over Tom Shaefer, I doubt anyone would complain. He's a dick. And he can't play clarinet for shit."

It takes me a few moments of unhelpful navel-gazing to comprehend that Elsie is actually here, in front of me, not hurrying away or averting her eyes. I gather what remains of my wits before I lose my nerve.

"Elsie, I'm sorry," I say in a rush. "I never meant to lie to you. I know I'm useless, and I still don't even really understand what happened, but I know I did all the wrong things. I hurt your feelings. I'm so, so sorry. For that, and for everything. I'm a terrible friend. Worse than that chemist who injected his assistant with gonorrhea."

Elsie's eyes are fixed somewhere in the maple trees above us. She snaps them back to me with a huff.

"I just don't understand why it had to be such a secret!" she blurts. "I tell you everything, Sophia. I thought that you trusted me the same, but clearly you don't." Her whole face collapses, and my insides twist in response. She is not yelling. But two fat tears roll silently down her cheeks, and somehow they are worse than anything.

"I never thought you saw me as just another moron you had to tolerate. I know I could never keep up with you. But I still wasn't ready to be left behind."

"Elsie, but, you know that's not true! I trust you more than anyone."

She tugs her hair distractedly out of its topknot, waves

cascading down her back. It looks a little lanker than usual, like her complex haircare routine has fallen by the wayside. It's that, more than anything, that makes me feel like complete and total crap.

I try to order my thoughts, but I'm terrified I won't ever be able to articulate them, that I will stand here struggling uselessly to make myself understood while my best friend walks away. So I just open my mouth and let words pour out. "Elsie, I didn't tell you everything because you know me better than anyone. You know the me that everyone thinks is defective, and I know you see all of that too, but you've never tried to fix me. You know the me that maybe I don't always want to *be*. Sometimes, Elsie, I really, really want to be able to leave that person behind. But I never can when you're around, because you never let me forget who I am. And sometimes I love you for that. And sometimes, I really don't."

Elsie sits down on the nearest bench. The maple-strewn courtyard is quiet now, only a couple of stragglers still trickling out of the building. A few people glance at us—Elsie in her too-short uniform, angrily swiping at her tears, and me looking, I'm fairly certain, like some expressionless, brown garden ornament. I ignore them all.

She crosses her arms. "I don't understand. You are all sorts of incredible. You know that? I've never been jealous, not exactly, but d'you know how badly I wish I could do even a bit of what you can?"

I sit down beside her with a sigh. I still feel shaky, and so bone-tired, like the last half hour has drained whatever reserves of energy my body has been using to function. "Elsie, you know, I have these moments when I'm sort of… proud of myself. There are so many things I want to do. But then I think, like—why? What's there to be proud of, if other people only see the faulty bits? What if all I am is the problems that need fixing? You know, Perelman's mentor said that if this was still the Soviet era, he would've been forced into a psych hospital by now—"

"Argh, this guy again? Sophia, seriously, when did you get so fixated on a morose personality with a beard? Maybe you should check if Mr. Grayson has a nephew?" She sniffles, wiping her nose on her sleeve. "That Russian guy—who's to say that things aren't going as planned for him? Okay, so maybe no one else gets his plan, but why do they need to? What difference does it make? Why would you want to *not* be you?"

I hug my knees to my chest. "I don't. Not all the time, anyway. I just wish I wasn't such a giant freak with all the rest of it too."

Elsie pivots on the bench, turning around to face me. "Sophia. I *don't* think you need fixing," she says, her voice adopting that measured, low-octave doctor tone that I'm starting to suspect she's been practicing. "But I do think you need help. You need to talk to someone, and I mean, properly talk. You need to be honest with your folks and with your counselor… you don't have to pretend to be okay, Rey."

I clutch my knees even tighter, the sharp points of my patellas digging into my forearms. "Elsie, I think… I know." The words, inexplicably, seem to lift something heavy and burdensome from my chest. "I know I'm not okay. And I know all of my stuff has stopped you from doing normal things too. I never meant to hold you back—"

Elsie brushes a stray strand of my hair behind my shoulder. "That was a shitty thing to say to you. I've never regretted pulling you out of that corner in grade-four music, not for one second. And if you and I have maybe been a bit... well, isolated, it's not really fair to blame you." She snorts. "Believe me, I've done a bang-up job of keeping people away all on my own."

I sigh. "Christ, Elsie. We really are hopeless, aren't we?"

She grins. "Yeah. But maybe social competence is overrated." Her cheeks flush, a peculiar deep crimson. She tugs uneasily at her hair. "Trust me, snogging Marcus Hunn did nothing to improve my social skills, though I think at least 50 percent of the responsibility for that is on him," she says in a tumble of words. "I mean, dude, be less insipid, you know? I might as well have been practicing with a cantaloupe."

"Elsie!" I hiss, dropping my feet to the cobblestones with a thud. "*Marcus*? When did this happen? And why—"

She waves a dismissive hand. "It was nothing. Momentary insanity. Well, y'know, three moments of insanity. I don't know what I was thinking." She gives me a sheepish grin. "Maybe I just didn't want you to outperform me in everything. But I realized... well." She shrugs. "We've done okay together. Haven't we?"

I smile. "Yes. We probably won't leave here with dozens of signatures in our yearbooks. But I've just... always been glad that you picked me to be your friend."

Elsie is silent, a quiet smile on her face. She knocks her knee into mine. "So. Do you wanna come over tonight? We can watch the SyFy channel and make fun of technical inaccuracies. You can throw Pringles at the screen every time someone explains the physics of a wormhole wrong."

"Not sure I'm in the mood for bad science, Els."

Elsie looks at me hesitantly. "Well then, do you maybe wanna tell me about this boy? 'Cause something tells me he's sort of been significant?"

I sigh. "I'm not even sure where to begin. And it's not something I want to talk about while—" I gesture at the doorway, where two year eights are sucking each other's faces like the Hodge Conjecture proof might be hidden in one of their tonsils. I glance at my best friend. "Can I just come over and hang out? I promise I'll tell you everything. And maybe... you can fill me in on what's been happening with you? With America and, you know. All that stuff."

Elsie throws an arm around my shoulder, then lets go of me just as quickly. Then she launches into an account of the latest episode of *The Bachelor*, and it all feels so familiar that, if I were a crier, I think I might have bawled.

I am confident of many things.

I am confident that I can solve cube roots as quickly as a calculator and comprehend complex number theory without breaking a sweat.

I am confident that I will someday attempt to prove the Riemann hypothesis, even though there's a strong chance I'll end up nothing more than a footnote in an obscure journal, or a sarcastic meme on the Math faculty's Christmas party PowerPoint.

I am not confident that I will master much more than math. But for now, with Elsie nattering beside me and my heart beating at normal human speed, maybe that is enough.

Chapter Twenty

Before there can be wonders, there must be wonder.

—David Copperfield

I've never been a massive fan of escapologists. Weird, I know, 'cause they're kind of a huge deal among my people. But I dunno—like so much big, stage magic, it's all just a bit show-offy for me. There aren't many escape tricks you can do alone, not without a team behind you. And really, being able to get out of a situation where you're dangling in a straitjacket over a tank of sharks while someone shoots at you with a flamethrower—is that even magic? Or just pants-crapping panic?

But while I have no interest in busting out of an underwater tomb, I think maybe I'm starting to see the appeal. It's not the flash and bang, or even the possibility of drowning. It's the promise—the ticking clock, the terror of being trapped, and the exhilaration of working free.

Yeah. Kickarse metaphors aside, life is actually not the steaming pile of horse manure I expected it to be. I hang out with my friends. I pick up a bunch of extra shifts at Houdini's Appendix after Amy dislocates a shoulder at roller derby training, which, suffice to say, does not improve her mood.

Jasper takes to dropping by the shop and bringing her USBs of music and bags of Skittles, which *does* morph her frown from exasperated to mildly annoyed. It's mesmerizing, observing the two of them, like watching an iceberg trying to charm the *Titanic*. Sometimes I still wanna mash their thick heads together. But my interfering days are over.

I force myself to engage with exam prep, though that does involve a whole lot of staring and a ton of naps. I'm pretty behind, no surprises there. And I still have bugger-all interest in the finer points of Civil Law, or the details of molecular genetics, no matter how many YouTube videos Mr. Grayson subjects us to. But, you know—I'm present and accounted for, which is more than I've been able to claim in a while. I spend time with my sister, building a mini Eureka Stockade in our yard and fashioning period costumes from Dad's old fishing coveralls. It's the only way I can get Gilly to feign interest in her History homework. And, okay, maybe I spend a little too much time with my cat. But I'm good. It's not like I'm wasting away in a puddle of my own tears and my vaporized heart. I see Sophia at school, and I'm fine. I'm awesome.

Okay, maybe awesome is a tiny overstatement.

But I manage to pass the weeks in Bio without my eyes drifting to the back of her head—notwithstanding the time Damien shoved a pencil in my ear and hissed, "Dude, for god's sake, grow some gonads and talk to her!"

I dunno about the state of my gonads. All I know is: Sophia seems fine too. Solid, like some of her tumbling pieces are finally catching up with her amazing brain. I don't know why I ever thought she needed someone like me. Not even when Tom Shaefer, the ham-fisted git, cornered her in the hallway, and I found my feet moving of their own accord, possessed by this desperate need to—well, maybe give him a stern talking-to or something. But she didn't even need me then. Elsie will always have her back, no matter what.

I don't have the energy for magic anymore. It's stupid and childish, something I should've let go of a long time ago. I still get a buzz out of helping the kids at the shop—teaching them simple shuffles and reveals, seeing their little faces light up when they master something new. Occasionally my hands feel edgy and lost without a deck in them. Amy, in her usual graceless way, tries to talk me around by yelling at me till I take to wearing headphones at work. She even shows me this awesome variation on an Invisible Flight trick that I've been trying to get her to teach me for ages. But none of that matters. I need to move on. I'm never going to be anything other than average with it anyway. It's about time I grew the hell up.

The weeks wind down. Nights fall later and later, and the chill in the air that felt like it would last forever slowly disappears. Details of our graduation ceremony are revealed—a liturgy in the chapel, followed by an assembly in the sports hall, both of which I have as much intention of attending as I do of joining Damien in his planned using-weed-killer-to-burn-a-giant-penis-on-the-soccer-field, last-day caper.

Exam time finally lands on my doorstep. History is a breeze. Math is like being slowly wedgied with a cactus. But all in all, I think I'm doing okay.

By Friday afternoon after the Bio exam, I'm exhausted. I've ditched pizza with Damien and am instead lying on my bed, staring up at my shelves. I'm trying to decide whether I have the will to study or if I should tackle *Game of Thrones* from the first book again, when Gillian bangs open my door and barges in without knocking.

"Whatcha doing, J-bag?"

"What does it look like I'm doing, Gilly-bean? I'm chilling."

She drops onto my fading star rug, tugging off her school tie. "Uh-huh. Moping, more like it."

I toss a ball of socks at her. "Hey, not fair. I haven't moped in ages. No mopage here. Totally beyond that."

Gillian snorts. "You may have convinced yourself of that, big brother. You may even have convinced Dad—I haven't seen him look this pleased with you since you mastered a Left-handed Spring shuffle. Who knew you could make him so smiley just by cracking open a couple of college course guides at the kitchen table?"

I can't help but chuckle. Dad's been looking at me with that nostalgia-glow thing he gets periodically. It's typically followed by montage-y reminiscences about the day I was born. I've been trying my best to dodge these moments, but as the year winds down, they feel a bit inescapable. It's pretty disturbing how immune my father is to my best efforts at misdirection. Though, I dunno. I guess there could be worse things to deal with than the shine of his spotlight.

"Yeah, you may have convinced everyone else that you're a-okay," Gillian says, tracing a random pattern in the stars on my rug. "But you've been pulling off a pretty accurate melty-Olaf impression these last few weeks. Trying to smile while your arms and face slowly fall off."

I take off my glasses and rub my eyes. "Oh, for a day with no *Frozen* analogies." I sit up. "Okay, maybe I've been a bit... blue. But really, Gilly, I'm fine. Or, I will be."

She pulls herself up on my desk, short legs swinging. "Well, I know *that*. But the question remains—have you really given up on the girl?"

"Gillian. That's not... she made it clear she doesn't have room for me. I have to be okay with that. What choice do I have?"

Gillian shrugs. "Maybe no choice. But, you know, I reckon there's some unfinished business there, Joshie. You gotta deal with that stuff. Say what you mean, and then you can move on. Don't let things fester. It's not healthy."

I laugh. "TED talks?"

"Nah," she says sheepishly. "Might have been something Mum said."

My eyes drift to my dark ceiling. I think about all the things I wish I could have said to Sophia. All the things I wanted to tell her but didn't, because they somehow seemed too bare, too small and ordinary.

"Gilly. I think I already talk way too much."

She punches me in the arm. "Joshua, you are awesome. Why are you being such an arsecrack about this?"

I burst out laughing. The crappy thing is, even though I've got no hope left of anything happening between Sophia and me, I hate how unfinished everything feels. I miss talking to her, even though I know that words were never enough. I can talk a good game, but my patter is mostly meaningless. And Sophia doesn't trust words. It's proof that she's looking for, always facts and evidence. Maybe I went about it all wrong. But if I had my time again, all I'd want to say to her is that I think she's extraordinary. I may have bugger-all faith in myself, but I have faith in her.

Bammo.

"I see her. That's what I'd want to tell her," I say slowly. "I won't pretend that I see all of her, but... I think I see what she's afraid of. And I know I can't make it better—well, I know that *now*," I say in answer to Gillian's sharp stare.

Gilly's face relaxes. It's not even her usual cynical face. It fills me with the weirdest sense of hope.

Gilly leaps down from my desk and drops a quick kiss on my cheek. "I hope you get the chance, Josh."

I lie down again as the door snicks shut behind her. Narda walks around my head in a semicircle, her purrs a soothing rumble.

Proof.

Proof that I understand. Sophia never really needed my help. At least, not in the way I thought she did. But that doesn't mean I didn't—don't—want to try. But mostly, if I had my chance again, I'd want to tell her that I know it was never fair of me to hide in her shadows, relying on her amazingness, so I could keep being safe and small.

I sit up, dislodging the protesting cat. What I need is hidden behind a Philip Pullman box set, way up on my highest shelf. I drag the stepladder out from under my bed and scramble up, tunneling through the junk. My hands grab for an overflowing folder of diagrams and carefully sourced printouts.

I fall into my chair, pushing aside the pieces of a Comtoise clock that a dozen YouTube videos have not helped me fix. I flick madly through the folder till I find what I need—a schematic, formulated with Amy on the back of a Houdini's Appendix invoice one particularly slow Sunday and discarded soon after in irritation and resentment. With a notebook and pen in hand, I open Google Street View on my laptop, searching for Earth, Australia, Melbourne. I scribble a hasty version of the schematic on a blank double-page, crossing out the bits that look unworkable and adding in my own switches and modifications. Crazy, jittery exhilaration builds in my gut as the impossible takes shape before my eyes.

I stare at my sketches. I stare at the map. Crap on a stick, I think I can do this.

I reach for my phone.

"Blerg. Tell me this isn't another cry for help," says a sleepy voice. "'Cause if you're drowning in sad ballads again, I might have to send Adrian over to stage that intervention he's been gunning for. It'll involve chocolate and probably a Klingon war song."

"Sam, are you sleeping? It's four o'clock in the afternoon—what are you, a toddler? Wake up, man! I need your help."

A giant yawn rumbles through the phone. "Dude, I was *napping*. What do you need?"

"Lights," I answer.

"Lights?"

"Lights, Sam—I need lights. This isn't a complicated

request. You have access to that sort of stuff, right? I need lights. Big ones and lots of them. Jasper and those guys, they can get those, yeah?"

There is silence on the other end of the phone.

"Josh, unless you are shoring up your house against a vampire attack, I'm gonna need a little more information."

I take a deep breath. I know exactly how big a git I'm being and exactly how douche-y I'm going to sound. But I stare at my notepad and open my mouth, and my plan, unwittingly, pours out.

I run out of breath, tapering into a silence that's echoed on Sam's end. It's practically filled with the clunking sounds of his brain.

I stare at my watch. The silence lasts for what feels like an epoch.

And then laughter echoes through my phone, so loud I have to hold it away from my ear.

"Lights. Gotcha. You're going to have to give me some time."

"So you'll help me?"

I can hear Sam struggling to can his laughter. "Josh," he chokes. "There is no way in hell I am missing out on this. You are, objectively, insane. This sounds like the worst plan in the history of everything. Worse than the time Adrian tried to ask Annie Curtis out by sending his mum over to her house with a pot roast."

"That's not what this is about—"

"Yeah, whatever. Dude, I *need* to see this. Yes, I will help you."

I leap up, boosted by a sudden surge of adrenaline and

gratefulness. "Sam—thank you. Um, I'm gonna call Amy too, but I think I might need a few more hands—"

"Guess you're lucky our crew is full of hopeless romantics," he says dryly. "I'll make some calls. But hey, Joshua?"

"Yes?"

He bursts out laughing again. "Dude, you are *so* gonna end up as a character in one of my movies."

Chapter Twenty-One

The Limits of the Observable Universe

I'd almost forgotten how comforting Elsie's home is, with her dogs and cats and too-loud brothers, most of whom don't live here anymore but who nevertheless are always here. I wave at Ryan and Raj, who are in the midst of raiding the fridge and who greet me casually, like I haven't been missing at all. Colin is in the living room, feet up on the sofa, phone pressed to his ear while he shuttles handfuls of peanuts into his mouth. He winks at me without a pause in his conversation, lilting Hindi following me up the stairs. And when I'm curled up on Elsie's messy bedroom floor, the setting sun casting oranges and pinks through her window, it's like I can breathe properly again.

Elsie sits in front of me with her no-nonsense face on and methodically assails me with questions. I do my best to answer, laying out facts as succinctly as I can. But I'm fairly certain that, in this case, the facts only illuminate some of the story. Elsie wants me to talk about my *feelings*. And, like that floundering boy in so many of her romance movies, I stumble and choke on my words, not at all sure what I'm supposed to be communicating.

We exhaust every permutation of the Joshua conundrum till I beg for a change of subject. Just saying his name is making my heart falter. It is as disconcerting as it ever was, but I have long since given up trying to quash it.

Now Elsie is stretched out on her bed watching *An Affair to Remember* on her laptop while I, having abandoned any hope of gleaning usable information from her movies, am reading an article on Maryam Mirzakhani and her Fields Medal on my phone. Half my brain is on the symmetry of curved surfaces, the other half on... other things.

It's late. The only light in the room is from our screens and the string of butterfly lights above Elsie's bed. I'm yawning, waiting for my brother to give me a ride home, when my phone pings with a message. Like my errant thoughts have conjured him from the ether, Joshua's name appears on the screen. My hands start to tingle.

The message reads:

Sophia. I think I have made an important discovery. And I think you might be the only one who understands it. I know it's late, but can you meet me at school?

I don't know what Elsie has seen on my face, but she pauses her movie. She sits up and clicks on her lamp, swinging her legs over the side of the bed. Wordlessly, I hold my phone out to her. She grabs it from my hand and looks at the screen.

She stares at it, and then at me, for an absurdly long moment. And then she leaps to her feet and flings open the door. "Rajesh!" she yells down the stairs. A moment later, a flustered Raj appears in her doorway, Sunil Gavaskar wheezing behind him.

"You need to drive us to school," she barks.

"What, now?" he says, waving a hand at his Mr. Men pajamas.

Elsie grabs her denim jacket with one hand and my sleeve with the other. "Yes, now, dumb arse! It's an emergency."

I swallow, my eyes fixed on my phone. "Elsie—"

Elsie stops fluttering. She walks over to me, stopping a handwidth away. "Rey," she says gently. "What do you want?"

I glance at my phone as it pings again, twice in quick succession. The first message is from Toby, letting me know that he is waiting out the front.

The second message is from Joshua.

If you're coming, head toward the East Lawn.

I gather my thoughts. They're still half-circling through Mirzakhani's moduli spaces, and also, for some reason, the fact that the collective noun for a group of cats is a clowder. My phone feels hot in my hand.

"All right," I say decisively. "Let's go."

Toby pulls up in front of St. Augustine's and kills the engine, thankfully no longer protesting or demanding explanations. Elsie and Raj lean forward from the back seat. The four of us stare, silently, at the hulking buildings and shadowy lawns.

I turn around. I don't know what Elsie is pondering as her eyes roam over our school. I think what I'm seeing in her face is something like sadness.

"You know, Sophia," she says quietly. "Did you ever wonder if all of this isn't just some giant, pointless waste of time?"

I follow her eyes. "Pointless. Which part, specifically?"

Elsie waves a hand at St. Augustine's. "All of it, specifically. Like, so far, we've spent most of our years in buildings like this, and for what? What are we supposed to be equipped for when we're spat out the other end?"

Toby drums his fingers on the wheel. "I remember a heap of guff that'll only ever be useful for pub trivia—if I ever got invited to pub trivia, which I don't, because oh hey, my only friend is a weird Finnish guy who I'm pretty sure is stealing my clothes—" He takes off his glasses and rubs hastily at them.

I shift in my seat and consider my brother. He looks like the same Toby: crisp shirt and clean-shaven face. But there's something bubbling to the surface under his skin; it's like watching liquid on a Bunsen burner just before it boils. This unmoored version of Toby fits no part of my paradigm. It's alarming and yet oddly comforting.

Raj leans through the gap in the seats and punches Toby in the shoulder. They've never really gotten along; I think Raj is too loud, and Toby too grim, for them to be friends. I don't think Toby knows how to interpret the punch. He stares, frowning at the spot on his arm that Rajesh has smacked.

"So then maybe Pinky has the right idea," Raj says. "Lock yourself away in a lab or something. Stick to what you know. It worked for—I dunno, who was that guy who discovered oxygen? I read about him in History of Econ?"

Elsie wraps her hands around my headrest with a snort. "You mean Carl Scheele? You know he also liked to lick his experiments? This guy was supposedly a genius, but he couldn't figure out that sticking your tongue in a test tube of cyanide is probably not a great idea."

"He ended up dying of mercury poisoning," I add. "I don't think he's the role model any of us should be trying to emulate."

Toby snorts. The windows of the Corolla have fogged up, the glow from the streetlight above us barely breaking through. It should be claustrophobic. But sitting here in the dark beside my friends and my brother—who, by all accounts, has been saving all his words since the beginning of time to unleash upon me these past few weeks—I'm filled with an inexplicable sense of calm. I've only experienced it a few times in my life. With my head inside an equation. Whenever I'm in Elsie's presence. And, most recently, cocooned inside Joshua's tiny bedroom. I ignore the sharp squeeze in my chest at this last thought and unbuckle my seat belt.

"Guys, I'm the last person in the universe who'd have any useful advice." I run my palm over the windshield, clearing a space in the fog. The school looms in the distance. "Yes, some of this has sucked balls. But, you know, not *all* of it has been *that* bad." I jab my brother in the arm, and then let my hand linger experimentally on his shoulder in a way that I hope might be reassuring.

Toby glances at the dead weight of my hand. He rolls his eyes, grinning faintly as I hastily pull my hand away and crank open the passenger door.

"Anyway," says Elsie, "I suppose the alternatives are pretty bleak. If it's a choice between this or some kind of *Hunger Games* scenario, that is. Though how much simpler would it be if our only goal was to not die horribly?"

"Elsie, unless your dystopian scenario involves a race to solve a quadratic equation, or, like, a battle of the spreadsheets, all of us would be cannon fodder," I say. "I'm not sure the not-dying-horribly thing would be simpler for any of us."

I swing my legs out of the car and slam the door shut behind me. Three faces peer thoughtfully out at me.

Toby winds down the window. "So, what? You're saying we should just accept our limitations."

I shake my head. "No. I don't think I believe that. I think—well, say, take the Doctor. He has all of time and space at hand, and he *still* can't anticipate every outcome." I ponder this for a moment. "I suppose if you knew for sure which battles weren't winnable? You might as well just lie down and let the Daleks shoot you in the face."

Toby laughs again, that thin chuckle that makes him seem both wiser and younger. He smiles at me, and I think—no, I know—that he means it.

Elsie casts one more glance at the school. "You sure you don't want me to come?"

I lean in through the open window. "I'll be fine. I'll call you if I need you, okay?"

I turn around and walk away before I can change my mind.

As I suspected, the gates to the school driveway are padlocked shut. I look around, noticing that a small side gate has been left ajar.

There are no stars out tonight. I slip through the gate, pulling it closed behind me, and as I move into the school grounds, the light pollution from the street quickly disappears. The sole park bench on the wide strip of lawn sits abandoned under the blank, dark sky. For some reason, it makes me feel infinitely sad.

I hug my jacket close as I walk, St. Augustine's looming all around me. I recognize the pathways and the water fountains as I round the main building, following the path to the East Lawn. I pass the circle of benches that the year tens have claimed, and, just beyond them, I can make out the kitchen garden, the year-sevens' guinea pigs peering suspiciously through the wire grate of their hutch. The science labs look particularly shabby in the dark—the squat bunker seems less a center of wisdom and scholarship, and more a gray prison dormitory from a Siberian gulag. I *recognize* it all, in theory, but I can't seem to regain my equilibrium; there's an alienness to this place that daylight-me has mapped from memory. Odd what a little variation in light can do to something so familiar.

I walk beneath the covered walkways behind the main building. It's even darker here, with the maples towering overhead. I suppose some people would label my current predicament—wandering through an empty school in the middle of the night, with the wind whipping a sole salt-and-vinegar chip packet around me—as maybe a bit creepy. Luckily I'm not foolish enough to be freaked out by a little darkness.

I pause at the edge of the path, the wide plain of the East Lawn stretching in front of me. The dark is so thick here that my depth of field is all off. I know it's just a trick of the night, but the lawn seems larger than normal—and yet... there, in the distance, at the very edge of the grounds, it remains. A blot on the landscape, framed by a backdrop of identical, featureless trees. The double-story brick monstrosity that is the bane of my existence. The St. Augustine's Visual and Performing Arts Center, the building that is either representative of everything dysfunctional and impossible in my life, or just a repurposed convent with leaky toilets and the pervasive smell of wet dog.

It actually looks kind of small in the dark.

"What the hell am I doing here?" I whisper into the empty air.

Come on, Sophia, my brain supplies helpfully. *Stop ignoring the obvious. You know why you're here.*

"Fine," I hiss out loud as my feet take me forward. "But if this ends with Joshua from the future coming to tell me I'm about to get hit by a bus, I am going to be *so* pissed off." Strange how I fail to hear the conviction in my voice.

I know this is hopeless. Between the two of us we barely make one functioning human; forget about being two halves of a whole or any of that nonsense. Together, I think we might be more akin to a gene-splice experiment gone awry—the abominable creation of a mad scientist, with three left arms, and testicles where its ears should be.

But I can't deny that there is *something* that draws us together. Let's face it. If I can do nothing else, I can quantify data and weigh up evidence—

Fact: I miss him.

This is hopeless. I have zero chance of being able to match someone whose heart is so open. I'm not that sort of girl. I will never cry in movies, and, even after a year of practice, I still cannot laugh on cue. Nothing about us makes any sense. And yet.

And yet and yet and yet...

"There, I said it," I say out loud. "Are you happy now, brain?"

But the night air doesn't answer me, so I walk on, feeling like a dipshit for talking to myself.

I have no idea where I am supposed to go, but instinct propels me toward the Arts building. I'm partway across the lawn when I catch a glimpse of something over to my right, in the middle of the overgrown grass, flapping gently in the breeze like a beacon.

A single red flag, shiny and bright, standing right in the center of the decommissioned amphitheater.

I step into the long grass and head toward it.

I think the last time I ventured out here was in year seven at that infamous production of *Joseph and the Amazing Technicolor Dreamcoat*, watching Sanjay Khan and half a dozen teachers trying desperately to untangle his pharaoh wig from the mechanized stage gears. Three shallow circles of steps lead to the round stage, a few weeds, black in the night, growing through the boards. The metal box that houses the controls is locked tight with a rusted padlock. It looks exactly like what it is—a useless, broken amateur stage with an incongruous red flag on a pole jammed into a cracked board in the center.

I walk down the steps and up to the flag, searching for a clue.

It's made, not surprisingly, of a familiar red paper, thick and shiny. I examine it closely, but there's no writing or instructions of any kind, just a blank pennant taped to what I now see is a broom handle. The amphitheater sits parallel to the Visual and Performing Arts Center, the shadowy building in the distance directly behind the flag.

Something crackles in the atmosphere. I pivot in place, the red flag fluttering behind me.

A sharp screech echoes through the schoolyard.

And then music, grand and pompous, fills the air. It's all crashing cymbals and horns and brass. I frantically scan the East Lawn, but I can't see anyone. I turn back to the Arts building, bracing a hand unconsciously on the flagpole, and I'm immediately blinded by what feels like the blaze of a thousand supernovas.

I reel backward as the East Lawn is flooded with light. I throw up a hand to shield my face, the grandiose music increasing in tempo. In the distance, I can just about make out the Arts building, lit inexplicably from the outside.

I can't be sure—what with the eye trauma and the mild panic that at any moment a crowd is going to lunge out at me like some deranged surprise party—but I could swear the ground beneath me seems to *roll* just a fraction.

I close my eyes and grip the flagpole, heart hammering and eyes on fire.

And then, just as quickly as it began, the lights and the music die.

Spots dance beneath my eyelids. My ears are ringing in the now-resolute quiet.

I open my eyes again, still clutching at the flagpole. In front of me is the wide expanse of lawn, a row of identical pine trees standing peacefully along the fence.

A soft ring of lights, like the landing circle for an alien spacecraft, flickers to life. Slowly, the light intensifies, way out in front of me.

And the St. Augustine's Visual and Performing Arts Center is gone.

I blink… and blink again.

I rub my eyes. I must look like one of those cartoon characters, eyes popping out of my head, doing a comically exaggerated head-clearing shake.

I clock the row of trees, still, ostensibly, on the edge of the grounds. I see the overgrown grass, gently moving in the breeze, and the tall fence that marks our school boundary.

But the Arts building persists in its absence.

I take a single step forward, but that almost imperceptible rumble shifts beneath me again. I feel kind of dizzy.

There is a crackle and hiss, and the music resumes. The empty circle of light intensifies, till that blinding glow floods the East Lawn again. Despite my best efforts, I can't keep my eyes open. I squeeze them closed as a spotlight hits me directly in the eyeballs.

And all of a sudden, it is dark behind my eyelids again; only flickering entoptic remnants remain. I open my eyes. The lights have gone. The music has stopped.

And the Arts building is standing exactly where it should be.

My feet carry me backward until the backs of my knees hit the lowest edge of the amphitheater steps. I sit down heavily.

The grass on the stage floor is slightly trampled. The flagpole is a tad askew. The ringing in my ears from the music muffles any other sounds. I look, dazedly, around me, but, though I have the strangest instinct that I am not alone, there is no one here that I can see.

I stare at the Arts building, my brain spinning.

And I burst out laughing.

The sound rings through the schoolyard, unhinged and insane. I can't seem to stop.

"You're brilliant!" I yell. I stand and applaud, the sound of my clapping reverberating through the empty grounds. There's no reply, aside from my echo. I didn't really expect there would be.

The school is silent. The Arts building remains.

Just me and my nemesis, alone in the dark.

♥

Chapter Twenty-Two

The Duality Principle

I never did find Joshua that night. I don't think I was supposed to. I am almost certain that *that* was not the point. I want to tell him I understand. I want to tell him that I always believed, that I knew he had the potential to be *epic*. But the mental space I may have had for dealing with the Joshua conundrum is soon occupied by a somewhat more pressing matter.

I have actually put some time into practicing. I have read and studied and researched. I have even rehearsed my monologue in front of an unwilling audience of one, Toby looking all sorts of pained as he sits in a dining chair and is subjected to my thespian-ing. He refuses to offer any constructive criticism or advice. But it *is* the most I have heard my brother laugh since Dad accidentally backed his car over the neighbors' inflatable Santa.

It's mild today, so mild that I shrug out of my blazer as I head through the main school gates. It's the strangest feeling, this winding-up time. I recognize some of my classmates hanging around in odd configurations, either desperately engaging in last-minute cramming or conducting feverish postmortems of exams just completed.

The Arts building hasn't gone anywhere. It stands, still a brick-and-mortar monstrosity, carrying the weight of everything I fear within its fungus-encrusted walls. My heart has been pounding all morning, my skin almost feverishly slick with sweat. There's no point pretending otherwise; I know that my control over my anxiety is tenuous at best. There is every likelihood that I will end this morning curled in a ball on the smelly brown carpet or being carted out on a stretcher, still dressed in my Salvation Army costume and wig.

I square my shoulders, adjust my outfit, and march into the building with my head held high. I ignore the dust. I ignore the liquid sensation behind my kneecaps. I ignore the table of examiners and Ms. Heller and their various looks that I think are supposed to convey compassion and support. I ignore the thumping of my heart, the fight-or-flight response that is screaming for flight. I take the stage stairs. I am ready. I will do this.

And I do.

And—I suck.

Like really, spectacularly, Hindenburg-exploding-in-a-fireball-level suck. I open my mouth, and the words that I memorized months ago pour out; they might be in English, but at the speed that I am vomiting them, it's hard to tell. Perhaps my subconscious has absorbed more than I knew through my time at Elsie's, because at some point I realize that I have adopted an accent that sounds faintly, and possibly offensively, Indian. Midway through, I calculate that my seven-minute monologue will probably be done in one minute and thirty-five seconds. I will my voice to slow. But at the same time, I experience what I can only describe as a complete mental collapse and forget if my character is supposed to be happy or dejected, so I end up racing through a section about a dead grandmother with a perky voice and a smile on my face. At some point I glance over at one of the adjudicators, only to see him doodling what looks like a semi-pornographic sketch in his notebook. And when I turn to walk down the stage stairs, I trip over a lighting cable and fall into the orchestra pit.

I can't be certain, but I think I detect a collective sigh of relief when I mumble a "thank you" and stumble out of the building.

I pause beneath the Arts Center sign, blinking into the daylight. A couple of my classmates are milling nearby, Romy Hopwood and her friends frantically practice-emoting in the sunshine. I see Damien Pagono, looking relaxed and unperturbed. He gives me a grin and a thumbs-up.

I suck in a few mouthfuls of air, my body still trembling. I remove my wig and the too-big dress that I'd hastily shoved over my school uniform. I breathe. And I wait. The tangled feeling in my stomach doesn't abate. But strangely enough, it seems that I am not dying today.

I turn toward the main path and hurry across the lawn, through the covered library walkways and around to the front of the main building, following an inexplicable, GPS-like homing signal that I am fairly certain I will never be able to explain.

He is perched on the back of the park bench, wearing his black glasses and his old-man tweed cap. His hands are buried within the pockets of his blazer. I'm pretty sure it's no magic trick, and it's certainly no phenomena of physics, but the light appears to bend around him. Some unknown singularity seems to make him glow.

He stands when he sees me, whipping off his hat. He takes a few tentative steps in my direction.

"So?" he says.

"So," I reply.

He shuffles his feet on the grass, two even scuffs for each foot, that unconscious tic that appears when he's nervous. He adjusts his glasses, and I can tell that he's fighting hard against the desire to just blurt out everything that's in his head.

I take another step toward him. "I'm done. The Drama exam, I mean. It's over."

He seems to be holding his breath. "And...?"

I flop onto the bench and massage my aching shoulders. "And it was bad."

He swallows convulsively and sits down beside me. I notice that he leaves more than a handwidth between us, carefully angling himself so our knees don't touch. It makes something in my chest ache.

"Uh-oh, really? How bad?" he says. "Are you sure? Maybe you did better than you thought? I mean, I totally thought I bombed the Bio test but—"

I cross my arms and lean backward, breathing in the dry air. I ignore the hitch in his voice, the remnant of his lisp that's back in full swing. "Joshua, you know that I'm incapable of hyperbole, right? Keep that in mind when I say that I'm fairly certain my Drama exam may have been one of the worst things to ever happen in the history of everything."

His eyes widen. A small smile starts to play at the edge of his lips. He rests against the bench, turning to face me. I match his posture, tucking my legs beneath me. "Was it worse than the time Mr. Finkler opened the swimming competition with that 'Eye of the Tiger' banjo solo?" he asks.

"Oh, it was *so* much worse."

Joshua laughs, though he still looks confused. "*Okay*. But, Sophia, you don't seem to be freaking out." He runs his eyes over me. "Oh boy, you're not, like, repressing, are you? Tell me you're not waiting for a quiet moment to... well, you know..."

"Have a gigantic meltdown? No. I don't think so. I guess I've had time to think about things." I force my eyes to meet his, almost afraid of what I'm going to see there. But he's looking at me with the same soft expression, a little bit concerned, and maybe just a tiny bit hopeful. It will never cease to amaze me how clear his face is to me. I may not be brilliant at it, but I think I can read this person. His shuffling feet, his ceaselessly moving fingers, the catch in his voice that appears whenever he is uncertain. It sort of breaks my heart that I might be the cause of those things.

I reach out and touch the cuff of his blazer. "I've been thinking about lots of things," I say. I'm sort of proud that my voice comes out steady. Inside, my atoms feel like they're shifting and crashing.

"What did you think about?" he whispers.

I shuffle forward, my knees connecting with his. My skin tingles at the point of contact, and part of me still hesitates at the touch. I don't think I'll ever be the sort of girl who can throw herself with abandon into the arms of another person. I will probably never be effusive or demonstrative. And I doubt I will ever be the sort of girl who belongs inside a romance movie.

Joshua's eyes widen. He leans toward me, slowly, his hand curving tentatively around the back of my neck. It's trembling, but not moving to draw me any closer. I know he's holding back, waiting for me to meet him halfway.

I move inside the circle of space that separates us. My heart is pounding. My hands are shaking.

It's not a proper kiss—more like the suggestion of a kiss, a faint brush of his lips against mine. I stay still, his face so close that I can feel the radiating heat of him. It's not entirely comfortable, but I think, with time and practice, maybe it might be.

"Joshua?" I whisper, my lips not quite touching his.

"Yeah?" he breathes.

"I think I may have failed. Like actually, properly failed. I tried really, really hard. I did everything I knew how to do. And I still sucked."

He moves back slightly. His eyes flicker between mine. "And..."

"And, I'm still here. It was awful. I feel, well, kind of mortified. But I'm still here."

His eyes crinkle at the edges. "Yeah. You are." He swallows, his thumb brushing lightly against my neck. "And... this?"

I take a deep breath, filling my lungs till they feel like bursting. And then I exhale, slow and steady.

"Okay," I say decisively. I lean in to kiss him again. "This."

♠

Chapter Twenty-Three

Be natural and use your head.

—Dai Vernon

Somewhere in the distance, music is playing. It's coming from Mr. Grayson's Mazda; he's locked himself in for his lunch break and is blasting Beyoncé. Rumor is he's quit St. Augustine's. Apparently he's off to volunteer at a sloth sanctuary in Costa Rica. It doesn't matter. His music may as well be a bloody-great hallelujah chorus.

Sophia is kissing me. *She* is kissing *me*. It's delicate and cautious. It is, without exaggeration, the most awesomely perfect thing to have happened in the history of everything. But I know I need to rein in at least some of my excitement. I can practically feel the effort it's taking her not to bolt.

She pulls away again, and my lips are instantly bereft. Her face is, as always, impassive, though her cheeks are flushed a brilliant red. I guess I can see how some idiots might think her expressionless, but her eyes roam inquisitively over me, and they sparkle, all bright and intense. I know I'm smiling at her like some git on magic mushrooms, but I can't make myself stop.

Her hand is on the very edge of my fingers, like she's

trying to acclimatize to the sensation. I turn my palm up, letting her hand wander carefully over mine. She looks puzzled, like there's something she's dying to ask.

"What is it?" I say, kinda desperate not to break this spell.

She looks up at me again, those curious eyes probing. "So what did you decide on, in the end? What are you going to study?"

I link the tips of my fingers through hers. I wait till I feel the slight curl of her fingers in reply. I'm pretty damn proud of myself for not whooping like an idiot. "Is this okay?"

She nods impatiently. "Yes. Answer the question."

I'm so distracted by the feeling of her hand in mine that I almost forget what she asked. The question still spins me out a bit. But at least I have something approaching an answer.

"Arts. I'll probably pick up some History and maybe experiment with a couple of other things. I don't know what I'll do with it after, but I had this thought that maybe... teaching?" I shrug. I feel like I'm talking about a weird future that belongs to someone I don't recognize. "I dunno. I like kids. It's something I might be good at. I reckon even I can picture me as the goofy substitute teacher who fronts his classes with a cage full of doves or something? Maybe not. I might change my mind next week. I know it's not, like, huge or spectacularly exciting or anything. And, you know, hello—that cautionary tale over there doesn't exactly inspire confidence," I say, nodding my head at Mr. Grayson and eliciting a knowing eye roll from Sophia. "But I think—right now, anyway—I think I feel good about it."

"Teaching," she echoes. She smiles, her beautiful face all aglow. "I think, Joshua, you'll be a really amazing teacher."

"Well, I dunno about amazing. And it's going to be a while before I can set foot in a classroom again. High school burned a hole in my brain that's gonna take time to heal, you know?"

"Yes. You may not be the only one feeling the pain." Then she narrows her eyes a little, the subtle twinkle in them all cheeky and bold. "So, David Copperfield—what would happen if I asked you to tell me how you did that *thing*?" she asks.

I grin, gripping her hand just a little tighter. "Is that something you're likely to ask?"

"Well, I'm assuming mirrors and obviously lights plus some kind of holographic screen or projector or—"

I laugh. She rolls her eyes again. "Don't worry. I'll figure it out."

"Yeah, I have no doubt about that." I glance down at our linked hands. "So, Sophia, I think I figured out something as well."

"Oh? What mysteries did you solve, Joshua?"

My heart does that insane skip that it always does when she says my name. "I think I discovered that maybe some mysteries aren't mine to solve. Maybe it's not my job to, you know. Save you?"

She peers at my face, unblinking and thoughtful, with those eyes that seem to see the whole universe. "I have another theory," she says, her husky voice steady and sure.

"Oh?"

She grins. It's small and reserved. I'm not sure anyone else would even peg it as a smile. But to me, it lights up her whole face. "Yes. Perhaps neither one of us needs saving."

She kisses me again, just a gentle touch of her lips, and my heart takes flight like it's mastered a levitation trick all on its own.

♣

Chapter Twenty-Four

The Expanding Universe

I have a long way to go. I'll never be great among crowds, and I know I'll never be totally happy too far outside my comfort zone. I still have moments where my fears get the best of me, where I need to lock myself away, alone, and focus only on the math. Joshua seems to understand; sometimes it's not another person I need, just space to be inside my own head. But, as the poster on the Nayers' bathroom door advises, I am trying to find the wisdom to figure out which bits to work on and which bits to accept. I'm even starting to pay attention in my counseling sessions, though I feel... well, as Joshua would say, I feel like a bit of a tool. But I am attempting to be less skeptical. Some of the exercises even prove to be a little bit useful. Puppets. Who knew?

My anxiety waxes and wanes—peaking when I start college, retreating a little when I realize that the advanced subjects I'm taking might actually be a challenge, but one that I know I can handle.

Of course, there is still something that sends me into a spin, one looming inevitability that no amount of logical evaluation can conquer.

One of Elsie's favorite romance movies has this whole spiel in it about airports. Something to the effect that the departure gate of an airport is, like, a microcosm of all that is wonderful about humans. When we watched it, it made little sense to me, all cheesy music and slow-motion hugging. Though if I think about it, I suppose I can sort of see the point; maybe we're always searching for tangible evidence of what we know is basically indemonstrable.

I haven't flown much, but the international departure gate at 7 P.M. on a Sunday seems anything but romantic. It's loud, overly lit by banks of fluorescent lighting, crowded with stressed-looking people and bawling children, and has a preponderance of sunglasses stores that makes no sense, given that its patrons are all about to enter a climate-controlled aircraft and are not, say, boarding a glass elevator for a trip to the sun.

Elsie's parents are trying to corral their family in front of the duty-free store. All of her brothers are here, as well as a handful of aunts and uncles, her grandparents from both sides, and a gaggle of cousins, all of whom are talking over one another and posting airport selfies on Instagram.

Damien Pagono managed to beg a ride with Joshua and me. Joshua was concerned that Damien was planning some grand airport declaration to Elsie that would probably end with his arrest, but at the moment he is merely sitting in a plastic chair, looking dejected. Though he does seem to be sitting just a bit too close to Elsie's cousin Mira, casting occasional glances her way. He bumps her knee and flashes something on his phone. Mira, surprisingly, does not look disgusted.

I stand apart from the crowds. Even under normal circumstances, Elsie's raucous extended family is too much for me. Today, I fear that a misplaced question or errant touch might be enough to crack my carefully held equilibrium.

I keep my eyes on the departure board, even as I feel Elsie's presence lingering beside me.

"Elsie, you know you're on a fourteen-hour flight, right? *Sitting*, on a fourteen-hour flight?"

"Yeah," she says quietly. "So?"

I drag my eyes away and turn to face my best friend. "So—why are you wearing leather pants?"

Elsie peers down at her legs. The shiny leather is so tight it looks like it was sprayed on. And then she throws her arms around me and bursts into tears.

"I like these pants!" she sobs. "They're my favorite, favorite pants in the whole world! I've had them forever, and I can't stand the thought of leaving them behind. What am I going to do without them, Sophia?"

I wrap my arms loosely around her, feeling only a little bit twitchy. "Els, it's okay, you can wear whatever you want. Though I'm pretty sure they have leather pants in America—"

"I'm not talking about the stupid, goddamn pants!" she yells, just about rupturing my eardrum in the process. "Jesus Christ, Reyhart, you are supposed to be the smart one!"

"Your metaphors suck, Elsie," I manage to say. I feel her tears on the side of my face, her hiccup-y sobs against my chest.

I pull away from her. She drops her arms by her sides, but I can still feel the ghost of them around me. "Sure you're not going to change your mind?" I whisper.

She laughs, wiping her face on her jacket sleeve. "Probably, once I'm subjected to my first pep rally or keg party. I'm not even sure what a keg party is, but it sounds sucky. I'll probably change my mind every other day. I'm going to miss home like crazy. But I still want to do this."

"Okay. But will you... you'll Skype and email and keep in touch. Right?"

She rolls her eyes. "No. I will step on that plane and immediately subject myself to a brain wipe. Really, it's the only way I can erase the memory of seeing Lucas Kelly's wang in the Bio exam. Seriously, they really needed a class on how to work a zipper, just for him." Elsie must notice my expression, because she rolls her eyes again and adds, "I will text you as soon as I get off the plane. Okay?"

I take a deep breath. "Elsie, I wanted to say... that is, I've been meaning to tell you... I'm sorry if I ever made you feel like you were alone. I know I'm sort of self-involved. And I've probably been a crap best friend. But I want you to know that, well, I don't think I would have survived all this if it wasn't for you. I know I probably made things hard, but you being my friend... it was the least lonely I've ever been. I just wanted you to know that."

Elsie bursts into tears again. Her mum and Raj and Colin and an assortment of cousins and aunts suddenly surround her, all hugs and proffered tissues, and slowly, she is drawn away from me.

"Wait, wait," she hisses, untangling herself from her family. Rajesh swipes fitfully at his eyes, and Colin laughs at him, but he looks kind of misty too.

Elsie barrels back toward me and grabs the lapels of my dress. "I'll see you at Christmas, okay? We can watch movies and eat Tim Tams and, well, not catch up, because I'm going to Skype you every second day—but it'll be okay. Okay?"

"Okay, Elsie." I say. My eyes are dry, but everything inside me feels like it's dissolving.

"And take care of the boy," she says with a lopsided smile. "I think he kind of likes you."

"Is that code for 'stop being such a giant freakazoid'?" I whisper.

Elsie giggles through her tears. "I have a feeling it's the freakazoid-y bits he likes the most," she whispers back.

I can't help but smile too. "What am I going to be when I grow up, Elsie?"

She smooths back my hair and then takes a step away from me. "You, my friend, are going to be amazing."

She bounds over to Joshua, who is hovering awkwardly at the back of the crowd. She stands on her toes and throws her arms around his neck, and he hugs her back just as tightly. I can't tell what she says to him, or what he says back, but I think I can hazard a guess by the way they both glance in my direction.

There is a flurry of activity from Elsie's family, who seem to have descended en masse. Her dad gives her a couple of encouraging slaps across the back, and her mum smooths down her jacket while crying quietly into a handkerchief.

Elsie's brothers don't seem to be immune either—Raj and Colin and even stoic Ryan descend into the fray. Elsie disappears beneath a swirling mass of arms and hugs.

She gathers her carry-on bag and her jacket, looking through damp eyes at her family and her friends and finally me. She winks.

Then she squares her shoulders and, without a backward glance, walks through the gaping mouth of the departure doors. And just like that, Elsie is gone.

I don't need to turn around. I feel rather than see him move, his strangely familiar presence appearing in the space behind me. He doesn't say anything. I still can't make myself look away from the gate. I am aware of a giant space that has opened up somewhere beneath my belly, which I know won't ever be filled in the same way again. But I find myself moving backward, inch by inch, until I bump into the solid, reassuring wall behind me.

"Okay?" he asks quietly.

"No. Not even a little bit."

He rests his chin on the top of my head. He doesn't say anything, but his arms circle around me, and he doesn't let go.

"So. Anyone up for a kebab?"

I turn my head. Joshua's arm remains around my waist. With his other hand he clips Damien over the side of the head.

"What? It's proper depression food."

Rajesh appears beside us, still sniffling. "Yeah, I could go for some food. I wouldn't mind escaping this lot too. Auntie Therese is trying to set me up with the chick in the Sunglass Hut." He shudders.

Joshua takes my hand. He looks at me patiently.

I cast one last glance at the departure door. And then I look at my friends and at Joshua's hand still clasped in mine.

"Okay," I say, mustering a faint smile. "Let's go."

We pile into Joshua's dad's car, and after some truly awful roadside kebabs, we drop Raj at home and Damien at the tram stop. We leave Damien armed with Mira's phone number and a plan to catch up for pizza later in the week. He waves goodbye by jiggling his hands in front of his chest, as if he is gesticulating with imaginary breasts. I am still slightly confused as to how this boy became my friend.

It's much later, and I should be at home, but it's Sunday night and my best friend is on her way to a new life on the other side of the world, and I have nothing to do tomorrow but sleep and crack the spine of an Advanced Geometry textbook.

We're side-by-side on Joshua's bed, beneath the dark ceiling and his rows of bookshelves. I'm sitting cross-legged, fiddling with one of his new Japanese puzzle boxes, while Joshua stretches out beside me, cuddling a purring Narda. He runs his hands over the cat's soft ears, and he watches my fingers as I work the wooden pieces and pegs. I can see how to solve this puzzle, so I set it aside. Instead, I lie down and watch Joshua. I can hear the faint sounds of Gillian's music, but apart from the ticking of a few too many clocks, his room is quiet and still.

"You know what's weird?" he says eventually.

I glance at him. I let my eyes travel, deliberately, over his beloved collection of magic memorabilia, old and new, and over Felipe, Elsie's skeleton, that my best friend gifted to my boyfriend with great fanfare. Felipe reclines against the lowest bookshelf and is currently wearing Joshua's velour cape and tweed cap. The skeleton holds a gleaming fencing foil, a prop from Joshua's new obsession—the fencing club at his university. My eyes skim over the spilled innards of the carriage clock on his desk and the poster of Mandrake the Magician that has pride of place near his bed. I look back at him with a raised eyebrow.

He laughs and leans over to drop a kiss on my cheek. "Okay, weird being relative. But, you know, you never call me Josh? Only ever Joshua."

I prop myself on one elbow. "Huh. I guess I don't. I don't know why. Josh. *Joshhh*," I say experimentally. The word sits strangely on my tongue. I shake my head. "No. It's not right."

"Oh?"

"Well, it's just that, it's so small. Four letters. One syllable. It just doesn't seem *enough* for you. Does that bother you, *Joshua*?"

He smiles, flopping onto his back again. "Nah. I like it. When you say my name it always sounds..." He looks up at his blue ceiling. "Momentous," he says with a grin.

I roll my eyes. I think he will always be far more effusive than me. But then he kisses me with his eyes wide open, and I can't bring myself to mind.

I'm not sure where any of this is leading, what the future holds for either of us. I still want my neat ending, my elegant proof. I think I will always be searching for irrefutable answers. Maybe it's a good thing I have math for that.

I never did hear from Perelman. I can only speculate on what my beardy friend is doing these days, what led to his vanishing act. There are way too many unknowns to calculate. Maybe he is in the midst of some great new discovery, sequestered away while he figures out the answers. Maybe it was just too much for him, the burden of so much expectation. Or maybe he achieved everything he needed to achieve, and he is happily spending his days with crosswords and Netflix. Maybe he fell in love? Who knows. I hope he's okay, whatever he is doing. More than anything, I hope that math still brings him joy.

Joshua holds my hand, clasped lightly between us. Our knees are pressed together, our shoulders a little apart, and we're looking at each other but not saying a thing. His eyes are all soft and warm, those strange moo-eyes that, inconceivably, only ever seem to be aimed at me. It's kind of extraordinary, our moments like this, just quiet and still. Well, one of us is still. Joshua's other hand flicks distractedly through a crisp, new deck of playing cards, as always, forever moving.

He's told me before that the fundamental key to all magic is simple—supposedly, it's all about timing. I don't know about that. I think I can safely say that, by and large, my timing sucks balls.

But here's the thing.

I don't think I'm running out of it just yet. My time may

not be infinite; I doubt I will ever find my TARDIS, a way to cheat time and space with a wormhole inside a mailbox. But perhaps I have enough of it to figure out a few mysteries of my own.

In any case, I think that I will give myself the time to try.

♥

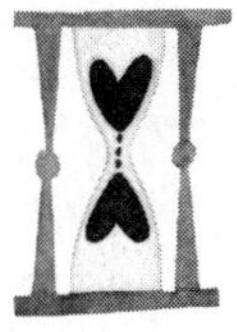

Acknowledgements

This book has been a long time in the making and would not have made it over the finish line without the support of my publishing team. As always, giant hugs and thanks to my superstar editor, Marisa Pintado, for shepherding this manuscript through the mire of my angst and self-doubt—I can't tell you how much your unwavering belief in these characters has meant over the past few years. Special thanks also to Penelope White, Vanessa Lanaway, and the fabulous Hardie Grant Egmont team.

Thank you to my writing group—Jo Horsburgh, Benjamin Laird, Nean McKenzie, Simon Mitchell, Jacinda Woodhead, and Kate Goldsworthy, and to Sophie Splatt and Frances Egan, who have both endured countless writing sessions listening to me lament at how hard it is to write a book—legends, all of you.

I have picked the brains of far too many math-nerd mates to list, but a big thank you to all the teachers and friends who have provided insight, inspiration, and research help over the past few years, with a very special thanks to my brilliant cousins for fielding my last-minute panicked queries. While I may not ever fully wrap my brain around the intricacies of the Poincaré conjecture, I highly recommend *Perfect Rigour*, Masha Gessen's excellent biography of Grigori Perelman. And a big thank you also to Kellie Jasper (Assoc MAPS) for your wonderfully nuanced feedback on teen anxiety.

And finally, a very special shout-out to the wonderful #LoveOzYA crew—the amazing fans, reviewers, festival organizers, booksellers, librarians, and my always-awesome fellow writers for your friendship, advice, encouragement, and support—I am so very blessed to be part of this world.

About the Author

Melissa Keil is a writer, children's editor, and compulsive book-buyer. She has lived in Minnesota, London, and the Middle East, and currently resides in her hometown of Melbourne. She was the inaugural winner of the Ampersand Prize, Hardie Grant Egmont's groundbreaking award for debut novelists. Her first two books—*Life in Outer Space* and *The Incredible Adventures of Cinnamon Girl*—have been published all around the world and have won several awards, including YALSA Best Books for Young Adults and the Parent's Choice Recommended Award.

You can visit Melissa at *www.melissakeil.com* *www.facebook.com/MissMisch77*, or come say hello on Twitter @MissMisch77.

Also by Melissa Keil

HC: $17.95 / 978-1-56145-905-6
PB: $9.95 / 978-1-68263-041-9

Alba prefers her quiet life of drawing comics and watching bad TV with her friends, but when a popular YouTube psychic prophesizes the end of the world everything turns upside down. It certainly doesn't help that Alba's small idyllic town is predicted to be the last place standing after New Year's. As doomsday enthusiasts flock to Eden Valley, Armageddon turns out to be the least of Alba's worries. Torn between her feelings for a boy who's just reappeared and one who's been at her side forever, Alba must decide if friendship is worth more than new romance.

"With a dash of swoon-worthy romance and a healthy helping of humor among the chaos, expect a wide readership to be thoroughly entertained."

—*Kirkus Reviews*

Sam Kinnison is on the bottom rung of the social ladder. With horror movies and World of Warcraft on his mind, nerdy Sam doesn't have time for girls. That is, until he meets Camilla. She's beautiful, friendly, and despite his attempts to ignore her, Camilla has decided she's going to be a part of Sam's life whether he likes it or not. Sam's geeky passions may have been fine before, but it turns out not everything Sam needs to know about dating can be learned from movies.

HC: $16.95 / 978-1-56145-742-7
PB: $9.95 / 978-1-56145-975-9

"A realistic piece of fiction that should enjoy broad appeal, particularly among younger teens. The central characters are complex and their stories compelling. Dialogue is believable and entertaining."

—*VOYA*